PITKIN COUNTY
library

inspire growth

D0021482

THE
Glass
Casket

ALSO BY McCORMICK TEMPLEMAN

The Little Woods

THE
Glass
Casket

McCormick Templeman

DELACORTE PRESS

Text copyright © 2014 by McCormick Templeman
Front jacket art copyright © 2014 by Leslie Ann O'Dell
Back jacket art copyright © 2014 by bblot/Shutterstock

Visit us on the Web! randomhouse.com/teens

Educators and librarians, for a variety of teaching tools, visit us at RHTeachersLibrarians.com

Library of Congress Cataloging-in-Publication Data
Templeman, McCormick.
The glass casket / McCormick Templeman.—First edition.
pages cm
Summary: After the brutal murder of her cousin, everything changes for sixteen-year-old Rowan, who must not only seek the evil forces responsible before they destroy her family and village, but also set aside her studies when she becomes betrothed to her best friend, Tom.
ISBN 978-0-385-74345-7 (hc)—ISBN 978-0-449-81315-7 (ebk)
[1. Fairy tales. 2. Supernatural—Fiction. 3. Murder—Fiction. 4. Community life—Fiction. 5. Witches—Fiction. 6. Love—Fiction.] I. Title.
PZ8.T25Gl 2014
[Fic]—dc23
2013001970

The text of this book is set in 11.5-point EideticNeo.

Book design by Angela Carlino

Printed in the United States of America

10 9 8 7 6 5 4 3 2 1

First Edition

FOR QUILL

Come away, O human child!
To the waters and the wild
With a faery, hand in hand,
For the world's more full of weeping
than you can understand.

—*W. B. Yeats, "The Stolen Child"*

PART ONE

1. THE WORLD

ONE BLEAK MORNING in the eye of winter, five horses and five riders thundered into the remote mountain village of Nag's End. Without ceremony or respect for local custom, they charged through the square and up the steep alpine trail that lay just beyond. Hazarding the rocky terrain, they weaved their way between snow-shrouded pines, climbing ever higher until they reached the icy plateau of Beggar's Drift—a place, it was said, that the Goddess had forsaken.

From the window of his father's tavern, Tom Parstle saw them pass, and although they rode with great speed, he was certain he caught the seal of the king's guard upon their breastplates. Few people of interest, and surely none so interesting as the king's soldiers, had ever passed through Nag's End, and in their wake, they left an aura of wondrous anticipation. For what could there be in such an isolated part of the forest to attract the attentions of the king?

Tom and his best friend, Rowan, were certain the arrival presaged the beginning of a marvelous adventure, but three days later, when the horses came surging down the mountain, barebacked and petrified, they knew that something had gone terribly wrong.

It was Tom who suggested the search party, and because Nag's Enders were a noble folk, the kind of people who saw even strangers as their brethren, volunteers gathered in earnest. After bidding farewell to his mother and to Rowan, Tom joined his fellows as they made the trek up to the forsaken place.

The higher they climbed, the more his lungs seemed to resist the harshness of the icy air, and when they neared their destination, Tom marveled at the fierceness of the tumbling snow. If the weather in Beggar's Drift was this brutal when the village below was calm, what must it have been like in the preceding days, when Nag's End had been hit with a gale the likes of which they hadn't seen for nearly a decade?

"It must have been death up here," his brother, Jude, whispered, as if speaking Tom's thoughts.

When they reached the plateau, Tom peered through the snowy haze to the bones of the camp stretched out in the distance. There was no movement, no sign of life, and yet Tom felt there was a strange pressure in the atmosphere—

a charged energy that made him feel as if he'd walked onto the scene of a massive celebration only moments after it had suddenly and inexplicably ceased.

As they approached, Tom saw something that astonished him. At the far end of the camp rose an enormous pile of wood, shattered and splintered as if heaved up half-digested from within the bowels of the earth. The monstrosity stood three men high and twenty men wide, and whatever its purpose might have been was lost on Tom.

"What in the name . . . ," Tom whispered, and started toward it, but then Jude grabbed his arm and pointed toward something in the near distance. One of the tents had been destroyed, a gash torn in its side, its rent fabric snapping in the wind. Upon seeing it, the men froze. Tom's father, Wilhelm Parstle, held up a hand to the others, but Tom and Jude broke into a run, as is the wont of teenage boys, toward the danger instead of away from it, and the others followed.

Tom reached the tent before his brother did, and when he stepped inside, his heart grew cold. The scene was utterly commonplace, and that in itself was unnerving. A flagon of wine stood on the table next to a half-filled mug of the same. A heavy coat lay on the cot, folded and ready to wear. The side of the tent had been mangled, and snow had swept in through the tear, marking time with its presence, but had it not been for that, Tom might have expected someone to return at any moment, finish his wine, and put on his winter gear before heading out for his day.

Tom jumped when he felt a hand on his shoulder, but he turned to find it was only his brother.

"Over there," Jude said, pointing to a journal that lay open on the table, a pen set neatly beside it.

Leaning down, Tom brushed the dusting of snow from its pages to find two words scratched below:

It's starting.

Down in the village, Rowan Rose stepped out into the afternoon light. She'd been hard at work on her translations all morning, and she needed to clear her head. Wrapping her cloak around her, she lifted her face to the sky, delighting as the falling snow kissed her cheeks. Nag's End got its fair share of weather, and while she might enjoy the wildness of summer and the quiet brooding of fall, she preferred the ethereal beauty of winter.

Rowan lived with her father and her housemaid, Emily, at the edge of the forest in a two-story stone cottage. Theirs was the only home in Nag's End with a gate surrounding it, and a thicket of thorns beyond that. But inside their yard was a beautiful garden, the crowning glory of which were twin rose trees that framed the front door, one bearing red roses, the other white. It was rumored that Rowan's mother had planted them, but no one could say for certain. Rowan had never known her mother. She'd died in childbirth–taken by the fairies, some used to whisper–but Rowan liked to imagine her mother's long, smooth fingers moving through the dirt, placing the seeds in the earth and nurturing the sprouts through sapling-hood.

Reaching out to touch the naked branches, she thought

how beautiful they would look when the snow melted and the rich buds burst forth. Lifting her sapphire skirts, she made her way along the garden path and stared out into the forest beyond. A bird lit on the stone wall, and Rowan smiled at its beauty. It was a bluebird—a rare thing in winter, when Nag's End seemed the exclusive domain of the large black crows that swept through the sky like terrible sirens.

Behind her, the front door opened, and Rowan spun to see her father emerging. Carrying a pile of books close to his chest, he moved briskly, his white-blond hair falling over his eyes. He looked worried, and when he saw his daughter lingering by the wrought-iron gate, he gave a start.

"I thought you were working," he said, a note of hesitation in his voice. "Glad to see you're taking the air. The life of the mind can lead to weakness of body."

"I've already had a morning walk," she said. "I went over to see Tom off before they left on their expedition."

Her father shook his head. "That search party is premature. You'll see, they'll find those soldiers hard at work up there, and then they'll feel the fools for wasting a full day on such a trek."

"Father," Rowan said, suddenly remembering the travelers who came to the door last night. "Who were they?"

There had been something about the trio that had riled her father, and even now, books pressed against his chest, he seemed more of a nervous schoolboy than the respected scholar he was.

He bit his lip and averted his eyes. "Yes, I've been meaning to speak with you about that," he said. "I rarely ask anything of you, you know that, but I'm making a request of you now. Do you understand?"

Taken aback by the intensity of his words, she nodded.

"Those people are dangerous, Rowan, and you are not, under any circumstances, to speak with them."

Rowan shuddered. "Dangerous?"

Her mind drifted back to the family of three that had appeared at their garden gates as if players in some distant dream. They were not from the mountain provinces; that was immediately clear. They wore bright colors and spoke with a strange accent that reminded Rowan of what it must sound like to hear the crash of the sea upon the shore. The man and woman were tall, and Rowan could not see much of them under their cloaks, but the third traveler was a girl who had thrown back her hood and stood gazing up at the sky, exposing the whole of her face to Rowan's eager eyes.

Roughly Rowan's age, the girl had been beautiful in the way that a crisp apple was delicious—almost too sharp, but with an underlying sweetness that makes its jaggedness seem merely bright. She was tall, with red lips and raven hair pulled back into a tight braid, and from where Rowan had sat perched in her window, the girl's dark eyes seemed to sparkle. Rowan's father had gone out to speak with them, but Rowan had been unable to hear his words. After a brief exchange, her father, clearly agitated, proceeded back inside and locked the door behind him.

"But what did they want?" Rowan asked.

"That's not your concern," he said, furrowing his brow.

"I'm hoping they've left the village by now, but if you see them about, I want you to avoid them."

Rowan opened her mouth to speak, but her father brushed past her. "We'll talk later, Daughter. I'm due to deliver some papers to Ollen Bittern." And with that, he strode out of the yard, his blond hair flopping in the winter breeze.

Rowan stood staring after him, disconcerted by his uncharacteristic brusqueness. Catching movement on the western wall, she turned, hoping to see her little bluebird, but there atop the stones, she saw an enormous crow, its wings frayed and its eyes black as night. It was said that before the crows came to Nag's End, fairies and wood sprites and other forest things lived openly in the woods. But death rode in on the black wings of the crows, for a fairy hatchling is a crow's favorite food, and it was upon the birds' arrival that the benevolent forest things began disappearing, wicked ones lingering in their stead.

Hearing footfalls coming through the snow, Rowan turned to see Emily stalking toward her, a stern expression on her face. Emily was only a few years older than Rowan, but she'd been acting like Rowan's nursemaid since she herself had been in milk teeth. Emily's mother, Antonia, had been Rowan's actual nursemaid, and since Rowan had grown up without a mother, Antonia had raised the girl as her own, the three of them eating dinners together at the kitchen table while Rowan's father, more often than not, kept to himself, translating texts in his study. But now Antonia was gone as well, taken the previous year by fever, and although Rowan adored her father, it often felt as

9

though she and Emily were the closest thing either had to a real family.

"You'll catch a chill out here. What are you doing, anyway? Waiting for Tom?"

Rowan shook her head. "He won't be back just yet."

"I heard your father talking to you," Emily said, concerned. "You saw that family last night?"

"I did."

Emily shook her head, disapproval in her eyes. "Strange, your father telling you not to talk to them."

Rowan nodded, hesitant. "He says they're dangerous."

"Does he?" Emily raised an eyebrow. "And did he tell you who the girl is?"

"No, though she was beautiful, wasn't she?"

"Like a rose, she was. But he didn't tell you who she is?"

Rowan set her hand on her hip, her patience growing thin. "Emily, don't be tiresome. Clearly you have something you want to tell me. Who is the girl?"

"She's your cousin," Emily said.

The words came like a jolt to Rowan's heart. Her cousin? Her father had never told her she had a cousin. Something felt very wrong. Trying to collect her thoughts, Rowan walked through the snow toward the northern wall of the yard. Behind them, ice-capped mountains climbed toward the sky.

She needed to speak with Tom. That morning, when she'd said her farewell, she'd told him about the mysterious strangers from the night before, but she hadn't known then that the girl was her own cousin. She wondered what Tom would make of it all.

Emily linked her arm with Rowan's and stared up
Beggar's Drift. "I have a bad feeling about that mo
I do."

"So do I," Rowan said.

From behind them came a cry and a tremendous beating of wings as the great black crow pushed off from its
perch and hurtled up into the sky. Rowan shuddered. She
had the strong sense that somewhere up on that mountain Tom was in terrible danger. She wrapped her cloak
tight against the winter chill, hoping for some sign that
everything would be okay, nearly certain that everything
would not.

† † †

Tom and Jude stared at the journal, neither sure what to
make of it. They could hear their father beginning to orga-
nize the men, and when he called for his sons, Tom set the
journal down and stepped outside, Jude in tow.

"Right. Fan out, everyone," his father said, sending
groups off in various directions. As the men dispersed, Wilhelm looked to his sons and lowered his voice. "Stay close,"
he said. "Something's not right here."

Tom nodded and started after the others, leaving
Bartlett the tailor to puzzle over the tear in the tent. Tom's
eyes swept across the landscape, white as far as he could
see, and up ahead to where the men were moving like animals, fear evident in their bodies. He turned to speak with
Jude, but there was no sign of him. No doubt he'd headed off
on his own as soon as the moment had presented itself.

In the distance, among the nearly naked trees, Tak Carlysle was waving his hands above his head, trying to get the others' attention. Tom set off running, and even before he reached Tak, he could see the trail of blood, crimson against white, leading into the trees beyond.

That was where they found the first body. It took all of Tom's restraint not to cry out when he saw the snow mingled with frozen blood and bone. He turned away and closed his eyes lest he lose his breakfast in the snow, but his father was watching, so he forced himself to look again upon the corpse. The man's tongue had been torn from his mouth, his eyes gouged from their sockets, and wounds of varying size and depth covered his body, as if he had been set upon from every direction.

"Animal attack," Dr. Temper was quick to say, for he knew their minds would drift somewhere worse given their whereabouts.

Tom's father cleared his throat. "We need to keep looking. We must find the others."

With no tracks to follow, the men set out through the trees in grid formation, Tom's belly clenching ever tighter at the thought of what might lie ahead. They had gone only a short distance when little Natty Whitt, no more than fourteen and a little slow in the head, began shouting for the others.

Natty stood over what appeared to be four sets of clothes, folded and stacked neatly. They were covered in blood.

Tom's father shook his head. "Holy Goddess. What happened here?"

That was when they heard Jude's voice ring out from behind a thick line of trees.

"Over here!" he called, and Tom gritted his teeth, not
wanting to see what his brother had found.

They were all there, the four other missing men, spread
out in the snow. They were naked, save for their under-
garments, and as far as Tom could see, they bore no injuries. It was almost as if they had disrobed and lain down in
the snow, where they had quietly frozen to death.

Tom looked away as Dr. Temper examined the bodies.

The cause of death was clear. They had been frozen
solid, victims of the elements.

"But this is lunacy" was all Tom's father could say. "No
man would allow himself to freeze to death."

Dr. Temper raised his eyebrows at Tom's father. "Goi
Parstle," he said, careful to use the honorific. "Are you
doubting my assessment?"

"Please," Wilhelm said, raising his thumb in apology. "I
meant no disrespect. But surely there must be some explanation."

"They must have been attacked," Paer Jorgen said, and
since he was the only village elder in the party, the rest of the
men fell silent. "Something tore into that tent back there,
and that first man, clearly he was mauled by an animal."

Bartlett the tailor, who had examined the tent at length,
nodded, wearing an odd expression. "About that," he said. "I
don't think something did tear into that tent. I think something tore out of it."

Tom shivered at the notion.

Wilhelm Parstle furrowed his brow. "You're certain?"

"It looks that way."

"Are you saying," Tom asked, his voice cracking, "that these men, they clawed their way out of that tent?"

"Yes." Bartlett nodded. "I think that's exactly what they did."

Paer Jorgen shook his head, fear evident in his eyes. "No. No, something is not right here. There is something we are not seeing. It must have been an animal—attacked while they were sleeping."

"The tent was torn from the inside," Bartlett insisted. "As if they were trying to escape something."

The men stared at one another as they considered this, all momentarily speechless.

"What was it they sought up here?" Jude asked, his voice cutting through the silence. The men turned to look at him—Jude seldom spoke, and when he did, he could be counted on to say something controversial. "Does anyone know? If we knew why they were here, perhaps we could figure out what happened to them."

Paer Jorgen shook his head. "They are royal soldiers. Their business is not our own. When it comes to the king's city, it is always best not to question. And I see no reason why we should. It was a wolf, plain and simple. Granted, we haven't had a wolf in these parts for years, but only this morning Mama Lune told me of a recent spate of moose killings up north in the old territories. With the mild winters we've had, it's possible that the population is expanding and venturing out of range."

"I'll give you the first man, but what about these others?" Jude argued. "They have nary a scratch on them."

"Mind your place, Jude," his father chastised before the boy could embarrass him further.

Jude balked. "I'm supposed to accept that a wolf did this?"

"You dare to argue with me?" Paer Jorgen's face was growing red as he spoke.

Jude raised a thumb. "Our purpose is the same, Paer Jorgen. I want to know what killed these men just as you do. Our people live at the base of this mountain. Don't you think it best that we explore every possibility before we cease our questioning?"

The old man took a step toward the boy, and instinctively the others took a step away. "And what experience have you with wolves? You were barely alive when the wolves took the Flywit children."

"I thought the Flywit children disappeared," Jude challenged.

"You will stop contradicting me. A wolf mauled that man."

Jude clenched his jaw. "And I suppose a wolf simply encouraged these men here to remove their clothes and lie down nice and still in the snow like that. You're right," he said, slinging his gun over his shoulder and walking into the woods. "That must have been it."

Tom moved to follow his brother, but then thought better of it. His gaze fell to the bodies, so pristine, blanched the same color as the snow. There was something wrong about the tableau before him, something he could not quite place. He leaned in to take a closer look but was pulled from his reverie when his father grabbed his arm.

"Tom, Paer Jorgen is speaking."

Tom looked to the elder, who was mid-argument. Something would need to be done with the bodies, and the men were already engaged in a dispute over what that thing was to be.

"... they may be the king's men, but it is our mountain," said Paer Jorgen, his lips pursing with anger.

"Yes," whispered Natty Whitt. "The Goddess would want them to rest."

"What does our mountain goddess care for the king's soldiers?" Goi Tate spat. "These same soldiers enslaved her people and drove her underground. I say send word to the palace city. Let them deal with the corpses. Theirs is a sea god. Let them have their ocean burial to sate him. They're not our responsibility."

"But we can't leave them out in the air like this," Bartlett said. "We can't leave them for the elements. Think of their bodies, what the scavengers will do to them."

"Think of their bodies?" said Paer Jorgen, eyes wide. "Think of their *souls.* No, these men must be put to rest, and waiting for the king to send more soldiers is a folly." He scratched his chin and looked over the bodies. "Of course, if it has been more than twenty-three hours, then they are unclean, and no rites can be said."

The old man looked to Dr. Temper, who winced. "It's difficult to tell with precision, but I would say they have been here a while. More than twenty-three hours. There's no way rites can be said."

"Then"—Paer Jorgen cleared his throat—"then we must burn them."

The other men nodded their assent.

"What will we do with the ashes?" Tom asked. "We can't offer them at the Mouth of the Goddess."

"You are right. That we cannot do," said the old man. He ran a hand across his forehead, and then nodded. "Yes, yes, that will have to do. The cimetière. We will bury the ashes out in there in the old necropolis."

The cimetière was a primordial place. To the east of Nag's End, beyond the confines of the village and through the forest a way, it was the ancient walled burial grounds of the old ones who'd lived and died long before man walked the earth. The thought of the place made Tom uneasy. He'd played there once or twice as a child, careful to skirt the wall that circumscribed the fetid place, never touching the ancient stones. The idea of burying anyone out there, ashes or no, gave him a bad feeling.

"Is that sacrosanct?" Wilhelm Parstle asked.

Paer Jorgen sighed. "If their bodies have turned, our hands are tied. Without the rites we cannot cleanse them, and unclean, they cannot rest at the Mouth of the Goddess."

"Their kin won't take kindly to a funeral pyre," said Goi Tate.

"It's the best we can do under the circumstances," said Paer Jorgen. "We must burn them, and then we must lay them beneath the stones. We cannot risk their spirits becoming restless. We cannot risk them rising again." The old man shuffled through the snow, stroking his beard, lost in thought.

"That wood," Tom said, remembering the confounding mass they'd seen upon arrival. "Perhaps we could use it for a pyre."

His father turned his gaze back toward the camp and squinted. "Yes, the wood. What in the name of the Goddess can it be?"

Paer Jorgen shook his head and turned to walk away. "Midday is upon us. We must get to work."

As Tom gathered the wood from the great mound at the center of camp, he tried to quiet the growing fear in his chest. Beggar's Drift was part of the Black Forest, a dense, wild place that surrounded Nag's End on all sides. As such, Tom knew it would be prudent to return to the village before nightfall. Although no one had seen a goblin or fairy for generations, the villagers were inclined to believe they were still out there, and while forest things might silently stalk a man by day, they were said to hunt them as prey only at night. Tom didn't know whether he believed the forest lore, but people who wandered into the woods at night did tend to disappear, and even skeptics like Henry Rose kept within the village bounds once darkness fell. Jude was the only person Tom knew who was reckless enough to brave the night woods with any frequency, but then his hunting skills were second to none. Tom liked to believe that if something was hunting his brother, the hunter would quickly turn prey.

Twilight was nearly upon them when Jude emerged from

a thicket of trees, his rifle at his side, a worried expression on his face.

"Where have you been?" Tom asked, lifting a bundle of wood.

"I was scouting the area. I wanted to see what was on the north slope of the mountain."

"Did you find anything?"

"I don't know," Jude said, his face still etched with concern. "The land up here is strange, unsettled. There are places where it looks as if something has erupted out of the ground. There are curious piles of ice and snow. I told Paer Jorgen about it, and he just mumbled something about wolves and sent me away. I don't know, Tom. Something happened up here. Something I can't for the life of me understand."

Just then, Tom heard his father call out for them. Bending to lift a final piece of wood before going to speak with his father, Tom noticed something small glimmering in the snow beneath a log. He scraped the powder away with a gloved finger to reveal an unusual coin. It was a circle enclosing a smaller circle. They were linked by seven spokes, empty spaces between them. He was leaning in to examine it more closely when he found himself suddenly queasy, as if beset by a noxious force. For a moment, he thought he might be sick. But he heard his father's voice calling him again. He slipped the coin into his coat pocket and hurried over to the older man.

"What is it, Father?" he asked when he reached him.

"You and your brother take Natty Whitt back to the

village. His mother will be missing him, and yours will need help with preparations for supper. An emergency council must meet when this business is done, and your mother will need the extra hands." Tom nodded, and his father continued. "Send up Maura King's boy, and that lout Olin Gent. Have them bring crates to fetch back the dead men's things."

Tom did not envy the boys their task, for he knew that as they packed the belongings, they would need to work quickly, making sure to avert their eyes lest they incur the luck of the dead.

"It will be dark soon," Tom warned.

His father nodded. "Then you'd better be quick about it, hadn't you?"

He gathered Jude and Natty, and the three trudged back down to their quiet village, Tom secretly glad to be missing the rites.

Once the fires were lit and the bodies slowly burning, the rest of the men would join them in the tavern, all but two—the pyre watchers—who would stay behind to guard the dead that night. At dawn the bones would be ground and mixed with ash before being taken to the cimetière and buried in the ancient clay, stones laid carefully atop.

Just in case.

2. THE EMPEROR

BACK AT HOME, Tom washed quickly and hurried down-stairs to help his mother, Elsbet. She was chopping forest mushrooms with a large butcher's knife when he came in, and she shook her head when she saw him.

"Awful business, this. Think of their mothers."

"Where's Jude?" Tom asked.

"Catching a rabbit for the pot." She motioned with her head toward the door that led to their backyard, and to the dense woods beyond. "Thank the Goddess there's some-thing he can do."

Tom disliked it when his mother spoke so of Jude, but he knew better than to argue with her.

"It was awful," Tom said, and picking up a potato, he began peeling.

"Natty said it was a wolf." Elsbet clucked. "What a crisis. A wolf is the last thing we need these days. I hope it's gone back north to the territories. What's wrong? Why are you looking like that?"

Tom sighed. "Mother, I'm not sure it was a wolf."

"Of course it was a wolf. And he said it must have been quite a one, to lay low five men like that. Must be these winters. They're breeding up there. And they come down here to fill their bellies, and just look what happens. Hasn't been a Nag's Ender killed by a wolf since before you were born."

"What about the Flywit children?" Tom said, still peeling, his mind wandering to the bloody twin caverns where the first man's eyes ought to have been.

"The Flywit children? No, they were taken by goblins. Don't you roll your eyes at me, Tom Parstle. It's many a human child that were snatched by hungry goblins before Mama Lune put up our village barrier. Thank the Goddess for her, I tell you. Not a wicked thing been through there since, but wolves are a different matter. Wolves are just like us—animals born of the Goddess. They don't care one whit about protection charms. Oh, what are we going to do?" She set her knife down, clearly upset.

Tom hated to see his mother distressed, and laying a hand on her arm, he tried to comfort her. "Don't worry, Mother. If it is a wolf, then it's probably gone north since then. Paer Jorgen said he heard something's been killing moose up there. Must have been our wolf."

Elsbet sighed and then picked up her knife and resumed chopping. "Sounds awful to say it, but I'm more than a bit relieved it was those soldiers and not one of our own. Could have been a child. Just think of it. Biddy Holmson lets those triplets run dog wild among the trees all day. Goblins and fairies may catch their prey by dark, but wolves eat when wolves are hungry. They'd likely eat a child for breakfast as not."

Tom nodded and remained silent, having learned years ago that when he didn't know what to say to his mother, it was best to say nothing at all.

"Fool men," she continued. "Going up to Beggar's Drift like that. Who does such a thing, and in the middle of winter? That's what you get." She shook her head as if to say that had she been in charge of things, such mistakes would not have been made.

† † †

That night, after the fires had been set and the dead soldiers' things stored in the tavern cellar, the men of Nag's End gathered at the inn. Decisions had been made up on that icy mountain, decisions that ran counter to the king's way, and now those decisions would speak for the whole of Nag's End.

Elsbet served the men rabbit stew and was more generous than usual with her pour. Wilhelm was among those who had made the decision to build the funeral pyre, and since Wilhelm wasn't used to any trouble, she worried for him.

"More ale, then?" she called to the men from behind the bar, but no one answered. They were all busy listening to Rowan's father, Henry Rose, speak.

"My good men," he chuckled, dabbing a napkin at the corner of his mouth. "All I'm saying is that Nag's End is steeped in mountain ways, antiquated beliefs—and although I worship at the Mouth of the Goddess, I'm afraid I do not believe in goblins, ghosts, and ghouls." A wave of murmurs swept through the room, and Henry Rose, who had been born in the palace city, once again recognized his place as a foreigner in his own village. "What I am trying to say is that just because you believe something does not make it so, and that just as you ask the king's people to respect your customs, we must admit to ourselves that we have violated theirs."

Paer Jorgen shook his head. "You may not come from the land of the Goddess, but you're in her province now. Her flesh and blood rests just below the surface of the earth. Her magic surrounds us. You have only to look about you."

"But that's just it," Henry Rose laughed. "I see nothing. No witch can produce a spell to impress me; no augur has proven accurate enough in my opinion to be rightly called divination."

"You say no witch can produce a spell to impress you?" asked Paer Jorgen, leaning in. "What about the protection that surrounds our village? The perimeter hasn't been breached for years."

Henry Rose rolled his eyes. "As far as I am concerned, there is no spell, only empty air defending us against

creatures that were never there to begin with." Henry, noticing the displeasure of his brethren, pushed a lock of
white-blond hair from his eyes and raised a thumb. "Please,
I mean no offense. I may not have been born in Nag's End,
but I consider you all my people. Truly, I am one of you. I
make the sign of the Goddess when a murder of crows flies
northeast to southwest. I am careful to cross the sash to the
left when I open the morning curtains. These are the ways
of the mountain folk, and I honor them, but let us think
clearly for a moment. Has any man among you actually
seen the dead walk? Or seen a Greenwitch turn herself into
a cat? I mean, we no longer believe in Greywitches, do we?
So why do we believe that their modern sisters wield any
real powers?"

"You go too far," Paer Jorgen protested. "I'll not hear a
single word against our Mama Lune. She delivered seven
healthy children for my Louise, and once drove an angry fox
spirit from my yard."

"Goi Rose has said nothing against Mama Lune," Wilhelm Parstle said, trying to keep the peace as usual.

"Placing a Greenwitch in the same sentence with a
Greywitch is a wicked thing to do," said Paer Jorgen, gri-
macing. "Besides, everyone knows all the Greywitches are
dead now—wiped them out at the culling, we did."

Henry Rose nodded and raised his thumb again.
"Please, I meant no harm. I bear Mama Lune no ill will. She
is a good woman, and a skilled healer, but delivering a child
and nursing the sick is not magic. You give her too much
power." He sighed and shook his head. "But this isn't about

our difference of beliefs. It is about the king and his soldiers. We must be prepared for some kind of backlash in the eventuality that a party is sent to find these soldiers. What I wonder is whether we might avoid a row by writing to the king's people, by telling them what we've done and why we've done it. I think we've the best chance of avoiding any trouble that way. So I am asking you, do I have your consent to write such a letter?"

After a moment, the three elders nodded in turn, although it was clear that none was happy about the idea.

"Now," continued Henry Rose, leaning forward. "Those men were sent here to find something. Does anyone have knowledge of what that thing might be?"

The Nag's Enders looked around the table at one another and shook their heads.

Henry Rose nodded again. "I'm wondering if before I write that letter, it might be wise to determine what these men sought. Perhaps if we know what brought them here, then we will be better able to defend ourselves against any accusations leveled at us."

"But how would we do that?" asked Wilhelm Parstle.

Henry Rose tented his fingers in front of his nose.

"Surely their possessions were gathered. We have simply to look through them and see if they provide an answer."

The men all stared at the scholar, each willing the next to speak. What Henry Rose was suggesting was tantamount to sacrilege, for it was customary to return a man's possessions to his people without so much as glancing at them. To look on a dead man's secrets was to invite disaster.

26

Henry Rose laughed. "Yes, of course, we're back here again, aren't we? Fine. I will do the deed myself behind closed doors, so that none of you will have to risk a thing."

Wilhelm sighed, glad that Henry Rose was brave enough to take on the task himself. "Their belongings are in the cellar," he said.

"Well," Henry Rose said, pushing aside his plate. "Please, take me to them."

"What? Now?"

"Yes, now. I don't see why not," he said, and then, unable to keep the scorn from his voice, he went on. "In the palace city, we used to divvy up whatever a dead man left behind. It's a wonder any of us is alive today."

Wilhelm led Henry Rose down to the cellar, and Tom bit into his beer bread as he watched them go. Something was surfacing in his mind—an image of the four frozen men on the mountain, their bodies naked, untouched. He looked to Ollen Bittern, who, despite his position as village elder, had said not a word during the meeting.

"Father Bittern," Tom said. "Are we certain we're dealing with a wolf? Might it not be something . . . something worse?"

"You speak of forest things, boy?" Ollen Bittern asked, his brow furrowed. "No, goblins are apt to steal a child for their supper, and fairies might bewitch one to drown in Seelie Lake, but this doesn't sound like their work."

Tom shook his head. "I don't mean goblins or fairies. I mean something worse, something unknown to us."

"No, it was a wolf. Of that I am certain." The old man's mind seemed somewhere far off, and when he spoke again, he did so slowly, choosing his words with care. "I am an old man who no doubt clings to the old ways, but I do not like the direction this meeting has taken. Five men died up on that mountain today. In my opinion, you men did the right thing by setting them alight. I stand behind you on this. Not a one of you will face punishment. We will take to arms before we let a distant king tell us how to lay out our dead. And yes," he said, raising his hand as if to stop any questions that might come, "I do consider them our dead. Those men came to our land, and they died on our mountain, and we are responsible for their bodies. Obviously, we weren't able to perform rites, and so we weren't able to lay them at the Mouth, but you did the best you could by them, and moreover, you did the best you could by us, by Nag's End. I'll not have some . . . scholar"—he spat the word as if it were poison—"telling good people they've done wrong."

He looked at the men who sat around him, and they smiled back at their elder, relieved to have someone defend their actions so vociferously. Seeing the admiration in the men's eyes, the other elders, Paer Jorgen and Draeden Faez, nodded their agreement.

"I think we three can stand together on this sentiment," Paer Jorgen concluded, raising a gnarled finger.

Tom, still unconvinced they were dealing with a wolf, spoke up again. "You say it was an animal born of the Goddess that killed those men, but then why were there no tracks around the bodies?"

Paer Jorgen narrowed his eyes at Tom. "There had been fresh snow. The tracks would have been covered."

"Of course," Tom said, the words seeming almost to slip from him. "The scavengers."

"What's that?" Paer Jorgen asked, growing increasingly cross.

"Scavengers," said Tom, unable to contain himself, for suddenly he understood what had bothered him up on that mountain. "Why was there no evidence of scavengers? If they'd already been up there several days, then why were four of the bodies untouched? And what of the winter rats? What of the snow beetles?"

The room grew silent, all eyes on Tom.

Tak spoke up. "Tom's right. There wasn't anything. There should have been something, but there wasn't. It doesn't make sense."

"Perhaps the snow provided a barrier," said Ollen Bittern. "Whatever the reason, we will keep it in mind."

Paer Jorgen cleared his throat. "Research will need to be done, of course, and oracles consulted, before we can speak more freely. We will need time."

The men agreed, and with that, they clinked their tall mugs and moved on to lighter topics, the meeting officially adjourned. When Henry Rose returned from the cellar, he was met with questioning eyes.

"Did you find anything, then?" Paer Jorgen asked.

Henry Rose sucked on his bottom lip.

"Nothing of interest, no. It's difficult to say, but as far as I could tell, there is nothing of use to us down there."

Paer Jorgen nodded. "It was nice to think that our mountain might conceal a secret treasure trove, but it is, alas, unlikely. A disappointment, yes, but then we are Nag's Enders. We are born of disappointment."

Henry Rose bid Tom farewell and thanked the Parstles for their hospitality before heading out into the night. What Tom did not see, what no man saw, was that inside his winter undercoat, buttoned fast against the wind and snow, sat the soldier's logbook, pressed like a lover's secret over the scholar's trembling heart.

It wasn't until the next day that Tom saw Rowan's enchanting stranger, and when he did, something stirred within him. He was passing through the village square when she caught his eye. Extraordinarily beautiful, she moved with the grace of a spritely fawn, and as she came to perch on the low stone wall that surrounded the village well, Tom felt certain he'd seen her somewhere before—as if she were a girl from a dream, or a story told to him long ago.

Tom was staring at her, his jaw gone slack, when the girl lifted her face to him. Her gaze now upon him, their eyes locked, each seemingly unable to look away. It was as if he were seeing an old friend for the first time in years.

Her face was gentle, confused, as she looked at him, and then suddenly the ridiculousness of their staring match was upon them, and they both broke into startled, unrestrained laughter. The intimacy of the moment—the shared intensity followed by the shared foolishness—did something strange to Tom's heart, and he found himself in thrall to the mysterious creature.

But then the girl's cheeks flushed crimson, and lowering her eyes, she turned away.

"Her name's Fiona Eira." A voice at his elbow startled Tom. He turned to see Rowan's big eyes peering up at him, and he had to smile.

"She's breathtaking, isn't she?" Tom asked, returning his gaze to the girl, who was now running her fingers along the smooth stones that lined the well.

"She's my cousin," Rowan said.

"Really?"

"Apparently," she said, her bluebird eyes squinting up at him through pale lashes.

Looking at Rowan, Tom found that despite the differences in coloring, he could see a definite family resemblance. Perhaps that was why the girl seemed so familiar.

"What's she like?" he asked.

"I don't know. My father's forbidden me to speak to her, but that doesn't mean I can't spy on her, does it?"

"It seems strange of your father to tell you to avoid her. That doesn't sound like him."

Rowan raised her eyebrows. "It's the whole family. He won't see them. He's instructed Emily not to let them in, and I'm supposed to ignore them should I meet them in the square. He thinks they're after money."

"But the girl is your cousin. Surely she can't bear you any ill will."

"Surely not," said Rowan, watching her cousin, black tendrils of hair framing her luminous face.

"Then you should speak with her," Tom said.

"Yes, Tom. I'm the one who wants to speak with her," Rowan said, and then she grinned at him with such knowing that he felt a blush rising in his cheek.

† † †

That evening, when Tom returned home to his mother, who was pouring ale for the men of the village, he found his brother reading in the corner, chestnut hair falling over his dark eyes.

"Jude," he said. "Helping out as usual, I see?"

"I caught your dinner." Jude grinned. "What else do you want from me? And while we're doling out criticism here, where have you been?"

"Out," Tom said, avoiding eye contact.

"Taking the air, then?" Jude asked, a mischievous smile playing on his lips. "Just having a walk down to the well? See something you fancied, did you?"

Tom laughed. "Fine. You've got me. I went to the square, and there I happened to see Rowan's mysterious stranger. She's quite beyond description."

"There's no need to describe her. I've seen her myself. What's more, I saw you and Rowan staring at her like she was one of those insects you two used to trap in jars."

"If you've seen her, then you know what I mean," Tom said, his voice soft, reverent. "A man could hardly look upon such a creature and fail to have his heart stolen."

Jude shook his head. "Alas, the slant of her cheek does nothing to move me. Rowan, on the other hand . . ."

"You don't even like Rowan."

"That doesn't mean I can't appreciate her beauty. Don't tell her I said that, by the way."

Tom rolled his eyes. "I'll ask you please not to speak so of my friend. She's a proper lady, one not meant for your wandering eye."

"Don't I know it." Jude smiled and returned to his book.

Tom turned to see that his mother was looking especially harried, her blond curls hanging limp to her chin. Concerned, he moved to help her.

"What can I do, Mother?" he asked, and he caught Jude making the motions of being ill.

"Ah, my boy, you can wipe down the counters, you can," she said, handing him a rag. "Was your brother giving you grief, then?"

Tom leaned against the bar. "The family that just moved into the village, have you met them yet?"

Elsbet raised her eyebrows. "The girl I haven't met, but I've met her mother. I dropped off a basket of scones this morning. The woman was very kind. She said she'd be over to see us as soon as she had a moment, but the glassblower, he couldn't see fit to come to the door for a simple hello."

"He's a glassblower?" Tom asked as he moved the rag in careful circles atop the oak bar.

"Mmm." Tom's mother nodded. "I've heard he's quite skilled—gifted, even—but what's that beside some common courtesy? Couldn't be bothered to say hello, though I could see him sitting right there by the fire. He doesn't seem to think we're worth his time. I can tell you one thing, though," she said, leaning into the counter. "The mother, Lareina's her name, she's quite lovely."

"She's the stepmother," Tom corrected, working his way down the bar.

"Neither is the girl's parent, my boy."

"Really?" Tom, surprised, set his rag down and sat upon one of the high barstools. "Rowan didn't say."

"Sure," Elsbet said, brushing the curls from her eyes. "The girl belonged to Rowan's mother's brother and his first wife, but that one died when the girl was small–sickness of the blood. And then only last year, he died as well. The glassblower is some distant friend of the family, swooped in to provide and protect, but he seems a rough sort to me. Not sure I'd want the kind of protection he could give."

"Mother, you don't even know them."

Elsbet shrugged, and picking up Tom's rag, she began pushing it along the counter in steady sweeps, going over what Tom had already done. "I know people in general, Tom, and that's worth more than knowing any one person any day of the week. Now be a love and gather some wood for me, will you? Don't stray too far into the forest, though. I don't care what your brother says. There are wolves breed-ing in those trees."

"Mother," Tom sighed.

"Get on, now. The stove won't light itself, child."

That evening as Rowan walked home, she kept her eyes on the trees. She trusted her father when he told her that the village beliefs were no more than superstitions, yet she could not deny that there was a magic to the forest—perhaps not goblins and fairies, but it held an otherworldly beauty for her, and even at dusk, she usually found herself taking the path that skirted its bewitching wilds rather than walking through the center of the village. She considered the woods her second home. And while she would never hazard them at night, she and Tom had spent most of their childhood running through the trees and combing the forest floor for insects. In the summers they would swim in Seelie Lake, and resting on its shores, they would gaze up toward Cairn Hill to the slate outcropping of Lover's Leap—perched as it was above the waters, it was where widows went to weep. But now the villagers were losing their heads over a wolf, the forest declared dangerous even during the day, and Rowan felt anxious and displaced.

When Rowan reached her home, she could see the candle lamps burning in the window of her father's study. As she stepped into the foyer, Rowan caught a whiff of a scent that always made her think of her mother. She knew there was no way she actually remembered her mother's scent—she'd died when Rowan was only hours old—yet sometimes, Rowan could have sworn that she did.

Rowan knew very little about her mother. Her father, still grief-stricken after sixteen years, refused to discuss her, and if Rowan ever asked any of the villagers about her, they would sweep their eyes away, not wanting to answer, not wanting to make a child pine all the more for a mother she'd never known. Her only knowledge of her mother was through her dreams. She came to Rowan when she was sleeping—of that the girl was certain. In her favorite dream, they were in her mother's room. The light from the window seemed to sparkle, and her mother moved her shining face close to Rowan's. In one hand, she held a wooden egg; in the other, a rope woven of pure gold.

Ah, that's better, her mother would say, and then she would kiss Rowan on the cheek, her lips soft as butterfly wings. Rowan would always emerge from those dreams feeling as if they were somehow more real than her conscious life.

Stepping out of the foyer, Rowan tried to put thoughts of her mother from her mind. She moved through the corridor and into the central hall with its high arched ceiling and heavy wooden beams. She was running her fingers along the carved rosewood panels that lined the walls when Emily emerged from the kitchen, spoon in hand, her cheeks splotchy from the heat. The candles in the mounted sconces played upon the girl's features, illuminating them with bursts of color.

"Late enough," Emily said, and scrutinizing Rowan's dress, she grimaced. "That's right wrinkled, isn't it? What have you been doing in that thing?"

"Nothing," Rowan answered as Emily's dog, Pema, bounded up to her. She ran her hands through the dog's thick black fur and patted her on the head. "That's a good girl," she said, her heart warming with just one look from the dog's watery brown eyes.

"Well, put it aside for me to work on," Emily said, already

turning to head back to the kitchen, Pema in tow. "And go in and say hello to your father."

Rowan gave a soft knock at her father's study door, and he called that she should enter. He sat at his desk, surrounded by books. Before him was a thick stack of papers.

"Working on something new?" she asked.

He set down his pen and smiled at her.

"I am. I've had a new shipment from the duke conservateur. Some really interesting documents coming into the royal library these days. One is a text that was only recently discovered in the hills of Montatrea, where they unearthed that massive trove of ancient texts. It's fascinating, really."

"Fortunately, they have you to translate it for them," said Rowan, who always took a quiet pride in her father's expertise.

He leaned back in his chair and laughed. "Well, it's not as if they have a choice. There are simply too few men trained in the Midway language these days. It's a pity."

"I can read it too, remember," she said, grinning.

"Don't say I never taught you anything. Have you and Emily had your supper yet?"

"Not yet, no. I was just about to go and see if she needs help in the kitchen."

"I'm sure she'll appreciate that."

"Father," Rowan said, looking at the shelves that lined the wall, at the endless stacks of books. "Those men who died. What killed them?"

He fixed his eyes on hers. "A wolf, naturally. But, Rowan, you mustn't trouble yourself about such things. Fear is the domain of the small-minded. You are to be a scholar, my dear, and scholars do not go around fearing the wind and quivering away at the thought of wolves."

Rowan smiled, knowing she was lucky to have a father like hers who so valued a girl's mind, who thought his daughter had the capacity to become as great a scholar as any son. In Nag's End, most girls were married off as soon as possible, and once married, they had no chance of being anything but helpmate to a husband. That was why Greenwitches never married. To yoke oneself to a man was to cleave yourself in two, so her father always said. He had told her many a time that if she studied, and if she attained the level of skill he desired for her, when the time was right, he would take her to the palace city. He'd once held a well-respected position there but had left the city upon meeting her mother. Sometimes Rowan sensed that her father, more than anything, wanted to return to that stunning place with its magnificent castle set high upon rocky cliffs.

Someday, she told herself, she would journey down the mountain passes that spilled from the north like spider veins, all the way to where the warm waters met pebbled shores, and see the palace city with her own eyes. She had heard enough stories, had seen enough artists' renderings to know that it was an enchanted place, a magnificent city pearled with sapphire canals.

Someday, Rowan told herself, someday she would see it with her own eyes, perhaps even live there. Her studies were the key, and she was capable of mastering them. Her father had said as much, and she hoped with all her heart that he was right.

As if reading her thoughts, Henry Rose held up a finger to her, and with his other hand rustled through some papers.

"Since we're speaking of Midway texts, I wondered if I might talk with you about your work on *The Book of Widows*," he said.

Rowan felt her palms growing sweaty. She had given her father her notes on a translation she was helping him with, and while she had hoped he might look them over before she continued with her work, she had not expected a formal review.

"Is . . . is something wrong?"

He furrowed his brow and smiled at her. "Quite the opposite, child. I was examining it this morning, and frankly, I am stunned. When I gave you the piece, I thought I might do so as a training exercise, but you've discovered something in here that I missed."

Rowan felt the anxiety draining from her as she processed his words.

"You're pleased, then?"

"To say that I am pleased would be an understatement. Tell me, though," he said, resting his chin on his palm. "How did you arrive at your conclusion?"

Rowan cleared her throat, trying to keep the excitement from her voice. "Well, I suppose it was instinct, mostly. After really looking at it, I just knew that a mistake had been made somewhere along the way. The version we have is in the ancient Luric, but the story itself reminded me of something I'd read about the Midway peoples and one of their creation myths. That made me wonder if it might have originally been composed in a Midway tongue and since then translated into the Luric. So I began looking for words that might have been mistranslated, and I found two. It all comes down to a simple homophone, really. *Lan Ce Sai,* meaning 'bloom colors' or 'colors bloom,' but *Ce Sai,* when translated into the dialect of the Midway peoples, is the word *tsvety,* meaning 'colors.' Since the word *tsvety* has the homophone *tsveti,* which means 'flowers'—I began to wonder if the word in the poem was not *colors,* but *flowers. Flowers bloom.* When you think about it, it seems rather obvious, and I don't imagine that it changes much, but I thought I should make a note."

Her father stared at her with a mixture of surprise and delight. He shook his head.

"Really, Rowan, I cannot tell you how impressed I am with what you've done. Whether the change is important or not is not for us to say. Our work is in the discovery. I'm going to send what you've done to the duke conservateur right away."

Rowan could barely believe his words. "You are?"

"I am." He smiled. "I am very proud of you, my child. Your gifts seem to grow with each passing moon."

"Thank you, Father," she said as she watched him set her notes to the side.

"Now," he answered, "why don't you eat with Emily. I'm afraid I won't be joining you. I have far too much work ahead of me."

Pride filling her chest, she left her father's study and went to wash up.

Supper with Emily was stew again, and although Rowan could think of little other than her translations, Emily seemed able only to speak of Fiona Eira.

"So lovely, she is. Tall for a girl. Funny, your being cousins."

"Why's that?" Rowan said, taken aback by the perceived insult.

"Oh, no, not that you're not lovely, Ro. It's just that you are so scrawny and pale. It's like you're all one color—like mashed potatoes—while her colors are so vibrant, all black and peach and red. She's almost like a painting. And hearty. She's got lovely curves, that one."

Rowan thought about her cousin long after supper and was still thinking about her, up in her room, as she dressed for bed. She resented her father for preventing her from speaking with the girl. Fiona Eira was family, after all, and they were practically the same age. She might make for a good friend; although, looking at the girl today down by the well, Rowan wasn't sure the two would have much in common.

She changed into her nightgown and turned down her bed. On her desk, beside the candelabra, sat the remainder of *The Book of Widows.* Perhaps just a little translating before bedtime would calm her. After lighting the candles, Rowan was gazing through the picture window and out into the woods beyond when she was overcome by a sudden chill.

She felt almost exactly as if someone was watching her. She stood still a moment and nearly moved to blow out the candles, but then she decided she was being ridiculous. Shaking it off, she pulled out her chair and sat down. With the lush green lacquer of her desk smooth beneath her arms, she lost herself quickly in the motion of the pen over paper.

She did not stop until she was satisfied with her work, and when she laid down her pen, she looked out the window to see the nearly full moon stretching high into the sky. But just as she pushed her chair in, she thought she heard something outside her window. She froze, peering through the panes into the moonlight-dappled darkness beyond. Pema, who had been asleep under the desk, jumped onto Rowan's bed, startling her.

"Pema, girl, you frightened me," Rowan said, but she knew it was not Pema that had scared her. The dog curled up at the foot of the bed.

"You're staying in here tonight, eh?" she said, petting the dog's head. "I suppose Emily won't mind." Pema hadn't heard the noise, Rowan told herself, and Pema could hear a northern squirrel scuttle up a pine from hundreds of yards away. Her mind was playing tricks on her, that was all. Nodding to herself, she climbed under the covers and blew out her candle. She lay there a moment, listening to her breath, until she could take it no longer. In a flash, she was up again and at her window. She drew down the curtains against the night, against the unknowable. Finally content, she climbed back into bed and drifted off to sleep.

3. THE EMPRESS

FIONA EIRA COULDN'T stop thinking about the boy in the square. When she'd looked up to see him, when her eyes had met his—it was as if something inside her had changed. There was a kindness to his face that she'd not often seen in young men, and when he'd laughed, it had awakened something in her, and she realized that their shared moment was the first time she'd laughed since her father had died. As she walked back home, she noticed that she still felt him with her, lingering in her mind's eye.

She wanted to meet him, but she would need to discover his name without Seamus, her guardian, finding out. She knew she ought to be grateful to Seamus for providing for her and Lareina after her father's death, but the truth was he made her nervous.

She walked on, concentrating on the ground beneath her feet, listening to the solid crunch of the snow and focusing on the scent of the rich oils of pine that lingered in the breeze. She filled her belly with air and softened her lungs, slowing the rate of her heart, which had crept ever steeper since thinking of her father.

Before he died, she had been a happy child, an uncomplicated girl. She loved her father and her stepmother almost as much as she loved swimming in the sea and playing chase with the village children. But when her father died, everything changed. Seamus Flint had shown up almost before the man's body was cold, promising money and comfort, protection. Lareina had no family, after all, and had a girl to look after now—a girl who wasn't even her own, he had said. How that had angered Fiona, for Lareina was her mother, if not by blood, then by spirit, and as Lareina often said, a woman need not birth a child to feel a mother's love.

Before their journey to the mountains, Seamus had told them that they were leaving to be closer to Fiona's family. He had intimated that her long-lost relatives would greet them eagerly and with open arms, but they had done no such thing. The scholar, her uncle, had turned them away with barely a word. And just now at the square, the look in her cousin's eyes . . . she recognized it. Her cousin had been told not to speak to Fiona—that she was dangerous. But what dangers could she possibly present?

As Fiona walked the forest path back to her new home,

her mind drifted to memories of her father. He had been a quiet man, a man not accustomed to showing affection, and yet he had been a good man, providing for her, always giving her a kind word when she was most in need. She missed her life by the sea—the warm winds and clear blue ocean swells.

Her heart ached when she thought about the morning walks she used to take with Lareina, their bare feet sinking into the sand still cool from the night. There, they would comb for seashells to string into necklaces that her father might sell at the weekly open market. In the afternoons, they would sit in the sand outside their cottage, the warm sun beating down on Fiona's shoulders as they worked. Lareina made a habit of setting the loveliest necklace aside for Fiona. Fastening it around her neck and kissing her on the cheek, she would say, *An ocean bloom for my ocean rose.* Those necklaces were gone now too. In the end, Goi Flint had sold even those. The past year had been a dark one, but Fiona was beginning to suspect that things might be changing. Perhaps her gentle stranger, that solid, earthbound boy, augured the start of a new kind of happiness.

Lareina looked up from her sewing the second Fiona pushed her weight against the heavy wooden door. Setting down the needle and thread, she smiled at her stepdaughter.

"Hi, Mum," Fiona said, and kissed her on the cheek. "You were worried, weren't you?"

Lareina laughed and shook her head. Fiona's eyes fell to

the knitting needle on the hearth, and a heaviness settled over the girl's face. Her mother, Malia, had died an agonizing death—sepsis—and the root of it had been the prick of a simple knitting needle. Such a small thing to destroy the lives of a woman and child.

When Lareina had first met the girl, she was barely a slip of a thing, ashen and traumatized, huddled by the hearth fire, in need of attention and serious grooming. She had been five, and it had been three months since her mother's untimely death. Her black hair had run wild, and her large coal eyes had pockets of gray beneath them. To Lareina, she'd looked like a withered and grieving old soul trapped within the body of a child. Lareina's first thought upon seeing Fiona was that she was somehow cursed—a witch's spell gone awry. The girl had looked at her new stepmother with unseeing eyes, and Lareina, being not much more than a girl herself, and not knowing what she could possibly do to help the child, had sat beside her, removed a comb from her bag, and had begun the colossal task of untangling the child's obsidian nest of hair.

Since that day, the two had engaged in this ritual whether or not Fiona's hair was in need of combing, and so the girl, now nearly a woman, undid her braid and sat at her stepmother's feet. Picking up the comb that lay beside her, Lareina lifted her stepdaughter's hair and ran the fine ivory teeth through it with care while Fiona rested her cheek on her stepmother's knee.

"How was the square?" Lareina asked, and the girl sighed.

"Fine, I suppose. Not much of interest, and no one will talk to me. They stare at me, though."

"That's to be expected, my child. You are growing to be quite lovely. People are bound to appreciate it," she said, but her heart was heavy at the prospect. She'd been noticing for a while that Fiona was no longer a child, that before her eyes she was transforming into a truly beautiful creature. Yet Lareina also knew that too much beauty could be a dangerous thing, and that often it was best to be just on the pretty side of plain. The pretty side of plain was no longer an option for Fiona, however, and now more than ever, Lareina wanted to keep the girl in her sights.

"I don't think they like me," Fiona said, staring into the fireplace, her eyes dancing along with the flames.

"They will once they get to know you."

"I'm not so sure. They look at me like I'm an infection," she said.

"You must be imagining things," Lareina said, massaging her stepdaughter's shoulders. "We will grow to like it here. I promise you. We just need to settle in."

"I'm afraid," Fiona said without really meaning to. Sometimes when she was with her stepmother, her heart opened up and unexpected things came spilling forth, things she herself did not know that she felt.

"Shhh, now," Lareina whispered. "Everything will be okay. You'll see." And sitting there by the warmth of the fire, gazing out the window and through the veil of snow, both believed that it just might be true.

† † †

That afternoon, Tom and Rowan walked south through the woods to Seelie Lake. *Wolves be damned,* she'd declared, setting off through the trees. When they reached the edge of the frozen lake, he and Rowan lay on their backs atop the cold rocks that stretched along the icy banks, and stared up at the clouds. Crows were gathering up in the branches of a high-reaching pine, and Tom couldn't help wondering if the birds were watching them as they seemed to watch all the forest creatures. If there really was a wolf about, the crows would know. Would the birds give them warning, he wondered? Or would they watch the humans be slaughtered on the shores of the lake?

"What did they look like? The men who died on the mountain?" Rowan asked, as if reading his thoughts.

"Oh, that," he said, cringing at the memory. "It was awful, Rowan. You don't need to hear it."

"Sometimes you can be so tiresome," she said, hitting him gently on the shoulder.

"I'm protective."

"You don't need to protect me," she laughed. "I'm older than you."

"By three months."

"A lot happened in those three months, Tom," she said, turning to face him, her clear blue eyes squinting at him through pale lashes. "I didn't want to tell you this before, but a lot of secrets were divulged. I was inducted into some really high-ranking societies, stuff you'll never

48

understand." Her lips quivered as she suppressed her laughter.

"Is that so?" Tom laughed. "This explains why you so often need me to point out when you've failed to twin your stockings," he said, pointing to her mismatched pair.

"Mine is a life of the mind," she proclaimed, making a grand gesture with her arms. "Let others worry about my feet! Now, please, Tom. My curiosity is killing me. Tell me about Beggar's Drift."

Tom's eyes grew dark. "Ro," he said. "What I saw up there, I don't know how to explain it. It's a bad place, everyone knows that, but if you could have seen that man . . . his eyes, his tongue—they were gone, torn from him. What could do a thing like that?"

Rowan cocked her head to the side. "But everyone's been saying it was a wolf. That doesn't sound like the work of a wolf."

Tom nodded, relieved to hear her speak aloud what had been troubling him. "That's what I thought. It seemed to me that it was something . . . beyond wild animals, but no one wanted to hear it."

"Something beyond? What do you mean?"

"I don't know exactly—something not born of the Goddess; something not of this realm."

"Forest things, then?" Rowan asked, trying to keep an open mind. "Goblins and the like?"

He shook his head. "I didn't get that impression."

"Well, what impression did you get?"

He thought for a moment, and staring out at the icy

expanse, he chose his words carefully. "Evil," he said. "All around me up there, I felt the presence of evil."

Rowan's features were knotted with concern. "Have you spoken with an elder about it?"

He sighed. "No one would listen. It's as if everyone wants to blame it on a wolf because although we fear wolves, we understand their ways. But whatever happened up there is beyond comprehension. It was something wicked, Ro, and I think the elders know it. Paer Jorgen was with us, and I think that what we saw up there, it scared him—scared him so much that they're lying to us about the danger."

Rowan shivered at Tom's words. She didn't know what to make of his theories, but it was clear that his experience up on Beggar's Drift had frightened him more than she'd ever seen him frightened. "But what do you think, Tom? What do you think killed them?"

He shook his head. "I don't know. But there's a reason no one goes up to Beggar's Drift. Whatever's up there, it's not the same as the forest things down here. It's like the land—icy and foul."

"You're talking as if you saw something."

"No," he said, shaking his head, his eyes distant. "No, it wasn't what I saw; it was what I felt. It's bad land up there." He ran his hands through his hair and shut his eyes as if to close them against the memory. "Tell me something, Ro. Tell me something good."

"What do you mean?" she asked, wanting to help him but not knowing how.

"I don't want to think about that place anymore." He sighed. "Tell me something silly and sweet and mundane."

She bit her lip, searching, and then raised her eyebrows. "Well, I think our Emily's going to marry Bill Holdren," she said.

"That's good news. Bill's a nice fellow."

"Yes, he's nice. That's not the point. I don't want him to take my Emily away."

"It's time enough," Tom said, starting to feel more like himself. "She's getting on twenty."

"But what will I ever do without her?" Rowan whined.

"More housework, I suppose." He laughed. "Those little scholar hands of yours might actually get a callus or two."

"I do housework," she snapped, feigning outrage.

"Chatting to Emily while she does housework is not in itself housework."

She stuck her tongue out at him, and he laughed. "Perhaps I'll leave."

"And go where?" he asked, surprised.

"The palace city," she said, sitting up. "I'd love to see it, to meet all the different sorts of people who live there."

"Aw, Ro," he said, gazing at her with pride. "They'd be lucky to have you. Anyone would."

"So let's do it, then. Let's run away."

"You must be joking." He snorted at the idea. "I'm never leaving Nag's End."

"You don't even dream about it, about seeing far-off lands?" Rowan asked, trying to keep the disappointment from her voice.

"Nag's End is good enough for my father, and it's good enough for me." Pushing himself up to sit beside her, he stared at the sky a moment, as if pondering something wondrous. "Rowan," he said, "do you think it possible to love someone upon first laying eyes on them?"

Rowan sighed and pulled her knees to her chest. The idea of love made her nervous, and she and Tom never discussed it. "Well, the poets certainly thought it so," she said, drawing on her scholarship, as she always did when she felt unsure of herself. "If they're to be believed, a woman's eyes can know a future lover upon seeing him, and if the man sees the fire in those eyes, sees himself there, then he can fall in love before they've even spoken a word."

"But what do *you* think?" he asked, a fervor in his voice. "Do you think it's possible?"

She considered this, furrowing her brow. "I don't know. I suppose I like the idea of some part of our bodies knowing and recognizing our futures even if our minds cannot. That appeals to me. But no," she said, shaking her head. "I don't think it possible."

"You don't?" he laughed. "Really? If your future husband came riding into the village one day, you don't think you'd recognize him immediately?"

Rowan shook her head. "I don't think that's how it works."

"How does it work, then?"

She was silent for a moment as she tried to untangle what she thought from what she felt. "I think in order to love someone, you must know their heart. You need to witness their goodness, and you can't know something like that unless you've known someone for a while. I think familiarity breeds love."

"That's not very romantic of you," he laughed.

"Isn't it?" she wondered. "I think there's something charming about couples who grow to love each other as they get to know each other. Why, didn't you tell me that your parents only married because their own parents wanted to merge families? Presumably they didn't love each other at the beginning, but now I imagine they feel all the more proud of their love because it wasn't easy to come by. It was something they worked at."

Tom snickered. "You can imagine all you want, Ro, but I find it highly unlikely that my parents love each other even now."

"No," she said, mildly troubled. "They love each other."

"They're familiar with each other. There's a difference. I'm talking about love, grand love—that thing that makes your chest feel like it's about to explode, that makes you feel like your knees are about to give way, that certainty that you've seen the essence of your future in a pair of red lips."

Rowan sighed. "Tom, beauty isn't the same thing as goodness; it isn't the same thing as love."

Tom smiled slyly. "Ro, just because you haven't experienced it doesn't mean it doesn't exist."

Rowan was growing increasingly uncomfortable. "You needn't play games, Tom. We both know you're talking about Fiona Eira. You might as well call her by name. But you haven't even met her—you've only seen her once. You're delusional if you think you know her."

"But my heart knows her," he said, not to be dissuaded. "She is my future. When I looked in her eyes, I saw my birth, my death, everything in between, as if knowing her so intimately in the future means that I already know her now."

Rowan noticed an unfamiliar tension in her shoulders. In their relationship, she was the one used to having the answers. She was the one who explained things to Tom, but here he was so confident, explaining things to her as if she were a child. She didn't like it.

"Tom," she said. "I know you want me to make the introduction. I know that's what you're getting at, but you'll have to ask another girl. My father doesn't want me speaking to her, remember? Can't your mother do it?"

"My mother won't do that, and you know it," he said. "She already thinks poorly of the glassblower. And besides, sometimes I'm not sure my mother is fond of the idea of me ever taking a wife, especially not . . ."

"Such a pretty one?" Rowan finished what Tom seemed unable to say.

Tom nodded. "The pretty ones are always ill tempered. I've heard her say it fifty times if I've heard her say it once."

"Let me guess, the lovely harlots are for Jude. You're meant for a dull girl with big cow eyes who knows her way around a broom."

"Exactly," he laughed, and then he reached out for her, placing a hand on her arm. "Ro, you have to help me."

She bit her lip and exhaled a long, painful sigh. "Fine," she said.

Hearing the words was like a cure-all. He sat up and took her tiny hands in his, unable to keep what he knew was a very stupid grin from his face. "Are you sure?"

She nodded. "I promised my father, but you going on and on about your one true love is beginning to nauseate me. I'll do it, but on two conditions."

"Anything."

"One, my father can never know that I disobeyed him."

"I'll not tell a soul," he said, a hand to his heart.

"And two," she said, grinning, "you must stop being so sentimental. It's making me sick."

"Oh, Rowan," Tom said, hugging her. "A person could not have a better friend than you."

She laughed and pushed him away. "What did I say about being sentimental? I'll go tomorrow, okay? And then I'll report back to you."

Tom squeezed her hands and looked deep into her eyes. "I don't know what I'd ever do without you," he said, and she laughed and pulled away, focusing her attention back on the frozen lake.

"I can't wait until we can swim again," she said. "Sometimes winter seems interminable."

He nodded, his mind drifting to the countless days they'd spent together in the lake as children, and he wondered if those would be able to continue now that they were grown. There was a game they used to play. His grandmother said that when she was a girl, water nixies had lived in the caves under Seelie Lake. They were fierce creatures, she said, that no one ever saw because they only came out at night. But, she insisted, were a man to go swimming by the light of the moon, the nixies would tear his flesh from his bones. Tom had told Rowan, and the game had been born. With the sun high in the sky, they would take turns swimming out to just above what they'd decided was the nixies' cave, and lingering there, they would try to count to ten before swimming back to safety. Tom knew the nixies were no more than a tall tale told to frighten children, but when he was alone in the frigid water, that knowledge did nothing to still his fear.

He would feel it start at his toes, and then slowly it would creep up his foot until it felt like an icy hand grasping the base of his ankle, sliding up, and soon he would start to lose his breath. Gasping for air, imagining a horrifying underwater death, he would propel himself up and out of the water, flailing and desperate to get to shore, convinced that the sharp teeth of the nixies were within severing distance of his feet. Consumed with horror, he would plunge farther and deeper into the water, as if this would somehow help him to clear the distance more quickly, when what was really needed was a light and steady stroke along the surface. But sometimes when you want something so badly that you will do anything to get it, a light touch simply isn't possible.

It was only upon seeing Rowan's calm face, her absolute certainty that he would make it, that he was able to steady himself and swim the rest of the way to the rocky shore. Sometimes he felt sure that had he attempted the same feat alone, he would have drowned. But the faith in Rowan's eyes had always been there to save him. Sometimes it still felt like that. And sometimes those days felt very far away to Tom. Nothing had actually changed since the previous summer, and yet he had a sense that their swims together might never happen again. It was almost as if they were perched on the edge of a precipice, and at any moment, one of them might simply slip off and disappear.

4. THE LOVERS

SEAMUS FLINT SAT in the corner of his workshop, an ache gnawing at his belly. He looked over the pieces he'd made since coming to Nag's End. They were good. He was skilled, and his work filled him with pride, but he knew that however much his pieces might fetch, it would never be enough. The money he owed was more than he would ever be able to make on his own, and there was only so long he could hide before collection time was nigh and the wolves were at the door.

When he'd conceived of the move, Nag's End had seemed the perfect destination. Nag's End was a forgotten place. It was difficult to reach and contained nothing of interest to an outsider. It would be at least a year's time before anyone would be able to locate him.

And then there was Henry Rose. Nag's End hadn't been chosen simply for its wild mountain beauty. Henry Rose was a rich man, a very rich man who ought to take pity on his orphaned niece. Goi Flint hadn't counted on the man being so unkind.

He rubbed his thumbs together as he thought. Fiona was his only hope. If she could make contact with Henry Rose or that mousy runt of his, then maybe the man might be made to see reason. There was still a way, he told himself, the sweat beading on his brow. There was still a way.

Rowan stood at the forest edge, watching Fiona Eira's house. She wanted to speak to the girl, but she knew she couldn't simply knock on the door. She could perhaps trust her cousin to keep a secret, but her parents were a different matter. Goi Flint did not seem a particularly warm man; instinct told her to avoid him. She knew this much as one knows to put on a coat when the wind begins to bite. And so she watched from behind a tree for nearly a quarter of an hour, carving her initials into the bark with a hunting knife. She had just begun to tire and was nearly about to give up when the door creaked open and Fiona poked her head out. Rowan noticed that her cousin appeared much less confident than she had originally thought. There seemed something frightened about her, something injured. Presumably that was what Tom sensed in her. Boys loved beautiful, frightened things. They loved to play the rescuer.

Fiona wore a red dress and a matching cloak, and her hair was pulled back in an intricate plait that showed not a single deviation from midnight. She carried a basket with her, a white cloth draped over its contents, and she glanced over her shoulder, back at the cottage, as if she were afraid not of something without, but of something within.

When Fiona chose the long wending path on the outskirts of the village, rather than the more direct route, Rowan saw her chance. She followed a few paces behind her cousin. Any mountain girl worth her salt would have known she was being tracked, but perhaps being a child of the sea made you careless. Presumably, on wide-open beaches, there was little to fear and few places to hide.

Rowan followed her cousin, watching the rich red of her cloak drag along behind her. It wasn't until Rowan grew impatient with the girl's lack of awareness that she allowed herself to relax enough to step on a twig. The snap finally pulled Fiona out of her reverie.

"Who goes there?" she yelped, startling like a frightened animal.

Rowan held out her hand to the girl, as she would to a wild thing—as if offering her scent would ease the tension—but the girl took a step away.

"I thought we might talk," Rowan said carefully. "May I walk with you?"

Fiona appeared to think the request over for a moment,

and then she nodded, more to herself than to Rowan. "I'm going to the square. I suppose we can go into town together."

Rowan shook her head. "I'll walk you partway there, but I can't go into the square with you."

Timidity turned to suspicion in Fiona's eyes. She cocked her head to one side. "Why not?"

"It's difficult to explain." Rowan smiled warmly at her cousin, to reassure her. "My father, he doesn't want me to speak with you. We can't be seen together."

The girl nodded, though she maintained her distance, and Rowan took a step closer. She moved to speak but found she could not do so. Up close the girl was even more lovely than she'd supposed, and there was something else. There was something about her features that Rowan recognized. And then she realized that it was her own features made more obvious—lengthened and plumped, opened up for the world to see, whereas Rowan had always felt that any loveliness she might possess was apt to fold in on itself, like a house boarded up for a winter storm.

"Why are you staring at me?" Fiona said finally.

"We look so alike, you and I."

"We are cousins," Fiona said, a blush rising in her cheek.

"So we are," Rowan said gently.

"But almost opposites," the girl said, now taking a closer look. "Even in our dress."

And it was true. Standing there in the snow, one raven-haired beauty wrapped entirely in crimson and one pale-haired sparrow of a girl swathed in white.

"We must look like a tragedy," Fiona said.

"What?" Rowan asked, taken aback.

"We must look like blood in snow. That's all I meant." And she shook her head, clearly unsure of herself. "I'm not smart," she said, beginning the walk toward the square.

"You oughtn't say such things," Rowan scolded, following the girl. "You seem smart enough to me. You shouldn't speak of yourself so, or others will start to believe it."

"It's true, though," Fiona said, keeping her cousin in her periphery. "People have always said it about me—*At least she's pretty. At least she has that.* And I do." She lifted her chin as if daring Rowan to defy her, to say that she was not, in fact, pretty.

Rowan smiled, charmed by the girl despite herself. "I'll not argue with that, but you could be both."

Fiona shrugged and stared at her cousin. "You're not like other girls I've met."

"I'm going to be a scholar," Rowan said proudly.

"You can read, then?" Fiona asked, astonished, for kingdom-wide it was exceedingly rare for a girl to be taught to read.

Rowan nodded. "In several languages."

Fiona furrowed her brow, and then her eyes grew wide as if some aspect of the world had suddenly clarified for her. "Do you think you could teach me?"

"Sure. It would be fun. You could come round to my house, and I could give you lessons."

"Really? You'd do that?" she asked, hope shimmering behind her black eyes.

"Sure. Only . . ." Rowan grew quiet as she remembered. "My father . . ."

"Why won't your father acknowledge me?" Fiona said, her excitement quickly replaced with hostility.

"I don't think it's you he wishes to avoid. I think it's your stepmother's new husband."

"But I am his brother's child, am I not?"

Rowan stopped and stared through the snow at her cousin. "But you can't be. You are my mother's brother's child."

"Are you saying I'm a liar?" the girl asked, fists balled at her sides, scarlet blooming in her cheeks.

"I'm just being logical. They can't have been brothers," Rowan said gently. "We have different names. You are an Eira and I am a Rose. Surely if they were brothers, they would have the same family name."

Fiona nodded and then grew shy again.

"It's a lovely name, Eira," Rowan continued, trying to lure her back out.

"Thank you." Fiona smiled. "It means 'snow.' Rose is quite nice too."

"Thank you. It means . . . well, it means 'rose,'" Rowan said, laughing at her obtuseness, and soon Fiona was laughing too.

Fiona shook her head. "Well, whatever your father's reasons might be, I wish he would see to it to change his mind."

"So do I," said Rowan.

Fiona now looked at her cousin, regarding her with an air of great seriousness. "If your father has forbidden you to talk to me, what are you doing here now?"

Rowan bowed her head. "I have a friend who wants to meet you. He wants an introduction."

The girl smiled to herself, and Rowan wondered how it would feel to be so completely confident of your own beauty.

"I know the boy," she said.

"You do?"

"Yes," Fiona said, walking again. "There are two brothers. They were both watching me. One was quite beautiful, but he wasn't interested in me."

"He wasn't?"

"No. He has other interests. It was the other one. He was less handsome, but he had a kind way about him. A little awkward, maybe, but special."

"Tom's not awkward," Rowan said, barely able to contain her shock at her cousin's vanity. "He's the best thing this village has to offer by a long shot."

The girl paused for a moment, a small grin forming on her lips. "You might be right," she said after a while. "You say he wants to meet me?"

"He does."

"And you're to arrange it?"

Rowan nodded.

"Well, if my own cousin is to arrange it," she said, a big, beautiful smile illuminating her face, "then how can I refuse?"

"Shall he come round to your cottage?" Rowan asked.

Fiona grew quiet for a moment, as if she were concentrating, trying to come up with the right answer. Finally, she shook her head. "No. He can't come by the cottage. That won't work at all. I will meet him here. Tomorrow. Do you think that will work?"

Rowan nodded. "I'll arrange for it. Can you meet him here tomorrow at this same time?" she asked, and Fiona agreed.

The two girls stayed a moment longer, staring into each other's eyes. And now it was Fiona's turn to sense something strange between them.

"You know," she said, "there's something so familiar about you. It's as if I've always known you. Tomorrow will you come too?"

The idea of seeing Tom and Fiona together caused a sudden painful constriction across Rowan's chest, and she began to wonder if she might be making a terrible mistake. She shook her head. "No. I know that would be customary, but I have other commitments."

"I see," Fiona said, not bothering to hide her disappointment.

And though Rowan could tell that this girl, so cold only moments before, wanted her to stay, wanted to talk with her, to make some sort of connection, she knew she couldn't let herself befriend her.

"Tomorrow, then," Rowan said, and turning, she made her way back down the path, her cousin, cloaked in cherry and crimson-lipped, watching as she went.

Back at home, Rowan found Emily busily preparing her mother's old wing for guests.

"Who's coming?" she asked, but Emily just raised her hands and shook her head.

"He's not telling me a thing. He seems very anxious that everything be perfect. He says he even wants Pema kept in the kennel while they're here."

"What?" Rowan was shocked. "No. It's too cold for her out there."

"That's what I said, and he nearly snapped my head off. He says she can't stay in my room because it's too close to the guests, and he fears she'll disturb them. You'd better talk to him yourself if you want something done about it."

"Where is Pema now?"

Emily put her hand on her hip, her eyes wide, revealing how ridiculous she felt the whole thing was. "I had to chain her up out there, didn't I? I didn't want to. I warmed some towels for her, but I still don't think it's a good idea. Like I said, he's not going to listen to me. You go talk to him."

Rowan took the back stairs two at a time and, running through the kitchen and out to the kennel, she wrenched open the door. Pema lay shivering on the cold ground. Emily had done her best to try to keep the dog warm. She'd put down towels like she'd said, but Pema had bunched them up at the edge of the cage, and she lay shivering at the other end. When she saw Rowan, she scrambled to her feet and bounded over to the girl, licking her hands and putting her paws on Rowan's shoulders, though Henry Rose usually scolded her for doing that.

"Come on, girl," Rowan said, leading her back into the

house. The dog scrambled off, bounding up the stairs, presumably to the comfort of Emily's bed, and Rowan headed down the hall to her father's office.

She pushed open the door without knocking, startling Henry Rose, who quickly shut his book and slid something into his top drawer.

"Rowan," he said, trying to hide his shock at having been interrupted.

"I should have knocked," she said, taking a step back. "I'm sorry I didn't. I wasn't thinking, I suppose. I was so upset, you see."

Her father stood, alarmed. "What's wrong, my child?"

"I've found Pema out in the kennel, although it's clearly too cold for her to be there."

"Is it?" he asked, seeming genuinely surprised. "I had Emily put her out there. Don't be cross with her. It was at my bidding."

"The fact remains that she can't stay out there. She can stay in my room. I'll keep her in there if you want while your guests are here."

Henry Rose stroked his chin. He was nervous, she realized. Rowan wasn't sure she'd ever seen him nervous before. "Mmm. I see. Yes, I suppose that would work. I'm sorry for not taking the weather into account. I have been distracted, what with the guests coming."

Rowan cocked her head. "Who are they, Father? Who is coming?"

He smiled, though the tension did not drain from his face. "You mean, you haven't heard already? I thought it would be all over the village by now. Why, the duke himself is coming."

"The queen's brother?" Rowan asked, unable to keep the surprise from her voice, for Nag's End had never hosted anyone of such high stature. "Coming here? But why?"

"I invited him. You will remember that he is not just the queen's brother. He is also the king's conservateur. He was eager to discuss some of the work I sent him, and when he heard about the death of the king's soldiers, he offered to come to Nag's End and serve as royal representative."

"But why is he staying with us?"

"Where else is he going to stay? At the inn?" her father laughed, unable to keep the unkind note from his voice. "No, ours is the only home fit for a member of the royal family. They will be staying with us."

"They?"

"Yes," he said, stacking some papers. "His ward is accompanying him. It seems Nag's End is to serve as a geography lesson of sorts. She's eleven—a little young for you, I know, but perhaps she'll be a friend nonetheless. We'll have to keep her occupied while she's here."

"When will they be arriving?"

"Late this evening, I expect. I will meet with him first thing in the morning, and I'm told the girl will need to rest in, so it is best if you keep yourself occupied tomorrow. Go early to the market, will you?"

Rowan nodded, smiling at the thought of a young guest.

"And tell Emily no listening at doors. Better yet, give her the day off. She can go visit with that boy of hers . . . Bill."

"I'll tell her. Oh, Father, how exciting this all is!" Rowan could barely keep herself from clapping like a child.

"Yes," he said, his voice straining. "Yes, it is that." And then he returned to stacking his papers, already occupied with plans for the morrow.

Rowan could hardly contain herself as she bounded up the stairs to her room. The duke conservateur coming here to Nag's End. She could hardly believe it. Rowan felt excitement building in her chest. The queen's brother in their house! And his ward as well! The idea of having the younger houseguest thrilled her. She had always wanted a little sister, someone to comfort and to guide. Since she was small, she had, in fact, always felt that something was missing from her life, as if she were constantly reaching for someone who wasn't there.

After retrieving Pema's food and water, she headed to her room to make a space for the dog up there, and then set herself up at her desk and began on her next stack of translations. She'd meant only to work for a short while, but time had a habit of slipping away from her, and when she happened to glance up again, she saw the dying of the light and realized that she had yet to speak with Tom. After putting away her papers, she took the stairs two at a time, but as she slipped on her cloak, she found her heart suddenly heavy with the task at hand. She had a suspicion that this meeting she had arranged between Tom and Fiona might mean losing Tom forever, and yet she knew she couldn't bring herself to deny him his happiness.

"Where do you think you're going?" Emily called as Rowan started out the door.

"Over to the inn."

"At this hour?" Emily raised her eyebrows and tucked her chin in disapproval.

"I'll be back soon," Rowan said, rolling her eyes.

"Don't stray from that path," Emily said. She turned then, and before sauntering back to the kitchen, she added, "This close to dark, forest things'll snatch a girl before you can say *crow's eyes.*"

† † †

Jude sat on the stairs listening to the men talk. When his father had seen the elders approaching, he had closed the place down and sent the boys out on errands, but Jude did not go. Instead, he waited for Tom to leave and then settled in on the back stairs high up enough that he might be hidden in the shadows and yet still see all below. He did not consider his father a smart man, but he was a good man, and Jude distrusted the elders.

Paer Jorgen, who was the most senior of the elders, stroked his beard and looked at his fellows.

"As we told you earlier, Goi Parstle, we are concerned about the safety of your clan. We have consulted the bones, and we have conferred with the witches, and there seems to be a darkness over this house."

"What?" Jude's father said, taken aback. "But mine is an honest house."

"We know this. It is why we've come here to speak with you this evening. We fear the impending visit from the duke. We worry for you."

"But why me? What does the duke have to do with me?"

Paer Jorgen nodded. "Only that he is coming here to look into the deaths of those soldiers up on Beggar's Drift, and our oracles point to something evil within our village, here, of all places, at your inn."

"But I have committed no crime."

Ollen Bittern cleared his throat. "You must understand, we know that none in your house is guilty of any crime, but we feel the need to warn you that every oracle we consulted seemed to refer us back to this house."

Wilhelm's voice shook when he spoke again. "What does Mama Lune say? Surely she must know my house is clean."

"Not exactly," Paer Jorgen said. "She held that you were a good man, and that it was unlikely you'd have done any wrong, and yet she sensed it too—something within these walls, something wicked. We worry that the duke may launch a formal death inquiry, and if he does, I fear we will have to tell him what our oracles have seen. Whether he accepts oracular truth or not, it is our way to let it be known—we are compelled to display the evidence."

From the darkness of the stairs, Jude saw what his father refused to see. If the oracles said there was something base beneath their roof, then perhaps there was, but that didn't have to mean it concerned their family. Theirs was a public place, a tavern frequented by all in the village. Perhaps there was an evil in their home, but if there was, it was a *visitor* to their hall, not a family member. He decided that from now on he must keep an eye on the door, and an ear to the ground.

Wilhelm Parstle swallowed, and when he spoke, his voice quavered with anger. "Are you implying that I, or one of my boys . . . that we murdered those soldiers?"

"Of course not. The very idea that we are looking for a man is absurd," said Paer Jorgen, unable to keep the disdain from his voice. "I was up on that mountain. I saw those poor souls. There's not a man alive capable of such brutality. It was the work of an animal—I'll not hear any different."

Ollen Bittern nodded. "We do not doubt you. We only tell you that the bones led us to your door."

"Well." Wilhelm sighed and ran a hand through his thick hair. "What do you suggest we do?"

"For now we do nothing. Perhaps the duke will make a quick assessment of mauling and exposure, respectively, and be on his way. This is what we hope," said Draeden Faez. "But we are pleading with you. If you, or anyone in this house, know what it is that the oracle points to, then we beg you to speak up. All of our lives are at risk."

Wilhelm nodded. "I will ask my boys about it, but I'm sure neither of them will know."

Jude had heard enough. He stood, and making barely a noise, he descended from his hiding place and left through the back door, the cold night air pulsing against his lips.

Snow was falling steadily as Rowan walked over to the tavern, and the hollowness of her heart did little to protect her from the cold.

Shivering, she tried the tavern door but found it locked,

which was unusual for suppertime. She peered in the window, but all was dark inside. Walking round the back, she heard someone cough and she froze. It was Jude's cough—she would know it anywhere. Years ago she'd learned to recognize any signs that Jude might be nearby. He was a year older than she was, but she was so small that he'd always seemed much older than that to her, and while she knew he was harmless, there was something vaguely frightening to her about that sly smile he always wore when he looked off into the distance as if she weren't there. If it had simply been that he ignored her, that would have been fine, but he didn't ignore her—no matter what he might pretend—because he always seemed to know things about her that no one else did.

When she rounded the corner, she saw him sitting on the low stone wall at the edge of the forest. He was carving something, his hair falling over his eyes.

"The tavern's locked," he said without looking up. "Father's in a meeting. He should open it again soon, I'd imagine."

As usual, her heart stopped when she saw him. There was no denying that Jude was handsome, but she didn't understand him, and something about him always made her nervous.

"That dress doesn't fit you," he continued, his eyes still on his work. She could see that he was smiling.

"Yes, it does," she said, trying not to stumble over her words.

"Look at you, you're swimming in it."

"It's none of your business how my dress fits," she said, unable to disguise her irritation.

He shrugged, still not looking at her. "I'm just trying to be helpful."

"Thanks, Jude. You're always so helpful. Is Tom around?"

"He'll be back soon," Jude answered. "He went to drop some things off to the Widow Bardell."

Rowan stood there, not knowing what to do with herself. The inn was practically her home, but she never knew how to hold herself around Jude.

"Do you mind if I wait here?" she said, feeling an idiot for asking, weak for not demanding her place.

"Suit yourself," he said, still focused on his whittling, the knife sliding slowly down the length of the wood.

She walked to the edge of the wall and sat down as far from Jude as she could.

"You have news, then?" he asked.

"Excuse me?"

"For Tom," Jude said. "You have news, I can tell. It's good news, I presume."

"I don't know what you're talking about."

"Sure you do. Fiona Eira, the girl he can't stop talking about. You've been to see her."

"How do you know that?" she asked, wary.

"Because there's something different about you," he said, still refusing to look at her, as if she didn't merit his attention. "You're sad. You're never sad. And you would only be sad if you'd been to see her and you had good news for Tom."

She stood up, her body feeling suddenly frail, as if she

74

were composed of only brittle bones and weak tendons ready to snap at a single blow from Jude.

"I'm not sad," she said. "And I don't look different. How would you even know when you've refused to so much as look at me?"

With that, he grinned and looked up at her, his heavy eyes lit with a boyish beauty. "Ah, Rowan. When will you ever learn?" Then he shook his head and went back to his work.

Staring at him, she felt rage burning in her chest. How was it that he could make her so angry? How was it that he always seemed to know how she felt without her saying a word? It was unfair. He had no right to her feelings. Her temper getting the better of her, she strode over to him, her hands clenched into fists, and took a single wretched swing at him. The force she'd put behind the blow was intense, but she never connected, for he caught her forearm gently in his hand, and looking deep into her eyes, he held her gaze.

"You're making a mistake," he said.

She wrenched her arm away from him and smoothed down the sleeve of her cloak.

"I don't know what you're talking about," she sneered, unwilling to let him see any more of her heart. "I've just come round to speak with Tom like I always do."

"Why? Why are you trying to marry him off? Surely that can't be in your best interest."

"Jude, you're not making any sense," she said, changing tack and feigning concern. "Have you been at your mother's ale again?"

"No, I'm just observant," he said, something like kindness in his eyes. Rowan recoiled at that more than she would have from a blow. Kindness from Jude was disorienting, and it could mean many things, but she was sure that sincerity wasn't one of them.

She took a step back but was unable to look away from him. His gaze seemed to pull her closer, to see deep within her. She wondered just how much he knew. "Why wouldn't I want Tom to marry?" she asked, testing him.

"Do you want me to say it?" He raised his eyebrows. "Out loud?"

She opened her mouth to speak but found that the words refused to come.

"I don't think you do," he said, and shaking his head, he broke eye contact and went back to his whittling. "I don't think you want me to say it."

She stood there, breathless. Her cheeks began to burn, and she started to feel that familiar dizziness that usually accompanied making the mistake of engaging with Jude at all. It was always the same. She knew he meant to make her uncomfortable, and that was the pain of it all. He always succeeded.

Turning on her heel, she walked away with short determined steps, all the while looking at her feet.

"Don't go," he said, and she could hear him stand up.

She turned, fighting back the tears, and saw him standing there, arms out to the sides, something like regret in his eyes.

"Rowan," he said. "I was only teasing. Don't act like that."

"Don't tell me how to behave. I will act how I want to act, and I will feel how I want to feel."

"Don't go," he said, his voice cracking. "Listen, I'll go, okay? You can wait here for Tom."

He didn't wait for her reply. He climbed over the wall and walked away, slowly disappearing into the trees.

Rowan stood there a moment, watching Jude go, wondering how two brothers could be so completely different.

Then, as she always did when she was nervous, Rowan began to pace, slow steps, her small black boots sinking into the snow. She liked to count her steps . . . fourteen, fifteen, sixteen . . .

Somehow things didn't have to be so bad. It wasn't as if the world were ending or anything like that. Tom liked a girl and the girl liked him back. A beautiful girl, yes, a bewitching girl, true, but that didn't have to mean anything so bad. Maybe he would get to know Fiona, and he would find her tiresome.

Seventeen, eighteen, nineteen . . .

Or maybe he would marry her.

And then there was a snap, a crack far out among the trees, and she found herself slowly backing away from the forest edge, staring into the darkness therein with eyes that didn't want to see. Surely, she thought, it was only a rabbit or a deer, but maybe it wasn't the right time to tell Tom after all. She found herself moving quickly out of the empty yard, back toward the sound of drunken voices on the other side of the inn. Soon she was out in the open again, Joel Proudy and Sarah Unger up ahead, laughing and smoking pipes. Rowan's shoulders, which she hadn't realized she'd been holding high and tensed, relaxed, and she fell into a comfortable stride, hoping the nascent and unexpected fear did not show on her face. Yes, Tom could wait. It was best to get home. It was best to get indoors.

5. THE MAGICIAN

IN THE MORNING when Rowan awoke, she sensed that the house was more full. There were extra noises, different smells. The duke must have arrived in the night, she realized. Market Day was Rowan's favorite day of the week, and there was a bounce in her step as she dressed herself and went downstairs.

As she walked down the hall, she could hear the quiet muffle of voices behind closed doors. She wanted to stay and introduce herself, but her father had told her to head straight to market in the morning. When she passed his office, she thought she could hear her father raise his voice. That gave her pause, and she considered listening at the door, but she wasn't a dishonest girl, and besides, she was eager to head out.

On Market Day, all the mountain folk of the smaller neighboring villages gathered in Nag's End to sell their wares, and to buy and trade with others. It was always a festive time, and since it was the main opportunity for young people to socialize, the girls tended to fix their hair and the boys tended to wear their finest clothes, while their parents did their best to push them off in agreeable directions. But Rowan had no interest in courtship, so she never bothered to dress up for the day or to plait a purple ribbon into her hair to display her maidenhood, not even to dab smudge grass behind her ears, as was the custom among girls of a marriageable age.

When she headed out her door and through the gate, she could already hear the market in full swing. Mountain folk were enthusiastic, if not especially gifted, musicians, and the air always filled with song at their gatherings.

When she came upon the market, her eyes searched for Tom, as they always did, but he was nowhere. She made her way through the stalls, and waving to friends, she tried to be cheered by their goodwill, but something started to overcome her, a strange sense of foreboding. She told herself that it was all due to the growing darkness of the sky and the sudden chill that whipped through the air, but she knew that couldn't be it. She felt very much as if she was being watched, and though she did her best to calm herself, she was growing increasingly uneasy as she moved through the stalls.

She leaned against a pole and tried to talk herself down from her bizarre flight of fancy. Surely no one could be watching her. She was not a girl whom people watched. But turning around, she noticed a woman staring at her from several stalls away, and quickly her fear turned to curiosity.

The woman was like none other she'd ever seen. Her skin was as dark as a winter storm, and her beauty alone would have caused her to stand out, but her height was so extreme as to be aberrant. She was taller than any man in Nag's End, and her ebony hair was piled on top of her head like a crown, white feathers and jewels woven throughout. Her gown, blue as the sky and made from exotic finery, gave the impression of royalty. It hung on the woman's frame as if it were made of cloud dust, falling from her high neck straight down to the dirt as if it had a life of its own. Yes, she looked very much like a queen, and for a moment, Rowan wondered if she might be part of the duke's retinue. She stared at Rowan like she knew her, and Rowan cocked her head as if to ask if she should know her as well, but the woman shook her head and smiled. It was a sweet smile, an inviting smile, and Rowan realized that she very much wanted to speak with this woman, whoever she was. But just then, Mama Lune came to stand next to the beautiful queen.

Rowan's father was certain that all witches were charlatans, and while Rowan agreed with him, she could not deny that there was something different about Mama Lune. No one knew how old she was, but physically she seemed to linger in the prime of her womanhood. Henry Rose attributed this peculiarity to some herb she must eat—something that grew deeper in the forest and which she fed on out of vanity. Whatever herbs the Greenwitches used, he reasoned, most likely could be used by a man with similar efficacy, but witches kept such secrets to themselves, using them as sources of power. Give Dr. Temper the same twigs and leaves, her father was fond of saying, and he could no doubt work magic as well.

Mama Lune slid her arm through the stranger's. Pale, with deep red hair flowing wild to her waist, Mama Lune did not exactly conjure images of castles and courts. Her simple green dress and her threadbare slippers seemed out of place beside her friend's finery, and yet there existed an obvious sorority between them. Suddenly Rowan realized what she ought to have guessed right away: the beautiful stranger was a Bluewitch.

As a child, Rowan had learned all she could about the different kinds of witches. Greywitches—often called metal witches because of their penchant for collecting and hoarding silver—had been wicked creatures. When they'd thrived, they'd been the scourge of the land, but the other kinds of witches—the surviving witches—were relatively harmless. There were Redwitches, who drew their power from passion, and Woodwitches, who lived like sprites in small forest colonies, and of course, Greenwitches were the healers. The Greenwitches often lived in the forest just outside a village, limning the space between the tame and the wild, always a short trip away from the birthing women and the quietly dying but far enough from prying eyes. Of all the witches, the Bluewitches had been Rowan's favorite. Bluewitches were diviners, and water was their natural medium. Like water, they tended to ramble, wandering as the water beneath the ground did, ever flowing, ever moving. They were also known to be especially beautiful.

Rowan was certain that the lovely creature before her was a Bluewitch, and while the novelty of it excited her, she had to remind herself that the woman was still a witch, and witches functioned outside the laws of man. They followed their own religion, and their own codes, and the fact of it frightened Rowan.

The two women looked at each other and then seemed to make up their minds. Before they took even a step, Rowan knew they were coming to talk to her, and deciding she most definitely didn't want to talk to them, she turned and started back through the crowds, moving at a pace that was neither customary nor polite. Turning her head, she saw that the two women were gliding along behind her—the crowd parting for them as people called out greetings to the Greenwitch and her enchanting friend.

Rowan's breath caught, and she fought the sensation that was slowly creeping up her legs, grasping at her heart, starting to squeeze. She looked over her shoulder again. They were only a few paces behind her, walking with that light and steady gait. Rowan knew she needed to escape them, and she plunged through the crowd. And then she felt a finger brush her shoulder. Out of the corner of her eye, she could see green lacquered nails, and she knew that the hand belonged to Mama Lune. She ought to turn. It was rude not to do so, but her father had spent her entire life warning her about this woman. Alone, she found herself without her armor. She could feel the witch's teeth trained on her, and she could barely breathe.

An arm caught her from the side, and she let out a yelp. She looked up to see Tom, his gentle face awash with concern.

"Ro, are you okay? You look scared to death."

Rowan felt a material soft as bog moss brush against her, and out of the corner of her eye she could tell that it was sky blue. She could feel the two women pass her by, and then there with Tom holding her arm, she was brave enough to steal a glance.

They'd started off on the path that led through the forest to Mama Lune's house, their colorful gowns sweeping behind them. The Bluewitch stopped for a moment and seemed to be consulting a tree in the most peculiar way. Nodding, she came to a decision and snapped a small branch from the young tree—a dowsing rod, for those were the tools of a Bluewitch's trade—and, as if sensing Rowan, the Bluewitch turned and smiled, then looped her arm through Mama Lune's again, and they continued on their path. Soon they disappeared into the heart of the woods, as if the forest had swallowed them whole.

"Are you okay, Ro?" Tom asked again, shaking her gently, his voice concerned.

She blinked as if to clear her head, and looked up at him. "I'm fine. I just . . . something weird happened, or I don't really know what happened, I guess."

Tom took her shoulders in his hands. "Do you need to sit down?"

"No," she said, slowly returning to normal. "No, I'm fine. Really I am." And then, looking at his heavy winter coat, she laughed. "Haven't you packed that thing away for the season? We're not in the midst of a blizzard, Tom."

"Your problem is you're not dressed warmly enough," he teased. "The skies have taken a turn, and you chose not to heed it because you prefer yourself in your autumn cloak."

"At least I don't look like I'm being swallowed alive by a dog."

"It's called foresight, Rowan. I saw the signs of an approaching storm, and I went up to the attic and got out my heavy coat. I'd only just packed it away after the trek up to . . ." Rowan knew he was about to say "after the trek to Beggar's Drift," but he winced and cut himself short.

"Tom," Rowan said, pretending she hadn't noticed his discomfort, "do you know who that woman was, the one with Mama Lune?"

Tom shook his head. "A Bluewitch, looked like."

"She looks like royalty or something."

"She must have come for a visit."

Rowan nodded. It was common, she knew, for witches to visit one another, sometimes staying on for protracted lengths of time. A few years back, Mama Lune had been visited by a round bean of a woman called Mama Saltana. She had a taste for liquor and would spend full days at the tavern, laughing loudly, her stringy blond hair resting in her beer.

"Do you ever talk to her, Tom, to Mama Lune?" Rowan asked.

"Sure, sometimes. She comes round to the inn when travelers are too sick for Dr. Temper to help them."

"What's she like?"

"A little cold, maybe. Likes to keep her distance from the villagers, but knows her herbs. When Jude had the fever last year, when we thought we might lose him, Mama Lune saved his life."

"I remember that. He was terribly ill."

"We thought for sure he'd die. Dr. Temper even prepared us for it, but Mama Lune came and stayed with him, treating him round the clock with plasters and tinctures and potions, and soon enough, he was on the mend. Jude knows her better than most, I think. Seemed to me they kind of bonded while he was ill."

Rowan looked out into the woods again. "It's curious. I had a strange feeling that they wanted to speak with me. I'm probably just being silly."

"Not silly," he said, throwing his arm around her shoulder. "I think you're wonderful. By the way, Jude said you came by last night."

"Oh," she gasped. She'd nearly forgotten. "I've spoken with Fiona Eira, and she's agreed to meet with you."

Tom's face went blank, and he removed his arm from Rowan's shoulder. He stared at her like he was afraid she might be lying. "You're serious?"

"Yes, I'm serious," she said, her voice growing quiet. "I spoke with her yesterday afternoon. She wants to meet you along the path between your houses in only a few hours' time."

"Already?" he laughed. "You must be joking. That was too easy."

Rowan did her best to smile. "You can pay me back when I fall madly in love."

Tom nodded. "I'll be sure to." His expression turned solemn. "Rowan, is everything all right? You seem upset."

"No," she said, looking away. "I'm not upset. I'm still thinking about the witches is all."

"Oh, Rowan, I can't tell you what you've done for me." He took her hands in his own, smiling brightly. "Thank you, my friend. You are a goddess, a queen."

As he held Rowan's hands, she was surprised by the ambivalence in her heart. "Well," she said, removing herself from his grasp. "Please, don't make a fool of yourself. She is my cousin, after all."

Just then, she caught sight of Jude strolling toward them, his cocky head held a touch too high, a jaunty step to his stride, and she let out a sigh. When he met them, he gave Rowan a playful grin.

"Hi, Ro," he said, but she only stared back at him, refusing to answer. "Mind if I borrow my brother for a minute?"

She nodded, and Tom slapped her on the back and gave her a conspiratorial wink. The two boys set off together toward the inn, and Rowan watched them go. She turned and started on the path home, her heart heavy.

Tom was right—it was growing colder, and it seemed to Rowan that the sky might open up at any moment, but near the eastern outcropping of the Black Forest, she witnessed the sun making its final stand. Streaming through the pines in defiant shafts of light, it seemed almost to animate the snow cover in sudden, sparkling waves. Rowan was smiling at its persistence as she rounded the last bend on the way to her house when something caught her attention. Near the ground, in the eye of a tree, was what looked like a bird fashioned out of bright blue paper. Kneeling down, she retrieved it. It was indeed a piece of blue paper intricately folded to create a beautiful bird. So surprised was she by the oddity that she nearly replaced it in the trunk of the tree, thinking that someone had left it there for some purpose, and who was she to interfere? But something deep inside her called out, and she knew that the bird was meant for her, and that she ought to examine it further.

Sliding a finger under its beak, she flipped it open to find a message written inside.

Someday you come see me, mmm?
I have something you want.
Blessed be,
Mama Tetri

Unnerved, Rowan refolded the paper and placed it back into the tree. Yes, Mama Tetri was probably the Bluewitch, but she couldn't be sure the note was meant for her. It was probably some kind of trick that witches played. Leave something like that—a lure, really—in the woods and wait to see who bites. Then, when the poor imbecile shows up at the door, besotted and asking for love spells, the witch makes him pay through the nose. But Rowan was smarter than that. She gave the bird one final look and set off around the last bend to her home.

Tom tried to prepare, but he didn't know if he was going to be able to speak to such a beautiful girl without making a fool of himself. He wasn't accustomed to fear, but now he was on the edge of trembling with it. He wondered if it might be better to arrive later, to make sure she was there before he was, so that he might not look so eager. Such thoughts were foreign to him, and he found them unsettling.

Attributing his insecurities to his breakfast sitting wrong in his belly, Tom shook them off and set out. He took the scenic path that ran along the edge of the forest, moving with long, deliberate strides, unable to calm himself.

He saw her before she saw him. She was sitting on a tree stump, her red cloak pulled tight around her body, hood up and covering her hair. He walked over to her and extended his hand. But she didn't take it.

"Hi," she said, looking up at him with eyes that might have been carved from a dark and ancient wood. "My name's Fiona Eira."

"Yes," he said, trying to look away from her, trying not to stare, but finding himself unable not to. "I'm Tom. My parents run the inn."

"I know," she said, and when a smile spread across her lips, Tom was reminded of raspberry jam smeared on a white tablecloth.

"You do?"

"Yes, I've wanted to meet you since I saw you in the square," she said, a blush rushing to her cheeks. "You know my cousin, then," she added, standing up and beginning to walk. Tom fell into step alongside her.

"She's my oldest friend," Tom said. "My best friend."

"That must be nice. I don't know that I've ever had a friend who's a boy."

"You haven't? I'd imagine you'd have lots of friends."

"No boys," she said, cringing. "The boys in my village were horrid. Not like you at all."

"Well, you don't know me yet. I might be horrid as well."

She laughed and shook her head. "No. You're special. I can tell."

He noticed she was beginning to shiver. "Are you cold? Would you like my coat?"

He was in the process of taking it off when something fell from the pocket. Quick as a cat, she crouched down and snatched it up from the snow. It was the strange coin he'd found on the mountain. He'd forgotten about it completely, and seeing it again gave him a bad feeling.

"I'm not cold," she said, staring in wonder at the glinting object in her hand. "What is this? It's beautiful. I've never seen anything like it."

"I found it up on the mountain," Tom answered. "But I forgot about it. I put it in my pocket and packed my coat away up in the attic. I should probably give it to my father."

"Oh no, please," she said, stepping away from him, eyes wide. "Must you? I'd love to have it myself. I can make it into a necklace. I had to give away all of mine."

Tom felt himself sway beneath the power of her beauty. "Do you really like it?"

"I do. I really do." She smiled, and her eyes seemed to glitter as she gazed at him.

Tom blushed. "Well, if your heart is set on it, I suppose you can have it."

"Oh, thank you," she said, her lips seeming to grow more full as she spoke. He found himself suddenly dizzy from their beauty.

She pulled a red ribbon from her hair, and concentrating, she slipped it between two of the coin's center spokes.

"Will you tie it around my neck?" she asked, and as she handed him the coin, something passed between them, and both were certain they felt a strange kind of connection—a bond. She smiled at him and then turned around. Gently lifting her hair, he laced the red ribbon around her neck and tied it with careful fingers. The deed done, she turned back around, beaming, and looked up at him with the eyes of a fawn.

"Beautiful," he said. And it was.

Before Tom could realize what was happening, she put her lips to his cheek and quickly gave him a kiss. "Thank you," she whispered, and then slowly walked away.

Tom felt dizzy from the lingering energy of her lips on his skin as he watched her step off the forest path and cross the village barrier. Did she know where she was going, he wondered?

"We ought to turn back," he said, catching up to her.

"Why?" she asked, such innocence in her eyes that he

wanted with all his heart to protect her. To keep her safe. Always.

"They're saying there are wolves about," he answered.

"Wolves?" she laughed. "I'm not afraid of wolves."

"Well, you should be. Have you ever seen a wolf?"

"Of course not. We don't have wolves where I'm from."

She paused and sat down on a tree stump.

"No?" he said, relieved that she'd stopped walking. "What do you have where you're from?"

Placing her hands behind her, she leaned back, her head tilted to the sky. "We have birds."

"We have birds as well," he said, and unable to keep from smiling, he took a seat beside her.

She wrinkled her nose. "No, you don't have birds. You have great terrible flying things. Monsters. Black as soot, and mangy. We have real birds the color of lily pads, the color of sapphires. And their songs are beautiful. None of this yapping and yammering I hear from your winter birds."

"Yapping and yammering? That's the proper term, is it?"

"Yes." She nodded. "That is indeed the proper term. Oh, if you could only see our birds, the way they glide out over the sea. And the sea itself. It's a color . . . well, it's a color you don't even have here. It's a shade of purple that is only at my sea."

"Maybe someday I can see it," he said, and she smiled at him, a twinkle in her eye.

"Maybe someday you can."

And without thinking, he leaned in and kissed her on the cheek.

† † †

Not twenty yards away, Rowan leaned against a tree. Watching them. Watching him. Watching his lips touch her cousin's cheek as they would never touch her own. An unfamiliar sensation rising in her chest, she held a hand to her mouth as if to silence a scream, and soon hot tears streamed down her face, burning her cheeks, as if the very act of her heart breaking had turned her tears to acid. Unable to stop the flow, she backed away, suddenly aware that she was making enough noise that they ought to have noticed and seen her. But they did not. They were so absorbed in each other that she couldn't have made them realize she was there had she wanted to. And so she turned and ran, gasping for air as if the atmosphere could soothe the rupture in her chest.

† † †

When Tom came home that evening, it was immediately apparent that something was different about him. He seemed to bounce in the door, and the color in his cheeks was a brighter red than normal.

"You look like a little girl in love," Jude said, and his mother swatted him with a dish towel. He swerved out of her reach, ignoring her.

Tom brushed past him and moved into the kitchen to see what might need washing or chopping before supper, Jude on his heels.

"You've been to see her." Jude smiled, leaning in and feigning coquettish interest, batting his eyelashes. "Was she everything you hoped–everything you dreamed she would be?"

"You joke," Tom said, unable to contain his enthusiasm. "But she was all that and more. Once you talk to her, you'll see. She's amazing. Smart and funny, and . . . I can't explain it. Interesting, I suppose. She's not like girls around here."

Jude grew serious. "Are you going to ask her father for her twine, then? Do I smell a blessing wreath?"

"It's a bit soon for marriage, don't you think?" Tom said, although he barely believed the words himself.

"I don't know," Jude said, taking a bite of bread. "Mother is keen to marry one of us off, and it isn't going to be me."

"True," Tom laughed. "She wants a barmaid."

"So better this beauty of yours than one of the local girls."

Tom shrugged. "I've only just met her. I'll not be binding her wrist anytime soon. But I can tell you this. There is not a girl for a thousand miles who is fit to touch the hem of her garment. She is special. She is somehow more than a girl ought to be. I don't know. It's overwhelming."

"Well, I can't wait to meet her. You must bring her round for supper soon."

Tom nodded. "I will. I promise I will. As soon as it seems appropriate, I will have Father ask her family over, and we shall all break bread together."

"I'm happy for you," Jude said, and for once, he seemed to mean it.

"Thanks." Tom smiled, and quiet joy flooding his veins, he picked up a knife to help his mother with the supper.

6. THE MOON

As soon as Fiona walked through the door, her mouth began to water. Lareina had cooked a rabbit. She was just setting the table, and she looked up with worried eyes.

"Where have you been, my child?"

"Out," Fiona announced, blushing. "Is supper ready?"

Fiona's head was still swimming, and instinctively her hand went to the place on her cheek where Tom had been bold enough to kiss her. She'd found herself doing so for the entirety of the walk home, and now in the warmth of the house, she could almost still feel his lips there.

"I've been holding it for you," Lareina said. "Seamus is in his workshop. Why don't you call him, and we can start eating."

Fiona avoided her stepmother's eyes. She wanted to keep Tom a secret, and she knew that Lareina would know she was hiding something. Fiona moved past her stepmother quickly and skipped to the back of the house, opening the door to the workshop without a knock.

"Suppertime," she called, and the glassblower looked up from his work. His eyes lingered on her a moment, a strange expression on his face.

"You look . . . different," he said, and then he smiled at her, an unnerving kind of smile, a smile she'd only ever seen him bestow on her stepmother. She didn't think much of it, because her head was so filled with thoughts of Tom—the way he smelled, the sensation of his skin against her wrist—that she could barely see for all her joy.

Doing her best to avoid Lareina's curious eyes, Fiona helped serve the food, and when she sat down, her heart seemed a hundred miles away from her. They ate mostly in silence, Seamus staring at her all the while, that same strange look in his eye, and she noticed that Lareina seemed distracted as well, glancing back and forth between her husband and her stepdaughter, concern on her face.

They know, Fiona thought to herself. They know everything I've done. Wishing to curry favor, she decided to tell them about her interaction with Rowan. She knew Seamus wanted her to try to meet the girl. She knew he was looking for any possible way to make contact with her uncle.

"I've met my cousin," she said after swallowing down a crusty piece of bread.

"You have?" the glassblower said, grinning. "Well now,

that's fantastic, it is. What did you talk about? Did she ask about us? Did she say why her father won't see us? Did she invite you over?"

"Darling," Lareina said, laying a hand on her husband's arm. "Why don't you let her speak?"

They looked to Fiona that she might go on.

Fiona shrugged, trying to seem calm and detached, but inside she felt frantic, doing anything she could to keep them from noticing the unfamiliar stirrings of her heart.

"She seemed nice enough. We didn't talk long. We met on the path, and she introduced herself. We talked about the weather, and I told her some of what it was like back home."

"Did you make plans to speak again?" the glassblower asked eagerly, and though they had not, Fiona had a feeling that such an answer would not be acceptable, so she nodded.

"Yes. We've not planned a specific time. She just said if we met again and neither of us had chores to do, that we might walk and talk some more."

Goi Flint rubbed his hands together and smiled proudly. "That's a good girl," he said. "I knew you could do it." And then he cocked his head and stared at her. "You look different."

"Do I?" she asked, raising a hand to her cheek as if to hide the kiss she wore there.

"You do," he said. "Older somehow. More lovely. You know, Lareina," he said, a twisted grin on his face, "I think it's true. Fiona Eira is now even fairer than you."

97

Lareina, not knowing how to reply, nodded, and picking up their plates, headed to the kitchen. When she was out of sight, she set them down on the first space she saw and leaned her back against the wall. She was shaking, trying to catch her breath, trying desperately to quiet the dread that was slowly swelling in her breast.

When Rowan returned home that night, she found Emily in the kitchen, washing dishes.

"Where are our guests?" Rowan asked, eager to finally meet them.

"Gone out," Emily said, raising an eyebrow to show her disapproval.

"Gone out?" Rowan said, disappointed. "But it's night. Where could they have gone?"

Emily shrugged. "No business of mine. If the lot of them catch the chill, it's not my doing."

Rowan was confused, but she was also hurt. Her father had kept her from the guests all day, and when she returned, they were gone? Was he ashamed of her? Did he not think she was good enough for his guests?

"That seems odd," she said, looking out the window into the snow beyond.

Emily leaned into the counter. "You want to know what seems odd? I'll tell you what seems odd. This duke, I ask you, how many servants do you think he brought with him?"

Rowan opened her mouth to speak, but then she was

struck by the utter quiet of the house, and she began to see what Emily meant.

"Not one!" Emily proclaimed, unable to hide the frustration in her widening eyes. "I'm supposed to look after you lot, and the brother of the queen, without a bit of help? It's downright disgraceful. Rude, it is. What kind of nobleman doesn't travel with a valet or a lady's maid for his ward? 'Oh, don't mind us,' he says. 'We take care of ourselves. We're not like the others.' I'm supposed to believe that?"

Emily turned back to the dishes, and Rowan could feel the anger radiating from her. She had to admit it seemed exceedingly strange that the duke had not brought his own people, but then, she'd never met a duke before.

"If you need help . . ." Rowan tried to choose her words carefully, for she knew how offended Emily could get about anything she perceived as criticism. "Give me chores, and I shall do them."

Emily softened, and setting aside the dish she was drying, she held a hand to Rowan's cheek. "Aw, sweet, I know you will. You're a good girl. Always have been. I'm just testy tonight. I saved your supper over there. You must be starving."

"I'm sorry for missing supper. I lost track of time."

"You didn't miss much," Emily said, turning back to her work. "Listening in on them, I swear you would have died from boredom. And the three of them certainly ate enough. They must have gone though a week's worth of my supplies, I tell you."

Rowan took a piece of raw carrot and popped it in her mouth.

"What were they discussing?"

"Goddess, I don't know. It seemed to be mostly about what happened up on Beggar's Drift. How you can spend an entire dinner discussing such things, I don't know. Surely that can't be considered polite."

Rowan laughed and reached for another carrot, but Emily slapped her hand away.

"Like I said, yours is over there. You eat it up in your room. I've had all I can handle down here tonight."

Rowan took a plate from Emily and began drying it. "What are they like? Is the duke as handsome as everyone says?"

"Well, I have my Bill, of course." Emily lowered her voice and smiled. "So I'm not one to say, but I can tell you they make their men mighty pretty in the palace city."

"Emily!" Rowan laughed.

"He certainly lovelies up the place, I'll give him that."

"And the little girl?" Rowan asked. "What's she like?"

A glorious smile spread across Emily's lips. "Oh, she's a doll. I could eat her up. You're going to love her, Ro."

Rowan was more excited than ever to meet the girl. She had visions of taking her on long walks, maybe even reading to her.

"Did you find out how long they're staying?"

Emily cocked her head. "Oh yeah, sure. The queen's brother rushed right into the kitchen to tell the servant girl all his business." She handed Rowan another plate to dry.

Rowan laughed and started drying the plate, but her thoughts drifted as she gazed out the window. Snow was coming down heavy now, and somewhere out there her Tom was dreaming of a girl that wasn't her.

Fiona Eira was preparing for bed when a knock came at her door. She wore only her white nightgown but assumed it was Lareina, so she called for her to come in. She tried to disguise her surprise at seeing Seamus, for he was not accustomed to visiting her room. Instinctively she crossed her arms in front of her and nodded to him. He looked strange, and he stank of ale. He closed the door behind him.

"I thought I might speak to you a moment, girl," he said.

He took a seat on her bed and motioned for her to sit beside him. He smiled at her strangely, almost as if he were leering at her.

"Fiona," he said, his breath coming in malodorous waves. "I thought it might be a good time to have a talk, you and I."

"A talk?" She inched away, confused by the way he looked at her.

He smiled, baring his teeth, and then he put his hand on her knee. It took all of her strength not to recoil.

"You're a pretty lass, you know that, don't you?"

Slowly his hand began to slide up the inside of her leg. She gasped, then froze, horrified. She felt as though she were drowning. She stared straight ahead, her insides gone suddenly numb. She could feel tears slide down her face as she concentrated on the grain of the wood on the wall in front of her.

"You keep real quiet now," he said, and his hand continued up her leg.

And then the door opened wide, and pulling away from her, he lurched to his feet.

Lareina stood in the doorway, staring at him, her face a mask of horror. He swallowed hard, but did not speak. Lareina looked to Fiona, then closed her eyes a moment, and when she spoke, her voice shook.

"Sam and Josiah are downstairs, Seamus. They've come to collect you," she said.

Refusing to look at either of them, he stood and stumbled out of the room. Lareina followed, and Fiona was left alone sitting on the edge of the bed. Below her she heard the glassblower speaking to the men, and then the door closing behind them.

Then she heard Lareina making a great deal of noise. She was opening and closing drawers, moving hurriedly. She was crying. Fiona Eira could hear all of this, but she didn't seem to hear it from within her own body. It was as if she were floating above herself, watching the terrified girl with her disciplined plaits sitting frozen on the edge of her bed while the world crashed down all around her.

She could still feel the glassblower's touch on her, and smell the ale, and her mind reeled, rebelling against her, trying to bury those moments before they became a part of her, before they became her fault.

She sat shaking, and it was only a moment later that Lareina rounded the corner, a travel bag in her hand. She looked at her stepdaughter with heartbroken eyes, and silently she began moving around the room filling the bag. The last thing she tucked inside was Fiona's stuffed lamb. When she had finished, she sank to her knees and took Fiona's face in her hands.

"My darling," she said. "My darling, you must forgive me."

"Forgive you?" Fiona whispered.

Her stepmother looked her square in the eyes. "You need to leave this place," she said.

"Leave?"

"Yes. Leave here at once." Lareina wiped tears from her eyes. "Before he returns. Our home is no longer safe. You will go to the woods. You will go deep into the woods to the Greenwitch. There you will wait for me, and in three days' time, I shall join you. Somehow . . . somehow I will secure money, and we two, we shall go together. This place is no longer our home."

And then she stood and wrapped her arms around her stepdaughter, and together they walked downstairs to the back door. It was snowing outside, and Fiona, still numb, still lost somewhere inside herself, opened the door and stepped out into the night. She looked at her stepmother, whose face was creased with pain as if she had aged twenty years in a quarter of an hour. Lareina took Fiona's hands.

"My wondrous child, how I love you," she said, and pulling her tight, she pressed her lips against her daughter's icy brow. "Now go quickly, and let no one see you."

On the other side of the village, behind the gate and past the thicket, beyond the rose trees, Rowan was just drifting off to sleep, her mind moving far from her body, when it was as if someone leaned in and whispered in her ear: *It's starting.*

And then there came a barrage of images, each more odious than the next, as if painted on the backs of her eyelids by a wicked hand. Wresting herself from the clutches of sleep, Rowan sat up in bed, hand to her heart, and stifled a scream. She tried to slow her breathing and calm her racing heart, but she couldn't still the sense that some vile creature was creeping ever closer, and that no matter what she might do, something terrible was about to happen.

† † †

The snow was coming down fast now, and Fiona moved on unsteady legs. What was happening to her? Where had her life gone? She longed for Lareina. She longed for her father. She had gone only a short way into the woods when she found that a crippling exhaustion bore down on her. There was something inside of her—something broken, and without it she was unable to move any farther. She climbed atop the remains of a fallen great oak, and letting her hair down, she watched as snowflakes slowly gathered in it, dotting the black with specks of glistening white.

She searched her emotions, but she found only fear: fear of her home, fear of life, fear of herself. Lareina had told her to go to the Greenwitch, but she found that she feared her too. How was she, a girl so unused to being by herself, so used to having all of her decisions made for her, supposed to find her way through the dark to the house of a stranger? Why should she trust her, this Greenwitch she'd never met? She put her face in her hands, and she wept.

And then suddenly she realized that maybe she wasn't as alone as she thought. Tom. She'd only just met him, but she trusted him. She would be safe with him; she was certain. Pulling herself up to stand, she ran through the snow, a wild gallop through the trees, and a few moments later, she was standing beneath what she hoped was his window. She threw a pebble, then another, and then a third and final one. And she waited there below, tugging her cloak tight against the cold.

† † †

When Tom heard the noise at his window, he thought it must be hail, but then he saw the gentle snowflakes falling, and knew it could be no such thing. No, someone was throwing pebbles. He stilled himself and then moved to the pane. Nothing could have prepared him for what he saw there beneath him. Her cheeks and lips were flushed especially red—crimson, even—and her dark eyes sparkling below seemed to call to his very soul. He opened the window.

"Hello," she said, smiling up at him like she'd always known him.

"Hello," he managed to say.

"Come down," she said, and then she moved quick as an animal, darting into the trees, and she was gone.

Breathlessly, he pulled on his trousers and slipped into

his boots. Grabbing his coat, he was off and out the door as if his very life depended on it.

The snow was falling in steady swirls. The weather, which had appeared docile from his bedroom casement, now obscured his vision and made him unable to see her footprints. He headed into the trees after her, and had run only a few steps when an arm shot out and grabbed him. For a second that arm seemed otherworldly, almost as if it were there but also weren't, caught between two realms, misshapen by his perception. And for a moment, the only thought that ran through his mind was of those men on the mountain, their bodies strewn about in the snow, and he screamed in terror. He could not help himself.

"It's just me," she said softly, and then he saw her again, the light of her, and moved to touch her, to press his lips firmly to hers, to crush her against him, but then he noticed that the skin around her eyes was red and swollen, and he stopped himself.

"Are you okay?" he asked, reaching out to her.

"I'm fine," she said, but in her eyes there shone a terrible sadness.

"You're not," he whispered. "Please, tell me what's wrong. Maybe I can help."

"Tom," she whispered, and then raising her hands to his face, she brought his lips close to hers, and kissed him deeply, truly, and in that moment, Tom felt certain he was coming home.

His head was still spinning a moment later when their lips parted, and stepping away, she looked up at him, the snow of her complexion now mottled with crimson and plum. And then he heard it—the sound of animals fleeing, hooves pounding against hard snow, wings beating furiously on winter birds who by their very nature were not prone to leaving. And then a noise. Deep in the woods, a rumble as something very large moved among the trees.

"We should go back," he said, gripping her hand. "These woods aren't safe."

She shook her head, sorrow returning to her eyes. "I can't," she said. "I can't ever go back."

But just as he was about to ask her what she meant, he was distracted by a great commotion—men coming out of the tavern, Goi Flint and his fellows.

Fiona froze, and staring in the direction of her guardian's voice, she began slowly inching away from the village, away from Tom.

"Fiona, please," he said, reaching for her. "We need to get back."

She looked at him with those lost eyes of hers, and she shook her head, and then suddenly she was gone, running, through the trees and into the darkness of the forest beyond.

It took a moment for him to realize what she'd done, but shaking off his confusion, he sprinted after. He yelled her name as he ran, but his voice seemed to disappear, swallowed whole by the forest.

And then that noise again—a movement through the trees too large to be any animal, punctuated by a scream, a bright and staccato scream that pierced the night. And then a snap. And silence.

He stood there frozen, stunned.

"Fiona?" he yelled into the darkness, but there was no reply.

Pushing off as hard as he could, he raced deeper into the woods, darting through the moonlight-speckled trees. His legs burning, the snow slipped out from under him, and he slammed his arm against a tree, but he didn't cry out in pain. He lifted himself up and pressed on. Ahead of him he saw a clearing, and he knew he needed to get there. He needed to see.

She lay in the snow, the moonlight illuminating the luscious pallor of her skin so that she almost looked like she wasn't there at all. Her dress and cloak were spread around her in an arc, and her hair was fanned out like a pitch-black corona.

He approached slowly.

"Fiona," he whispered, but still she didn't move.

He saw her chest, and his stomach lurched. It had been opened up, hollowed out. Flesh and blood mingled in stringy derangement. He looked and he saw, but he didn't really let himself see. He couldn't. Instead, he stared at her face, more perfect in death even than it had been in life. Her dark eyes were wide and fixed on the stars above—stars that seemed to have come out simply to witness her death, clearing the clouds aside that the moonlight might make her lovely one last time.

He knelt beside her and stroked her hair.

"Shhh," he said. "It's going to be all right."

He pressed his lips to her cheek. It was still warm.

"Everything will be just fine," he said.

He kissed her one last time, and then with fingers light as feathers, he closed her eyelids, and lay back in the snow waiting for it not to be true. Waiting to wake up from the dream.

PART TWO

7. THE CHARIOT

WHEN ROWAN AWOKE the next morning, she could tell that something had changed. Somehow the world was different, and the thought of it caused a gnawing pain to grow in her stomach. She nearly doubled over with it as she climbed out of bed.

As she dressed, she noticed that her clothes felt unusually heavy, and when she stepped out of her room, she sensed she wasn't alone. Turning, she saw a small figure sitting on the wooden bench at the end of the hall, down by Rowan's mother's old room—the room where her mother had died.

"Hello," Rowan said, and the figure sat up straighter but

made no move to stand. Rowan walked down the hall, trying to make out the child's face. When she came into view, Rowan was surprised by how hard the little thing seemed. Plain, with straight brown hair that curved to her chin like an obedient dog, the girl held her lips pursed tightly, and she stared at Rowan with a decidedly frigid air.

"I'm Rowan," she said, but the girl didn't smile. She just stared at Rowan, and after a moment, she raised an eyebrow. Just when Rowan was about to speak again, a man stepped out of her mother's room and smiled at her.

Emily had been right to describe the duke as beautiful, but she had neglected to mention how extremely young he was. Twenty-five at most, he was a tall, imposing man with dark green eyes and lips like bloodstains. He had a brightness to him that was immediately attractive. His chiseled face was smooth save for an odd scar he wore just below his left eye—three straight lines, almost like claw marks, that led down to one of his two disarming dimples.

Bowing her head and bending at the knee, Rowan curtsied, trying to hide how distracted she was by his beauty.

"My lord," she said.

"None of that, now," he said. On his left hand he wore an array of beautiful rings, and as he reached out to her, they glinted in the morning light. "I detest formality. While I am in your house, I am your guest and your friend but not your lord. Understand?"

He looked at her closely, his smile lighting up his dazzling eyes, and for a moment, she thought she might lose her footing. This man, she thought, was even more hand-some than Jude, and much better behaved.

"Yes," Rowan said, straining to find her voice. "I understand."

"And this," the duke said, indicating the girl beside him, "is my ward, Merrilee."

A strange smile played on the girl's lips as she stood and offered Rowan her hand. She wore a navy-blue dress that did not suit her, and black boots that appeared to cut in at the ankle.

"Nice to meet you," she whistled, air passing through the large gap between her top two teeth. "I'm sure we'll be the best of friends."

"I'm sure we will," Rowan said, decidedly disturbed by the girl.

"Rowan," the duke said, placing his hand on her shoulder and looking at her with kind eyes. "I'm afraid something's happened. Your father wants to speak with you. You'd best go find him."

Anxiety flooded Rowan's veins. She'd known something was wrong. She'd felt it upon waking. She only hoped her father was okay. "Thank you," she said, excusing herself. "It was lovely to meet you."

"We'll have time to talk later, I'm sure." He smiled.

The house was quiet when Rowan walked downstairs. The lights were off, and her father's study door was slightly ajar, but she could smell the lingering ghost of his pipe smoke.

"Father?" she called.

"Come in," he answered.

Slowly she pushed the door open the rest of the way. For the first time in her life, she was afraid of what she might see within. She had a brief vision of horrors, fires and blood, black smoke and silver-white teeth, but when she entered, there was nothing extraordinary about the scene. Her father sat at his desk, his hands fastened together beneath his chin, his brow tight with some indiscernible emotion.

He raised his eyebrows as if she'd awakened him from a particularly unpleasant dream. "I've just returned from Dr. Temper's. It appears there has been another incident."

Rowan felt her bones begin to chill, and a faint shiver ran along the nape of her neck. "What do you mean by 'incident'? You don't mean like what happened to the men on Beggar's Drift, do you?"

"I'm afraid I do. There's been another attack. Another death. Rowan, I'm going to tell you this because I don't want you to hear it elsewhere. This attack was particularly gruesome. This time the victim's heart . . . it was ripped from her chest. She appears to have died instantly."

"She?" Rowan asked, her voice breaking.

"Yes. I'm afraid it was your cousin, Fiona Eira."

Rowan felt the earth drop out from under her. Her forehead tingled with a shock that crawled over her skull and down her back. Suddenly she thought she might be sick. Gripping the chair, she stared at her father, trying to read his emotions, trying to understand where hers were coming from, and without speaking, she left the room. He didn't call out to her, didn't stop her, and she pushed herself to make it to the stairs, leaning against the railing as she mounted them.

By the time she reached her room, the nausea had passed, but still she felt awful. Only once she reached the foot of the bed and was able to lean into it did she understand what was happening. Grief—terrible, throbbing grief. She grasped at her chest as if to stop the pain, trying to understand why the girl's death paralyzed her so. She'd only met Fiona Eira once, but the loss tore into her, opened her up. Confused, weak, she climbed atop her covers, and curling up, she wept.

The funeral should have been the next day. It ought to have been. The village ought to have gathered in Fiona Eira's home, and the elders ought to have performed the rites. She should have been covered in the funerary shroud, hiding the sight of human flesh so as not to offend the Goddess. Her body laid up on Cairn Hill at the Mouth of the Goddess, stones carefully arranged atop her resting spot. These were the things that ought to have been done. But sometimes things don't go as planned.

Tom hadn't spoken much since the night before. Nor had he eaten, and Jude, worried, brought a bowl of oatmeal up to him in bed.

"I sprinkled sugar on top," Jude said as he set it before his brother, who didn't meet his eyes, who barely moved. Jude laid a hand on his brother's shoulder. "I'm sorry."

"The rites," Tom managed, his voice cracking with pain. "What time are the rites?"

Jude sat opposite him. "Well, that's the thing, isn't it? They're not being said tonight."

Tom sat up, his eyes suddenly clear. "What? What do you mean they're not saying them tonight? If twenty-three hours pass, she can't be laid to rest."

Jude shrugged. "Goi Flint is refusing to let them in."

"But the rites must be said."

"He's pickled in ale and extremely violent. He says he'll do what he pleases with her body, and that no one will stop him. No one's been able to reason with him. He gave Goi Tate a nasty black eye, and when Mama Lune tried to speak with him, he took a swing at her too."

"This is sacrilege we're talking about." Tom rose, his eyes dull as day-old bread. His brother put a hand to his chest to stay him.

"Listen to me, Tom. Goi Flint is a dangerous man. And he's gone completely mad with drink. He'll kill you. Someone should stop him. I agree, but it shouldn't be my only brother."

"Surely he can be reasoned with."

"They say you don't understand unless you've seen him. There's a rabid animal behind his eyes. He's practically murdered his wife."

"What?" Tom asked, surprised. "Is she okay?"

"I think so. She's inside with him now, apparently refusing to come out as well."

"This is lunacy. Surely the village elders can talk sense into him."

"They're shocked. They say there's nothing we can do—that we just have to hope he sobers up and listens to reason before twenty-three hours have come and gone."

"He must be stopped. He can't do such a thing. He can't." Tom moved to leave, but Jude held his brother at arm's length, his black eyes dangerous in their insistence.

"Sit," Jude said. "Eat your food. Rest some more, and this evening we will go and speak with him together. I cannot let you go alone."

Tom stared at his brother, uncertain what to say or do. He was frustrated by his own impotence and overwhelmed by his brother's loyalty. So he sat down and did as Jude asked.

"I'll be back for you in two hours," Jude said.

Rowan sat on the edge of her bed, her cold feet dangling as she stared out her casement window at the ceaseless snow. She had spent the afternoon in bed—had not even risen to eat, she who was usually so hungry, she who could never seem to get enough nourishment to sustain her small body. Her father had left her alone up there, and his guests had gone out. Only Emily had knocked, checking on her, a nervous quaver to her voice, but Rowan had been able to persuade her that she was ill and needed to be left alone.

She ran a finger over the battalion of goose bumps that

had risen along her arms. She ought to dress, ought to warm herself, but the cold felt good. She had no explanation for her reaction to her cousin's death. She hadn't known her aside from the conversation on the forest path. But now that she was gone, it felt as if someone very important had disappeared, and she had to keep her hands at her side lest they search blindly out in front of her for the warmth of a mother she knew she couldn't remember.

Bringing her palms to her spent eyes, she leaned into them, willing the grief to stop, willing herself to act in a recognizable manner. With great effort, she would put on her dress and her stockings and her heavy black boots, and she would wade through the snow to the center of the village to Fiona's cottage. She needed to pay her respects. She needed to see if she could be of service.

At the tavern, the men were fuming, caught up in the preparations, the thrill of the hunt infecting them all. Jude slunk in, trying to remain unnoticed. The last thing he wanted was to be given a weapon and dragged out into the wilds to fight a bloodthirsty beast, but he needed to know what was being planned.

"We'll do what has to be done," said Goi Tate, clearly relishing the chance to release some of his well-honed aggression. "We'll band together and hunt the thing down. Then we'll drag it through the center of the village and hang it up for all to see."

The rest of the men grunted in assent.

"Safety must be a consideration, of course," Wilhelm spoke up, his voice soft in comparison to the younger man's. "We'll need to go in pairs. We'll need to stay on our guard."

"We move tonight," Goi Tate said, pulling the focus back to himself.

Jude cleared his throat and got the other men's attention. "I don't think it wise that we should hunt this creature at night," he said.

"Don't be silly, boy," rasped Goi Tate. "It struck at night."

"That's my point exactly," Jude answered. "It hunts and kills at night, and if we send ourselves out into the darkness when it is at its most potent, we put too much at risk. It would be wiser to move at dawn, to catch the creature unaware, perhaps even while it sleeps."

"What does the boy know?" Goi Tate scowled. "He speaks from fear."

Paer Jorgen nodded. "He is right to be afraid. The creature we hunt, whether it be a common wolf or something . . . more, no man here is a match for it. Our best chance to kill it is to use our wits. We go at dawn."

Goi Tate raised his thumb. "Respectfully, I disagree. We need to slay the wolf before it can kill again."

"It was no wolf," a raspy voice said from the stairs, and Jude looked up to find his brother looking even worse than when he'd left him. The room fell silent, and the men waited for Tom to continue. "I was not twenty yards from it, and though I didn't see it with my eyes, I am certain it was no wolf. It was larger, I am sure of it—larger than any man, larger than any animal known to these woods."

"What are you saying, Tom?" his father asked.

He shrugged and leaned against the wall, a new kind of hollowness to his eyes. "I'm saying that anyone who goes out to find this thing is going to die."

The men laughed, rolling their eyes at Tom's dramatics, but Jude stared at his brother with utter seriousness, and when he stood, the men fell silent again. Their father cleared his throat and looked out the window as if to fully disassociate from his boys. Jude went to his brother, and taking him by the arm, he motioned to the door.

"We'll see you on the morrow for the hunt," Jude said as they left the inn.

Out in the snow, Tom pulled his collar close to block out the chill and gave his brother a wary look. "I hope you know I'll do no such thing. I'm never going into those woods again."

"You're not fit to hunt a squirrel. You'll stay home and rest. You were supposed to be resting now," he said, but Tom kept on trudging through the snow, his stolid face graying and blank.

"It was no wolf," Tom whispered.

"Then what was it?" Jude asked, growing impatient with his brother. "You must have seen it. You were twenty yards away. You said so yourself. And the moon was full that night. Surely you must have seen something."

But again Tom shook his head. "There was nothing to see. It was as if it was there all around me, but I couldn't see a thing. It was as if the forest itself came alive for just an instant, just long enough to destroy her, and then it disappeared back into itself, only trees and dirt, like it was never there."

When he spoke, Tom dropped the ends of his words, as if he didn't have the energy to finish his thoughts, and for the first time something awful occurred to Jude: Was it possible that Tom had done more than just bear witness to the girl's death? Was that any less possible than his account of the forest coming to life and swallowing her up? Unconsciously, Jude found himself edging away from his brother, just a touch farther down the path, a hair out of arm's reach, but then he caught himself and realized how ridiculous the thought of Tom harming anyone was. His brother was gentle. He was quiet and kind. He cared for the sick and for injured animals. He did good deeds every chance he got. There was no way he'd momentarily lost his mind and killed a girl with his bare hands. Still, Jude began to wonder if other people might start to find it suspicious that Tom had been the one to find her body, to report it back to the village elders. He'd withheld the fact that he'd been with her at the time of her death from all except his immediate family.

It had been at their father's insistence that Tom declined to tell that part of the story. The elders were already looking for malice beneath their roof. Connecting Tom any more closely with Fiona Eira's death would certainly feed their alarm, and so his father had begged him to twist the truth that he might not cast further suspicion on their family. Tom, who was never given to deceit, had had a difficult time with it, but had eventually come round to his father's point of view. And then there had been their mother's subtle push.

"Think of Fiona Eira," she'd said. "Think of what people would say if they knew she'd lured a boy into the woods like an enchantress. Dead or not, think of her reputation."

When the glassblower's cottage came into view, they were shocked to see a solitary creature standing outside.

"Is that Rowan?" Jude asked, wonder in his voice.

Tom nodded. "She's going to be difficult."

"Of course she's going to be difficult," Jude laughed. "She's Rowan."

As they reached the glassblower's cottage, Rowan held out a hand to stop them. And because Tom was given to doing what she said, a simple hand signal went a long way. The boys stopped in their tracks.

"Tom Parstle," she said. "You are not setting foot on this property."

"Step aside, Ro," he said, but she planted her palm firm against his chest.

"I've just spoken with Natty Whitt. He tells me Goi Flint's gone crazy. They say the man's gone mad—that he's dangerous. There's nothing we can do but hope he has a change of heart."

"If there's nothing we can do, then what are you doing here?" he asked.

Rowan furrowed her brow. "I don't know exactly. I just can't bring myself to leave."

"I need to talk to him," Tom said, distracted. "I need to convince him of the gravity of his decision."

"But, Tom," she said. "Natty told me that you were the one who found her, and that Goi Flint already thinks you ran off together. It sounds like he's this close to accusing you of her murder."

"That's ridiculous," said Jude, alarmed that someone else had considered the possibility.

Tom scowled. "They think I did this? I could never . . ."

"I know, Tom, but I'm begging you to go home. That man is dangerous—that house is dangerous."

"Rowan has a point," Jude said.

"But all of this . . . it's just insanity," Tom said, gripping his head.

"Exactly, Tom," she answered. "That's what I'm trying to tell you. He's gone mad. Onsie said he's been in his studio working all day, and when he does emerge, he babbles, says insane things. And his wife, she hasn't set foot outside all day. Some think she left—fled into the woods to hide from her beastly husband."

Tom's gaze shifted to the cottage. He stared, undeterred, and Jude placed a hand on his brother's shoulder as if to steady him. "Give the man until nightfall, and we'll see what he does."

"I won't abide it," Tom said, striding into the yard with such force that Jude and Rowan knew better than to stand in his way.

With a storm raging in Tom's head, and only emptiness where his heart should have been, he stalked through the snow toward the old oak door. For a moment, he had the oddest memory eclipse his thoughts—his grandmother serving him hot juniper tea and cinnamon cookies. She sat opposite him, smiling at him, and he remembered the scent of her skin, how sweet it was, how welcoming. She had died when he was only five, and he had no idea how he could have retained such a clear memory of her, much less why it was surfacing now as he walked up to Goi Flint's door.

He couldn't help but pause a moment and smile, standing there in the snow like a fool. And he realized he was fighting back tears.

"Tom?" he heard Rowan call. "Are you okay?"

"You don't have to do this," Jude said.

But Tom was a million miles away, and he knew with a hardened certainty that he did need to do this. It was his duty.

Tom stomped up the steps and pounded on the front door. There was a moment before anything happened, but as soon as the door opened, the man flew at him with all his bulk, and together they toppled over and collapsed into the snow. In an instant the man was astride him, the cold steel of a blade pressed flush against Tom's neck.

Tom gasped for air, and suddenly he started laughing, hysterical. Rowan and Jude moved in to help him, but Goi Flint shouted that they'd best back away if they didn't want him to slit Tom's throat.

It must have looked a horrific scene, and Tom knew that, but from where he lay in the cold snow, this monster threatening to kill him, he suddenly felt that the entire situation was completely and utterly absurd.

"I don't want to kill you, boy," the man growled, but Tom continued to laugh, unable to stop himself.

"Stop laughing, Tom!" Rowan cried. "You'll only make him angrier."

"Leave us alone, you hear me, boy?" Seamus Flint demanded.

But Tom couldn't stop laughing even as his mind's eye was beset by horrific images—the moon in the night wood, Fiona Eira laid out in the snow, bathed in her own blood.

"For the love of all that is holy, will you shut up!" he heard his brother yell.

Goi Flint pressed the knife harder against his neck, and then Tom saw Jude above, holding a large plank of wood. Then he saw him bring it down hard on Goi Flint's head. The beast of a man flinched and sprang off Tom, turning all of his aggression on Jude, who took off running, disappearing into the darkness.

Tom, free now, scrambled to his feet, and Rowan grabbed his hand. The two of them ran off, following Jude. The glassblower stood in his yard, the snow tumbling down around him, and long after the three had reached the safety of the tavern, he still stood there, holding his knife aloft, wailing into the night.

8. THE HIGH PRIESTESS

ARLENE BLESSING WAS the first to see it. As usual, she was up before dawn, and dressed in her warmest winter cloak, she set off for her morning stroll around the village. The snow was falling in gentle flurries. She walked her normal route, along the line of row houses, near the bakery, where, she could smell, they had already begun their day's work. She walked past the inn, and down by the glassblower's cottage—where that young girl had died.

At first she didn't understand what it could be—a sculpture of some kind, but no, that couldn't be right. The man was an artisan, and he worked with glass, but surely he would not spend the evening of the girl's death creating a massive sculpture to display in his front yard. Arlene's feet carried her forward, her curiosity forcing her to press on and gain a better look—but all the while her heart was twisting within her chest, urging her to turn around.

Slowly, she approached, snow crunching beneath her boots. Whatever it was, it was longer than it was tall, and made of crystal clear glass, peaked at the top into a harsh angle. It was up on a wooden stand, and there appeared to be something inside.

She stood at the edge of the glassblower's property, unable to believe what she was seeing. A step closer, and there was no mistaking it.

It was a coffin. A glass coffin, intricately carved, and set out in the yard for all to see. Inside it was the girl, her black hair splayed out around her, her lips like rotting cherries set against a newly ashen complexion.

Her body had been swaddled in white mourning cloth, but it was possible to see that she was no longer a full person. Flowers of blood bloomed where her chest should have been, and there was a dip to the torso that intimated she'd been all but hollowed.

Arlene's hand flew to her mouth.

And then the world seemed to spin, and a deafening cry rose up in Arlene's ears, surrounding her, threatening to swallow her up, and she lost her balance, her feet faltering in the snow. It was only when she caught herself that she realized that the scream had been her own.

Fighting back tears, she turned and hurried out of the yard.

† † †

By the time Rowan awoke, the news was all over the village. The grieving glassblower had done the unthinkable. By then the hunt had been called off—there were more pressing matters at home—and everyone had seen her, laid out in the snow like a memento mori. It was beautiful work, some of the younger people whispered amongst themselves. The glassblower had produced a piece of art unlike anything the villagers had ever seen. Too bad, Billy Bribey had chuckled to Onsie Best, that he was only able to access that talent in the wake of a tragedy, and wasn't it a pity there weren't more upon him that he might build them a magnificent glass cathedral. Rowan had been standing behind the boys, her face pinched with sorrow, and she had slapped Billy Bribey's hand so hard that red swelled forth.

Everyone agreed that something had to be done. Displaying the dead was a gross offense against the Goddess. Sacrilege like that would surely invite disaster. They needed to get the girl out of that casket. They needed to burn her corpse, and like the unfortunate soldiers, her ashes would be placed east of the village in the old cimetière where the ancients used to lay down their dead.

That morning, though, before anything could be done about the poor girl, when only a few villagers had gathered to see if what old Arlene Blessing said was true, the door had swung open, and the glassblower had emerged with a large shotgun in his hand. He didn't look at the villagers;

his eyes seemed to be propped open by the sheer force of insanity, voluble as tops all set to spin.

Upon seeing him, the villagers took cover, but it soon became clear he meant them no specific harm. He didn't even seem to see them exactly. Rather, he walked over to his glass coffin and stroked it like one might a cherished pet.

"That all might see," he babbled. "That all might see her beauty."

Eyes wild, he threw the gun strap over his shoulder and began pacing, slowly encircling his creation, guarding it.

He had been walking thusly for hours now, refusing to leave his gruesome post for even a moment. He circled it like a lion gone mad, keeping the spoils for himself as he stalked around his freshly killed gazelle.

"Where is Lareina?" people were heard to say. "Surely she can reason with him."

But no one had seen Lareina since the previous day.

Slowly throughout the day, the villagers gathered weaponry. "There's naught to do but put him in the gaol," Goi Tate said, and it was as if his proclamation made it so. They waited for the glassblower to show a moment of weakness before they would set on him. Their chance came finally when Goi Flint put down his shotgun to remove his heavy overcoat. Tom rushed him as soon as the man's hand lost contact with the weapon, and when Tom threw Flint to the ground, Rowan grabbed the shotgun.

"Oh, holy Goddess," Tom cried when he noticed the blood. His hands, which had a moment earlier been on the mad man's torso, came away sticky and streaked with red.

He jerked away, and several men who had come to help yanked at Goi Flint's coat, opening it to reveal undershirts soaked through with the red.

"Are you hurt?" Goi Tate asked, but the glassblower shook his head, and with a great howl, he bent forward into the snow, crying out with what they were beginning to realize was grief. From his spasmodic crouch there on the ground, he pointed back to the house.

Rowan's hand flew to her mouth as she came to understand.

"Lareina!" she screamed, and ran for the front door, only to slip in the snow and fall, smashing her lip on the front step. Ignoring the pain, she pulled herself up and opened the door.

Lareina Flint's body lay not three feet from the entrance, her throat slit, her soulless eyes wide, her mouth contorted into what must have been one final scream. Behind her was a trail of blood, the path she must have traversed as she'd crawled to the door.

"She was here all along," Rowan wept, blood from her lip mixing with tears, the acrid sting the only thing that kept her from fainting. "She was just behind the door this whole time while we were on the other side. Oh, great mother, what has become of us? What has become of us all?"

As the villagers dragged Seamus Flint through the snow to the gaol, the man keened like an animal. But when they opened the cell door and shoved him inside, he only bowed his head, smiling like a child.

Later that evening, Elsbet busied herself wiping down tables at the inn. "When are they saying the rites for Lareina?"

"Tonight," Wilhelm said, his head bent over a fresh pint. "They'll lay her up at Cairn Hill in the morning. Once that's done and the girl's unclean corpse has been turned to ash, we might all rest. Goddess knows we're all eager for this to be over."

"Just keeps getting worse, doesn't it?" Elsbet said, and her husband nodded in agreement. "And our Tom, how lost he seems today. I put it down to Jude, you know. Nothing but a bad influence, that one."

"Elsbet," Wilhelm sighed, for it pained him when she spoke of their boy as if he were a stranger.

"There's wickedness in that one, Wilhelm. I tell you there is." She paused, waiting for a reaction from her husband, but when she got none, she changed the subject. "Mark me, Wilhelm, an evil has come to our village. First those soldiers, and now that girl and her stepmother together like that."

Her husband nodded and stared into his ale.

"Maybe . . . ," she went on. "Maybe it was Goi Flint who killed those men up there. Maybe he killed the girl as well. Seemed mad with guilt to me, he did. We should kill him ourselves. Hang him from the old beech tree and watch him die."

Wilhelm shook his head. "Goi Flint was here in the tavern when the girl was killed, and what he did to his lovely wife was born out of madness and grief. We're in no danger from him."

Elsbet set a hand on her hip. "So seven people dead, and we're not a village in danger?"

"I didn't say that. We are very much a village in danger, just not at the hands of Goi Flint."

Villagers started trickling in, and Elsbet began pouring ale. The men would have a big night ahead of them gathering wood for the pyre, and they would need their sustenance. Elsbet was having a word with Goi Tate about what she liked to call *proper tavern behavior* when the double doors burst open and the duke marched in. Quickly the villagers bowed to him, but he waved them off and strode to the center of the room. All eyes followed the great man, and the room fell silent as he cleared his throat.

"I hear there has been talk of burning the bodies," he said, his voice booming.

"Just the girl," said Goi Tate, who stood a little straighter against the foreign lord. "The woman is clean, but the girl's corpse is tainted. Burning's the only thing for it."

The villagers nodded, but no one spoke.

"You'll do no such thing," said the duke, and a murmur rose among the crowd. "While I understand that these are your customs, I do not share them. I am from the royal city, where, as I'm sure you know, we worship the sea god. We do not burn our dead. Poisoning the air by emolliating rotting flesh is something that, I'm sorry, I simply cannot allow.

You've already burned my soldiers, reduced them to nothing. I shall not stand by and watch you do the same again. I will not breathe the fetid air."

Wilhelm Parstle felt obligated to speak. "Sir, if you'll excuse me, but that is how we do things in the mountains. If the rites can't be performed because the allotted time has passed, then the bodies are unclean. They must be burned, and their ashes laid at the old cimetière."

The duke squinted. "That's where my soldiers' ashes rest?"

"Yes. It's just outside the village, to the east," Paer Jorgen said, his voice quiet but clear. "It's where the ancients used to lay down their dead. They dug holes there and put them below ground. It's not our way. It's the old way, but we figure it's better than naught. We did the best we could for your soldiers. We laid some river stones atop to bless them on their journey."

The duke put a hand to his forehead and closed his eyes as if to still the anger within him. "Of course that's what you did." He opened his eyes, fresh fire burning there. "And the result is that I have no bodies to bring back to those soldiers' families. I cannot hand them a pile of ashes to push out to sea. They would call me a monster."

"Please understand, sir," said Paer Jorgen. "We meant no harm."

"No." The duke shook his head, and his voice grew quiet. "Of course you didn't. But listen here, this will not happen again. If you can lay the ashes in the cimetière, then you can lay this girl's body there too. You'll do it at once."

"But we can't do *that*," Draeden Faez nearly yelped.

The duke's shoulders slumped, and seemingly exhausted, he asked, "And why not?"

The old man stumbled over his words. "The ground is unquiet there. We . . . we can't put her there unburned."

"But that's where you put the ashes."

"That's different," said Tate. "Ashes can't very well rise, can they?"

The duke groaned. "Fine, then it seems your only other choice is to put her up at your Mouth of the Goddess."

"That we could never do," said Draeden Faez, solemnly shaking his head.

"And why not?" asked the duke, his face growing red with frustration.

"I don't know how you do things with your sea burials," continued the old man, "but up here, the dead are holy things. They are prepared and offered up to the Goddess. To give her something so unclean would be worse than sacrilege. With that ghoulish display, that coffin of glass, we're already at risk. Mountain folk or sea, displaying a corpse goes against the laws of the dead. You have to admit that."

"Of course." The duke nodded. "We would never do such a thing. Like you say, we send our dead out to sea. It is clean and simple and does not leave room for all these complications."

"So you see," said Draeden Faez, "we can't lay her at the Mouth of the Goddess."

The duke sighed. "Very well. What about my way? What about a water burial? There's a lake nearby, isn't there?"

"Seelie Lake," said Paer Jorgen. "But that's fairy business."

The duke couldn't keep from laughing. "Surely you people can't still believe in fairies."

"Fairies or no," said Tak Carlysle. "The lake is frozen now. Lot of good it would do to set her out there in a boat atop the ice."

"Listen to me," the duke said, clearly tired of arguing. "You will bury her at this cimetière you speak of. It may not be your Mouth of the Goddess, but it's a burial ground at least. If it was good enough for your ancients, it's good enough for you."

"But—"

The duke raised his hand. "It's not as if I'm asking you to bury her in the village square. I'm telling you to lay her in a burial ground. You will do this. If I find out anyone has other plans, if anyone strays from my command, the offense will be punishable by death. Do you understand?"

The room was quiet. Dark eyes watched him, and slowly the villagers nodded. Without another word, the duke turned back around and strode out through the heavy wooden doors.

† † †

For Lareina Flint, the rites were performed, her body put to rest up on Cairn Hill at the Mouth of the Goddess with as much pomp as the people of Nag's End could muster. But things were different for Fiona Eira.

The cimetière was a dark place. Through the wood

and to the east, where men did not often walk, it was an ancient place, surrounded by an archaic stone wall. It was commonly believed that the spirits of the old ones lingered there, polluting the air. The ground in the cimetière never froze. No one knew why. It wasn't the kind of thing one wanted to spend much time contemplating. The soil there was thick and gray, an unchanging claylike substance that remained malleable despite the weather. No one but an elder was allowed to walk the grounds of the cimetière. It was said that to stay there too long could cause a man's legs to wither, and his lungs to slowly fill up with blood.

A small group gathered, and Rowan was surprised to see the witches among them. They kept to themselves, though they did look her way once or twice. The day was not without incident. The corpse, already desecrated by its placement in that glass abomination, suffered further sullying when one of the pallbearers tripped, sending Fiona's body tumbling to the ground. The calamity caused the shroud to unravel, and her body landed faceup in the dirt at Mama Lune's feet. The villagers gasped, and some covered their eyes, but Rowan noticed a look of fierce intensity—almost horror—on Mama Lune's face as she stared at the body. Rowan tried to follow the witch's eyes to see what was causing her such distress, but by then the pallbearers had collected the body, and there was nothing to see. Rowan looked around her, and while people seemed rattled by the chaos of the tumbling body, no one appeared particularly distressed—no one except Mama Lune. She watched the Greenwitch whisper something in the Bluewitch's ear, and then Rowan turned her attention back to the proceedings, her heart heavy as she saw the enshrouded body carried through the stone arch to the center of the burial ground. When she looked over to where the witches had been standing, she saw that they were gone.

Inside the burial ground, the elders performed the modified rites over Fiona's body. They watched her corpse sink into the ground, and when it had disappeared from view, they laid the stones atop, although those too were quickly swallowed up by the hungry clay. By the time the elders were finished, the small funeral crowd outside the wall had dispersed, and Rowan was alone with Tom, gazing at the decaying necropolis that housed her sleeping cousin.

Ollen Bittern looked mournful when he hobbled out through the arch. "Terrible business."

The other two elders followed, their solemn eyes downcast. They nodded to Tom and Rowan, and then the three old men, their duty done, started back to the village.

Tom bit his lip as he watched them go, and Rowan could tell he was trying to keep himself from crying. There was no use hiding his grief. Rowan could tell he was being ravaged by it. His face was swollen and discolored, and his eyes were red and lifeless. Rowan had never seen him look so bad.

"You haven't been sleeping, have you?" she asked, taking his hand as they walked home.

He shook his head and looked off into the trees. "I don't know what's happening to me. I didn't even really know her. People aren't supposed to react like this. I feel so foolish."

"No, you're not foolish," Rowan said. "I didn't know her either, but for some reason, I've been sick with grief as well."

He nodded. "If she'd died normally, it might be different, but to go like that—with such violence. And then everything since has been so warped, so gruesome."

"It's true," Rowan said, a heaviness settling on her chest. "It's as if a plague has descended on Nag's End."

Rowan watched as the crows flew overhead, northeast to southwest, and she was quick to make the sign of the Goddess.

"Things will be okay," Tom said, that blank look still in his eyes. "I just need to get back to normal. I'll pitch in more around the tavern. Work will help."

"Do you want me to come visit you tomorrow? We could go on a walk."

He turned and smiled at her—a genuine smile, the first sign of life she'd seen from him since Fiona's death. "I'd like that."

When they started back on the path to the village, Rowan heard something coming toward them through the trees. Since they were outside the village barrier, she was especially uneasy, and she tensed at the noise, but relaxed when Jude came into view. Tom groaned.

"What?" Rowan asked.

"I don't want to see him right now."

"He saved your life the other night. I have to say I didn't expect that from him."

"Jude is Jude. No one knows why he does what he does.

Anyway, he's driving me crazy lately—always pestering me to sleep or eat."

"How awful of him," Rowan laughed.

When Jude reached them, he was breathing heartily. "Father wants you at the inn," he said to Tom. "Come on, let's go."

Rowan was offended that Jude didn't bother to acknowledge her, and Tom looked to his friend with sympathy. "I'm going to walk Rowan home," he said. "We're past the village barrier."

Jude tossed back his head in annoyance, and finally making eye contact with Rowan, he gave her a quick smirk. "Tom," he said. "Father needs you right now. It's about tonight's hunt. He told me to fetch you as fast as I could. Rowan will be fine. She could take on a wolf any day of the week."

"Jude," Tom said, losing patience. "I'll be home after I walk her."

"Fine," Jude said, closing his eyes in frustration. "*I'll* walk her. Just hurry up and get home, will you?"

Tom seemed to think it over, and then he looked at Rowan. "I'll see you tomorrow?" he asked. Rowan nodded, and he set off quickly back through the shortcut to his end of the village, leaving her to walk with Jude, a wide berth between them.

"I have a message for you," Jude said when they were alone.

She turned to look at him and saw that he was grinning at her.

"What?" she asked, barely able to believe her ears. "What can you possibly have to say to me?"

"It's from Mama Lune," he said. "She needs to talk to you. She says it's an emergency."

Rowan stopped in her tracks and looked at the strange, handsome boy she considered anything but a friend. "You must be joking."

"I'm not," he said, his dark eyes awash with wickedness. "Why do you think I had Tom run off like that?"

Rowan balked. "You mean your father doesn't really need to speak with him?"

Jude shook his head. "The run will do him good. Clear his head. And I'm to take you through the woods to Mama Lune's."

He reached for her, and as he took her hand in his, she felt a strange electricity, a connection passing between them. Suddenly his eyes widened as if he'd felt it too, but Rowan pulled away.

"What does she want with me?"

"Did you not get the note from Mama Tetri?" he asked, and Rowan nearly stopped, she was so surprised. "She's come to Nag's End specifically to see you. Did you not know?"

"What?" Rowan asked, a sick feeling in her stomach. The idea of the witch traveling all the way to Nag's End solely to speak with her filled her with foreboding. She knew for certain that she did not want to hear whatever the woman might have to say. It wasn't that she believed in magic, but Bluewitches were diviners. What if this one had actually seen something about Rowan's future? What if she knew something about Rowan that she herself did not want to know?

"If she wants to speak with me," she said, clearing her throat, "she can come and knock on my door."

Jude groaned. "You know she can't do that."

"Well, why not?"

"Your father hasn't been exactly friendly to witches. And Mama Lune hasn't liked him ever since he tried to have her sent away from the village."

"My father did no such thing," Rowan said, outraged.

"Sure he did. Back when we were small. She told me so."

Rowan spoke deliberately, as if she were trying to explain something to a child. "Understand me now, Jude. I don't care what that witch has to tell me. She's no friend of mine, and I refuse to go off into the woods alone to seek the council of a charlatan."

Jude laughed and shook his head. "I can assure you she's no charlatan, and you won't be alone. I'll be with you."

Rowan closed her eyes. "Jude, listen to me. The only thing I'd like less than spending time with a witch is spending time with you and a witch. Do you understand me?"

A dark wave passed over Jude's exquisite features. "Fine," he said, and taking a step away from her, he started walking back toward the woods. "Suit yourself."

Rowan turned and started walking away from him, but after a few steps she turned back and was surprised to find he'd actually gone. She was alone, outside the village bounds, and night was drawing near. Whether goblins and fairies existed—and truth be told, in her heart of hearts, she thought they might—there was no question that a dark force was afoot in the Black Forest, and quite suddenly she was terrified to be alone outside the village barrier. And then she thought she heard something move somewhere back behind the trees. Wrapping her cloak tight around herself, she hurried along the path, keeping her eyes on the woods as she went. She did not relax until she felt her hand on the heavy oak of her front door.

Despite enthusiasm, the hunt turned up nothing—not so much as scatological evidence of the creature they sought. Jude went along with the others, pleased that he'd success-fully convinced Tom, who was in no shape for a hunt, to re-main at home. Yet as he made his way through the trees, Jude felt certain that while there had been something in these woods very recently, it was no longer there. He knew long before the hunt was over that their efforts would come to naught. But he also knew something else: whatever he'd sensed out there, had been sensing in the woods for some time now, a group of villagers—no matter how rich their weaponry—were no match for it. When he finally settled down to sleep at the break of dawn, weary from the night's hunt, he felt a strange emotion—something he'd not felt since childhood. He tossed and turned, trying to quiet his heart, trying to comprehend the source of the heaviness there, and then he understood. He who had walked the night woods hundreds of times, he who had seen things out there that would make a grown man cry, was suddenly and utterly afraid.

The next morning, Rowan awoke early and went downstairs to find the duke in the sitting room beside a fresh pot of coffee. He was examining a thick stack of papers, which Rowan realized with some trepidation were her translations.

"Good morning," she said, bowing.

Startled, he nearly spilled coffee on himself. Putting his things down, he stood to his full height and beamed at her. His smile made her feel quite unusual—as if she were standing directly in the light of the sun, absorbing all the warmth it had to offer.

"Va Rose," he said, bowing. "What a pleasure it is to see you."

"I thought you didn't care for formalities," she said, grinning up at him.

"I don't," he laughed. "But I have been reading over your translations, and I must admit, I am stunned by your abilities. You are gifted, and in the presence of such a gift, I cannot help but use the honorific."

Hearing such praise, and from someone so respected, Rowan felt herself nearly swelling with pride. "You think they are good?"

"Good?" he said, guiding her to sit across from him. "They are magnificent. You must tell me, what are your plans for your future? Have you ever thought of coming to the palace city? You should really think seriously about visiting my library."

"I . . ." Rowan started to speak but was so overwhelmed with the possibility of leaving Nag's End that she couldn't find the words.

"I'm sorry. I must sound foolish," he said, his smile deliciously vibrant. "But please understand. I am so excited by your work. I feel that if I could spend some time with you, and really train you with all the palace city has to offer, that there'd be no end to what you could do. Together we could work wonders. I'm certain of it."

Rowan could barely believe him, and yet he seemed so genuine, and she wanted so terribly for it to be true. She smiled. "I am proud of my work, but it can't be more skilled than that of the king's scholars."

He looked away for a second, as if trying to decide something, and when he met her eyes again, there was an intimacy there that surprised her. "I have certain projects . . . certain personal projects that I like to keep separate from the king's affairs. And these projects, they need a fresh eye, someone whose mind is open and sharp, ready to make connections that wearied minds can't see."

Rowan considered. "And my father would work with you as well?"

"Of course," the duke said, clapping his hands together.

Rowan leaned back in her seat and observed him for a moment, his golden locks and dark green eyes, the slant of his jaw and the slope of his chest, and she thought that it wouldn't be so bad to work alongside such a man. More importantly, her father could finally fulfill his dream of returning to the palace city.

"That sounds wonderful," she said, and a beautiful grin spread across his face.

A noise at the door pulled her attention away from him. Emily stood at the entrance, carrying a tray of scones and looking back and forth between her and the duke. Upon noticing Emily's presence, he pulled himself up to sit straighter, and he lowered his eyes. Rowan thought she could see a faint blush rising in his cheeks.

"Your father'll be down in a minute," she said to Rowan, giving her a meaningful look. "Why don't you come help me in the kitchen?"

Rowan, suddenly flustered, stood and followed Emily out just as her father, anxiously shuffling papers, bustled into the room, barely acknowledging her as they passed.

When she reached the kitchen and the door had swung shut behind them, Emily set down her tray and grabbed Rowan by the shoulders.

"What do you think you're doing?" she whispered crossly.

"What do you mean?" Rowan asked, trying to hide her embarrassment.

"I saw you two in there making eyes at each other. What are you playing at, Rowan? That man is the queen's brother."

"So?" Rowan wrenched herself away from Emily's grip. "He's a good man."

"You don't know that. You don't know anything about him. Stay away from him, Ro. He's dangerous."

Rowan laughed. "Now, Emily, *you* don't know *that*."

"I do," Emily said, standing up tall. "They're all of them

dangerous, that lot with their sea god and their riches. He's a member of the royal family, Ro. You don't want to mess with those people."

"I'm not messing with anyone. He was just asking if I might like to come and work there for a bit. He wants me to work on some translations."

"Translations, eh?" Emily said, and putting a hand on her hip and thrusting out her jaw, she gave Rowan a look that could have withered an elder. Then she turned her attention to the sink.

Feeling strangely guilty but deliciously giddy, Rowan turned and left the room. She was set to meet Tom that morning, and she figured she'd better be on her way. As she walked by the sitting room, she caught sight of the duke again and smiled at him before she left. She couldn't help notice his eyes following her as she went.

Rowan found Tom inside the tavern, wiping down the bar. He still wore his grief, but she was pleased to see that the color was beginning to return to his cheeks. The work, it seemed, really was doing him good.

"Hello, you," he said.

"Are you ready for our walk?" Rowan asked.

"Nearly," he said, and then, after really looking at her, he squinted. "Are you sure you're okay going into the woods? I don't want to put you in any kind of danger."

Rowan's mind flashed to the way Jude had left her on

the path back from the cimetière the previous evening, and she wondered what would happen if she told Tom. She knew he would probably beat his boorish brother to a pulp, and for a moment, she considered instigating just that, but then she shook herself from her musing.

"It's daytime, and we can bring along a weapon if you like. It's just through the woods a way to Seelie Lake. We've done this walk more times than I can count. I think we'll be fine," she said, leaning into the bar. "But what about you, Tom? Are you okay after . . . after everything that happened? If anyone has a right to be frightened of the woods, it's you."

He sighed. "That's the thing, though, isn't it?" he said, setting down his rag. "I am afraid of them, and I don't want to be. Those woods are part of my life. I can't go on hiding from them."

"I'll be there with you," she said, her heart breaking to see him so distraught.

Smiling at her, as if he were slowly filling back up with life, he nodded. "Let's go."

The walk out was pleasant, and though steel-gray clouds lined the sky, the day wasn't very cold, and it seemed to Tom that the forest was especially alive. Northern squirrels scuttled alongside them, and deer crossed their path more than once. Birds followed them, their song breaking the stillness of the air and reminding Tom that the forest at its heart was a beautiful place—his place.

He was excited to return to Seelie Lake, to the place of childhood comfort, but when it came into view, stretching out like an icy maw, Tom fought the urge to recoil in disgust. It was as if someone had replaced a close friend with a terrible creature, a monstrous thing.

Tom stood there, considering the tableau—the icy gray nothingness before him, the bleakness, and suddenly he knew there would be no return to the kind of innocence and simple happiness he'd known before Fiona's death. For Tom the world had changed, and he had changed with it. Inside, he was as much a wasteland as the icy landscape before him.

But Rowan seemed unaffected by it. She danced along the rocks and took a seat in their regular spot.

"You coming, slowpoke?" she called.

It seemed to Tom that Rowan stood somehow apart from the tragic emptiness of the place, as if she were lit by a different source. She appeared to glow, so full of life she was, and when she smiled at him, he realized that it wouldn't get any better than this. Something inside him had died, and he now knew it was never coming back, but there was always Rowan and the happy strength that radiated from her. As long as he could be near that glow, life didn't have to be completely bleak.

It was later that day that he spoke to his mother about marriage.

"You're sure?" she asked, her eyes bright.

"I know it's unexpected."

"No," she said, smiling. "No, it's not unexpected at all. I must say, I've been waiting for this day . . . hoping for it for years."

"You have?" he asked, surprised. "Then you think I should do it?"

"Yes, of course I think you should do it. Oh, my boy," she murmured, wrapping her arms around him. "I can't tell you how happy you've made me. Oh, my blessed boy."

When Rowan arrived home that afternoon, she found the house to be uncharacteristically cold and quiet. Walking past her father's office, she noticed that although the door was wide open, the room was empty. She stepped inside and saw that his desk was cluttered with papers, which was very unlike her father. Curious, Rowan made her way over to the desk to see what he could have possibly left out, and she was struck by what she saw. The top two pages—the ones her father must have been examining earlier—bore strange images. Pencil drawings. One was of a cage of some kind set upon wheels. For Pema, she wondered? To transport her to the palace city when they eventually set out? She lifted the page, and examining it, she saw that the dimensions were enormous. She set it back down and then focused on the other drawing—a circle within a circle, and between the two circles, seven spokes. She was lifting the paper to scrutinize it further when she was startled by her father's booming voice.

"Put that down," he snapped, and rushing over to her, he snatched the sheet away, quickly collected the other pages, and shoved them inside his desk.

Rowan, shocked by her father's behavior, took a step away from him. "I'm sorry," she said. "I didn't know."

"You never," he said, turning on her, red-faced, "*ever* go through my things."

At first she thought he was giving her a directive, but then she realized it was an observation, and that mixed with his anger was some other emotion. Fear?

"Father," she said, "I'm sorry."

His brows arched with worry. "Not once," he sputtered. "Not once have you gone through my papers. Why now, Rowan? Why?"

Inside, her emotions were warring. She wanted to go to him, to apologize with all her heart for the wrong she'd done, but for the first time in her life, she was afraid of her own father. And yet he too seemed afraid. What could he possibly have to fear?

Dropping his eyes from her, he shook his head. "Go to your room," he said. "Do not speak of this again."

Rowan was stunned. She wanted to beg for her father's forgiveness, but instinct told her to do as he asked—to leave quickly, and to try to put the unhappy experience from her mind.

Turning, she headed out of the room and down the hall. She took the stairs two at a time, and as she was rounding the corner to her chamber, she saw a small dark figure looming over her desk.

Merrilee stood very still, staring through the legs of the silver candelabra out to the woods beyond. What was she seeing there? Rowan wondered, but her curiosity was overwhelmed by frustration that the girl had entered her room without permission. The fact that Rowan had just been chastised for the same offense only added to her ire.

"What are you doing in here?" Rowan snarled.

The girl stepped away from the desk and turned to Rowan, grinning at her. Rowan began to wonder if she might be slow-witted.

"You've a lovely room," Merrilee said, and after adjusting one of the pearl buttons on the navy dress that fastened clear up to her throat, she clasped her hands behind her back.

"That doesn't mean you can explore it whenever you like," Rowan said, trying to seem taller as she strode into the room.

The girl looked up at her with her half-moon eyes. "I just came to see if you might want to play a game of cards with me."

"Do I seem like I want to play cards with you?" Rowan snapped. "I'm not a child."

Merrilee, her face suddenly contorted with disappointment, bowed her head and started toward the door. "I only want to be your friend," she whimpered.

Rowan was hit with a wave of guilt. She stopped the girl. "Look," she said. "I'll play cards with you later, I promise. I just want to be alone right now." Merrilee, seemingly on the verge of tears, nodded, and Rowan felt even worse. She realized she knew nothing of the girl's past, but that it couldn't have been a happy one. Otherwise she wouldn't be a ward. Rowan took a step toward the girl and placed a hand on her little bird shoulder. "I promise I will play with you later.

I'm sorry I've not paid more attention to you since your arrival. I know you must feel out of sorts being in a new place. Tomorrow we shall spend some time together. Would you like that?"

"Yes," the girl said, and a shy smile crept onto her lips. She turned to leave, but Rowan, a question suddenly upon her, stopped her just as she reached the threshold.

"Merrilee, what was it you were so intent upon when I came in?"

"Excuse me?" said the child, clearly confused.

"You were looking out the window. You seemed very focused on something."

The girl seemed at a loss for words for a moment; then she shrugged. "I thought I saw something—something moving—among the trees."

A cold shiver of fear swept over Rowan. "I see," she said, and the child turned to go again before Rowan called out for her once more. "Merrilee," she said. "Be sure to lock your door tonight."

The child nodded and then disappeared around the corner. Quickly, Rowan went to the window and gazed out into the forest. But all was still. Whatever Merrilee had seen out there, it was gone now. Rowan shuddered to think that she and Tom had been deep in the woods only an hour earlier. From now on she would be extra careful about going into the forest—daylight or no.

Rowan was stepping away from the window when she noticed smudges all over her candelabra. The girl had clearly been fiddling with it while she was looking out the window. Rowan sighed with frustration and started cleaning the prints off with the sleeve of her blouse. She would try her best to be nice to the girl, but she had to admit the child did not make it easy.

Rowan stayed in her room and worked on her translations for the rest of the afternoon. When she thought she might be ready to speak with her father, she went downstairs to join him in his study, but when she reached the door, she found him playing cards with Merrilee. The girl gave her a sad smile, but her father avoided her eyes, and the scene irritated and hurt Rowan so, she decided to spend the remainder of the evening in her room. Feigning illness, she took her supper up there, and although she wanted to speak with the duke again, wanted to discuss her trip to the palace city further, she didn't dare interrupt when she heard him below talking with her father late into the night, their voices rising like smoke to her room, their words just out of reach. And when she heard the duke ascend the stairs to his room, she extinguished her candles with a heaviness in her heart.

9. TEMPERANCE

IT WAS LATE afternoon the next day when Tom made his intentions known to Rowan. They were walking around the perimeter of the village when he stopped and held a hand to her cheek.

"Rowan," he said. "Good old Rowan."

She pulled away, unnerved by his behavior. He spoke like a drunk man, only he hadn't been drinking, which somehow made it worse.

"Are you okay, Tom?" she asked, and he nodded, smiled even.

"I'm great. I've never been better." He ran a hand through his hair and looked out into the trees. "I've been stupid, really. Mooning around over a girl I didn't even know. I see that now. You can't fall in love with a stranger. You can't build a family, a home, with a girl when you don't even know how her mind works or what goes on inside her heart."

He looked to Rowan for confirmation, but she didn't know what to say. She wasn't sure where this was going, but she was increasingly aware of a sick sensation swelling within her belly.

"Do you understand me?" he asked, looking more lost than ever. She shook her head, and he covered his eyes for a moment as if the action might help him to think. "I'm saying that I know you, Rowan. I've known you longer and better than anyone else in my life."

She took a step back, and uncovering his eyes, he sank to his knees before her in the snow. When he opened his hand to reveal a thin strip of red twine, she shook her head, certain it couldn't be for her.

"Rowan," he said. "I want you to be my bride." With those words, he took her left wrist, the wrist that led to her heart, and tied the twine around it with gentle fingers.

She stared down at the red twine with horror. With one simple action, Tom had just destroyed any chance she might have of being a scholar. Wives could not be scholars. Wives could not travel at their leisure, nor could they study in the libraries of the palace city. From now on, she would go where Tom went and help him with whatever it was he chose to do, which Rowan knew meant a life spent at the inn with Elsbet barking orders at her and drunken oafs puking on her boots. And what was worse, she was now bound to a boy who would never love her, could never love her—not how she wanted to be loved—because his heart would always belong to another.

He looked up at her with a broad smile, and yet his eyes were completely lifeless—empty, even—and she realized she needed to try to smile. She loved Tom. He was her best friend, and when she had thought she might lose him, she'd realized that her feelings ran deeper, but marriage was something she couldn't consider.

And what of the boy who had cried love at first sight? Where was he? Fiona Eira's body was barely cold, and here he was tying a nuptial band round Rowan's wrist. She gazed down at the scarlet twine, bold against her pale skin, and she realized that she was nothing but a consolation prize. He had done what his mother wanted. He had chosen with his head instead of his heart because his heart had been ripped from him the moment Fiona Eira's had been ripped from her chest.

She felt the warmth of tears flowing down her cheeks, felt the sting as they glided past the cut on her lip, and Tom smiled up at her, and mistaking her grief for joy, he took both her hands in his. If it had been in her power to refuse, she would have done so. She no more wanted this for him than she did for herself. But he already had her family nuptial band. Her father had given consent, and she had no choice in the matter. She bit down on her lip to staunch the flow of tears as she wondered how her father could have done this without talking to her first.

Laughing now, crying too, Tom stood and took her face in his hands.

"I will take care of you," he said, and then leaning forward like he might topple over at any moment, he placed his cold mouth against hers. Politely, she met him with ruby lips, her heart breaking, and then she pulled back and nodded.

"I have to get home," she said, and he looked confused.

"Now?" he asked. "Don't you want to celebrate? My mother is eager to see you."

She held a hand to her stomach. "I feel unwell. I need to go home. Later . . . later we will celebrate." And with that, she turned and started off onto the forest path.

"Ro," he called after her, his voice anxious. "Are you sure you're okay?"

She turned and smiled at him. "I'll be fine," she said. "We'll speak later."

He nodded, and she held his gaze for a moment, and then headed out. When she knew she was hidden from sight, she veered from the path and delved deeper into the trees, the sky spinning above her, the crows circling as if waiting for her to trip and fall and split open her head. When she was certain no one would come upon her, she knelt on the ground and wept. She wept until she thought she might vomit. She wept until she thought there was nothing left inside her anymore. She wept for the girl she once was and for the girl she would never be, and inside her a rage began to burn.

When she had calmed herself, she wiped away the tears and walked home. As she approached her house, she could see that her father's light was burning in his study. Once inside, she didn't call out for Emily, as was her custom, but rather went straight to her father's office. She didn't bother knocking. She threw open his door, and he flinched, quickly closing the heavy leather book he was consulting, and stuffing a second—a thin black book—into his drawer.

"Rowan," he said, clearly unsettled by her presence. "What is it, child?"

She thrust out her wrist to him, displaying the red band that now yoked her forever and always to Tom.

"Ah, then." He smiled. "He's told you. What a joyous night. I'll have Emily fix something special."

Rowan stood aghast. "How could you?"

Henry Rose shook his head, appearing to be genuinely surprised. "You're not pleased?"

"You expected me to be pleased?" she asked, unable to keep the anger from her voice.

"Of course I did, my child. I would never want for you to be unhappy. It's been apparent for some time that you have feelings for the boy. When he came to me, my suspicions were confirmed. He'll make a good and faithful husband."

"He's mad with grief. He was in love with Fiona Eira. He doesn't love me."

"He will grow to love you. It is now his duty."

"I don't want loving me to be someone's duty," Rowan cried, tears threatening to flow. "I don't want to be someone's second choice, and I don't want to live my whole life in Nag's End. I want to be a scholar. Please, Father, you have to call it off."

He looked to the window and shook his head. "I can't do that," he said.

"Please, Father," she begged, desperation breaking her voice. "I can't do this. I'm meant to be a scholar. Please don't take that away from me. I can't marry Tom. I don't want to."

"Silly child, you're in love with the boy," he said, averting his eyes. "And times are dark. You need a husband to keep you safe. It's for your own good."

"Have you lost your mind?" she screamed, her world no longer making any sense. "We were going to go to the palace city with the duke—you and I. What of that?"

"You will not be going to the palace city with the duke or with anyone else. You will be staying in Nag's End with your husband," he said, looking down at his papers. "This is the best path for you, Daughter. I will not discuss it further. This is my final decision."

Rowan blinked and tried to focus on the ground, solid beneath her feet. Surely she must be dreaming, but she knew she wasn't. Her father was really saying these things to her. And all at once, she saw herself as her father must see her, as Tom must see her—weak, small, and useless. Beautiful in some fragile way, but what good was beauty? It had done Fiona Eira no favors.

She felt trapped, as if she might suffocate. But something else swelled in her chest, something hot and burning, similar to the anger she'd felt earlier but more intense. It was sharp and spiked, and pointed directly at her father, and she knew without a doubt that she hated him. Hated him more than she'd ever hated anyone. More even than she hated the Goddess for taking her mother from her all those years ago.

She cleared her throat. "Yes," she answered, trying to keep her voice from shaking. "I understand."

"Good," her father said, then stood and, walking around the desk to her, hugged her close to his chest as he had done a thousand times before, and she was astonished at how something that used to feel so warm and human could suddenly feel so dead.

She turned from him, and doing her best to keep from breaking down, she opened the door, the coldness of the metal knob like a knife against her skin. When she stepped out into the hallway, she was stunned to find Merrilee standing there, leaning against the wall, her tiny navy dress blending into the darkness. Had she been listening? The girl smiled at her, then turned and raced up the back stairs.

† † †

Tom tried to put his misgivings behind him as he approached the inn. Surely he was imagining things. Surely Rowan wanted to be his wife. There was no one who knew him better, no one who loved him more. So why had she reacted as if he'd proposed a double suicide?

He burst into the inn and found his mother setting up for the supper crowd.

"Hello, my boy," she called, looking up from her washcloth.

Jude sat in the corner, a piece of paper before him. He seemed to be puzzling something out. He glanced at his brother, and then folding up the paper, he put it in his pocket.

"Hey now," Jude said. "You look well for once."

Elsbet smiled at her youngest son. "You've done it, haven't you?" she squeaked.

"I have," Tom said, ebullient. "Just now. I'm to be married."

Jude stared at him, stunned.

"My brother," Tom said, hands on the table in front of Jude. "I've taken a bride."

"What?" Jude laughed. "Who? I thought you were . . . excuse me here, but I thought you were in love with Fiona Eira. I thought you said no other girl was fit to touch the hem of her garment."

Tom drew back, seeing Fiona's smiling face in front of his once again, smelling her breath on his neck, and then, as quickly as the vision had come, it was replaced with the image of her splayed out like meat in the slickening snow.

"Jude," Elsbet spat. "Show some respect for the dead. And for the living."

She moved closer to Tom and gave Jude a self-satisfied smile. "I'm going to have a daughter finally. I'd hoped you might be a girl, Jude, you know."

"So who is she?" Jude asked, beginning to warm to the idea of a sister-in-law taking the brunt of his mother's wrath.

"Why, our own Rowan, isn't it?" Elsbet said.

Jude froze, and Tom noticed his brother's face grow pale. "You're joking," Jude said.

"Not a bit," Elsbet chirped. "Tom's finally seen the light. Seen what was right in front of him."

Jude shook his head, anger slowly distorting his features. "Crow's eyes if I've ever heard such a thing," he seethed, his gaze boring into his brother.

"Jude!" Elsbet yelped. "I'll not have language like that in my inn. I've thrown men out on their ear for less."

Tom stared at his brother, his defensiveness piqued. "Do you have something you want to say, Jude?"

But his brother just glared at him.

"If you have something you want to say, by all means, say it," Tom urged.

Jude opened his mouth as if to speak, but no words flowed. He simply shook his head and stared at his brother with a hatred that seemed to reach into Tom's very being.

"You don't like Rowan, is that it?" Tom said.

"You know I don't," Jude said, looking away.

"Well, you're going to have to get used to her. She'll be moving in with us in two months' time. Soon she will bear my children."

And with that, a color rose in Jude's cheeks. "It must be very convenient for you to be able to change your heart so readily."

"I've done no such thing," Tom said, looking away. "Rowan has long been my closest friend, and she'll soon make an honorable wife. That is the most I can ask for."

"And I suppose you're the most she can ask for?" Jude said through gritted teeth.

"Jude," Elsbet snarled. "You watch it, boy."

"You're a hypocrite," Jude said, his eyes trained on his brother, and Tom saw that every muscle in Jude's neck was taut. He looked feral, like an animal waiting to tear flesh from bone.

"That's enough!" Tom yelled. "You will show respect to me and to my bride-to-be, or so help me . . ."

"So help you what?"

"You may be older, but I'm bigger than you, Jude, and I'm not afraid of you."

Tom moved closer, confident in his ability to hold physical master over his brother, but when he was within a few steps of him, Jude suddenly stood and, in one quick and terrifying movement, flipped the old oak table over, missing Tom's leg by inches. Elsbet screamed as Jude pulled himself up to his full height, and though he was slight of build, his rage seemed to lay claim to the whole room.

The two boys stared at each other, the animal within each pushed to its extreme—Tom ready to physically harm his brother, and Jude seemingly poised to kill.

Elsbet's hands flew to her face, and she backed away in horror from what she had created.

The moment hung like the blade of a guillotine, ready to drop with startling finality.

And then Jude stepped away. Tom relaxed his shoulders, and Jude turned and walked to the back door as if nothing had happened. Tom and Elsbet exchanged a look, the same one they'd been exchanging for years, as if to ask what they had done to deserve such a relation. But just as Jude was about to step outside, he turned back and stared at his brother.

"I just want you to know. I'll kill you before I let you marry her."

And then he was gone, the door slamming behind him with a heavy clash of wood against steel.

Arlene Blessing had set the hearth fires to burn low for the night. She had tidied up, and had drunk a cup of willow bark tea. Things were quiet now, different since the world had taken her William from her. It had taken her babies too, years ago—decades now. And though she'd loved them truly and with all her heart, she'd only known each of them a few days before the fever took them. The grief had been so great that she'd decided she couldn't bear another pregnancy, and she and William had been careful ever since. Still, she bore a constant ache in her heart for her children—Lily and Tim, she'd called them, but it was different to lose her William. She'd spent a lifetime with him—married a week after her fifteenth birthday they were, and now he was gone. One full spring and a summer he'd been gone, and now they were closing in on yet another spring. It wasn't sadness exactly that she wore in her heart, it was an emptiness, as if everything inside her had shut off, and now she moved through her life waiting, half hoping that every cough might develop into something more, wondering each night when she lay down to sleep whether things might be better if, when the dawn came, she simply didn't wake up.

And so it was that night as she dressed in her nightgown, as she brushed her hair, as she stared at the blank wall that she and William had painted together. Sometimes she thought she caught a vision of him, out of the corner of her eye. Sometimes it startled her, and she went so far as to turn, sometimes to even call out his name. She set her brush down and closed her eyes, the emptiness inside her more than she could bear. Then she shook herself out of it, turned down the bed, and climbed inside.

It was a moment after she blew out her candle that she sensed the presence. When you live alone in a house, you can hear things, feel things that you don't when you live with other people. And Arlene had lived in this house without William long enough to know that there was a stranger in her home. She was also wise enough to know that this tiptoeing stranger meant her harm, but she didn't move from her bed. She did nothing to arm herself. Rather, she lay there, clutching her sheet, and much of her wanted to close her eyes against it, whatever it was, because in the end, who wants to see the thing that kills you? But she couldn't keep them closed. She had to see. She opened them wide, a child's only defense against the dark, and when the door to her bedchamber opened, and when the shadow, slick as midnight, slipped into her room, she took a deep breath.

It seemed to linger there over her, as if deciding what to do with her, as if it wanted to play with her as a cat might do with its prey. And then, faster than Arlene could even process, the thing was on top of her, biting into her flesh, gnawing into her bone, and the pain was overwhelming. It was only then that Arlene cried out, but by then it was too late. The last sound she heard was the smothered gurgle of her own broken windpipe as the blood filled her mouth and her life slipped away.

Shafts of sun streaked out from behind dark clouds, and the snow was beginning to melt as Rowan walked into the center of the village. As she trudged through the slush, it seemed to her the scent of mountain pine hung somehow heavier in the air. It was an odd day, but then, she thought, maybe it wasn't just the day. Maybe it was the world itself that was growing increasingly odd. Since the deaths on the mountain, things had felt wrong to Rowan. The scent on the breeze was just slightly altered; the water tasted different. And her life was no longer her own.

Rowan was just heading over to drop some papers off with Ollen Bittern when she rounded the corner to see Mama Lune standing outside of the Widow Boone's cottage. The old woman leaned into her cane, listening intently as the red-haired witch explained something to her. Mama Lune held a small jar of what looked like flowers and earth, and seemed to be telling the widow how to prepare it.

Mama Lune turned and looked at her, and Rowan cursed herself for staring so long. Gathering her skirts, she began walking quickly away.

"Rowan," she heard the woman call out, and then behind her, she heard the shuffle of feet. In no time, the witch was in front of her, her green eyes seeming to draw Rowan in.

"What do you want?" Rowan asked, trying to maintain her distance.

"My guest, Mama Tetri, is wondering if you got her note?"

"Yes," Rowan said. "Yes, I think I did."

"She's eager to speak with you. She has some very important information for you."

Rowan smirked. "How can she have information for me? She doesn't even know me."

Mama Lune's eyes grew very wide. "Oh my. You have no idea, do you?"

A chill ran down Rowan's spine. "What do you mean?"

Mama Lune closed her eyes and tilted her head as if listening to distant music.

"It is for Mama Tetri to tell you, my dear, and I'm afraid she is away just now—following the water. Dark days these are, do you not agree?"

Rowan took a step back from the woman and nodded. "She's a Bluewitch, isn't she?"

"Mmm." Mama Lune nodded. "She water-witches. The water tells her things. Not my way, you understand. I could stand over a basin of water for a hundred years and not come away the wiser for it. Dirt is my business. But I'm sure even you know that."

"That's very interesting," Rowan said, ducking away from the woman, her fear turning to irritation.

"You will come, then? When Mama Tetri returns, you will come and speak to her? I fear bad things may happen to you if you don't."

Rowan turned and stared at Mama Lune. "Are you threatening me?" Rowan asked, doing her best not to seem intimidated.

"I am simply relaying a message, my dear. Mama Tetri is your elder, and she has something she wishes to tell you. I suggest you come and hear her out."

"And why should I?" Rowan asked. "She may be my elder, but this woman is a stranger to me."

Mama Lune's eyes widened. "Oh!" she gasped. "But you do not know even *this,* do you?"

"Speak plainly," Rowan snapped. "My patience is growing thin."

"Mama Tetri was your mother's closest friend." Rowan's head went numb as she tried to take in the information. This could not be, she told herself, but the woman looked at her with utter seriousness. "It is true, my child. Your mother and her brother, Pimm, grew up with Mama Tetri. Your father never told you?"

Rowan took a step away from the woman and shook her head. "You're lying."

"I tell you the truth, my dear. Mama Tetri is your soothmere. She said sooth when your mother was pregnant with you. She has come to speak with you. That is a bond that must be honored."

Rowan jutted out her chin defiantly. "If she's so eager to talk to me, why hasn't she come by the house? Why must I come to her?"

"She has called for you. It is you who must answer the call."

"No," Rowan said. "This isn't true. You're lying. My mother wouldn't have had sooth said while she was with child. She was a nonbeliever."

"Perhaps," the witch purred, "your father only wants you to think she was a nonbeliever."

"Excuse me," Rowan said, anger welling within her. "But I must be going."

"I look forward to seeing you, dear," Mama Lune said with a cold smile.

It was Emily who first noticed Arlene's absence. She was used to sharing gossip in the mornings with the older lady, and since the death of Arlene's husband, Emily had kept a protective eye over her. It had been a full day, and still she had not appeared in the village. Fearing she might be sick, Emily sent Onsie Best round to check on her while she and Rowan picked up bread for supper. The boy, who had been in the midst of skipping out on family chores when Emily had caught hold of him, was less than thrilled to have yet another thing to keep him from his favorite hobby of shooting at crows with his slingshot. Still, he was a good boy, and used to doing what he was told, so he went round to Arlene's, hoping that whatever he found there wouldn't provide much work for him.

He knocked on her door, but there was no answer. He knocked again before going around to look in the windows. There appeared to be no one home, though the curtains were drawn on the bedroom windows, so it was possible she had taken to her bed with sickness.

"Fantastic," Onsie grumbled as he climbed a tree so he might jump to her roof, and then down to a high window that he knew was easy to jimmy open because Arlene had had him do it once when she'd locked herself out. He pried the window open and then slid himself through, calling Arlene's name all the while, half fearing he might give her a start, but even more afraid that he might see Arlene in some state of undress.

He was in the hallway outside her closed bedroom door when he suddenly got the shivers. Something felt very wrong in that house, and for a moment, Onsie Best even thought about turning and running straight out the front door, but he knew he'd never live it down, so he swallowed his fear and opened the door to Arlene Blessing's bedroom.

Even from a hundred yards away, Rowan could hear his screams.

Turning to Emily, her body stiff with fear, she grasped the other girl's hand. "It's happening again," she said.

Rowan dashed off in the direction of Arlene's cottage, Emily fast on her heels. When Rowan reached the porch, she nearly crashed into Onsie Best rushing out, his face twisted in horror.

"She's dead," he said, with lips that were turning pale blue. "It's the most awful thing I've ever seen." And with that, he promptly fainted.

Emily, who had just reached the porch, breathless, crouched down and propped the boy's head up on her knee, keeping an eye on Rowan. "Don't you go in there."

But Rowan knew she had to. Without a thought for her own safety, she ran into Arlene's house. She flew up the stairs and rounded the corner to Arlene's room, but in the doorway she stopped abruptly.

"Goddess," she whispered, making the sign, and for a moment, she feared that she too might faint. Steeling herself, she moved to the body. The corpse was stark white, like a spider's egg sac. An enormous bite had been taken out of what had once been Arlene's neck.

Stepping away from the body, Rowan surveyed the bedchamber. The windows were closed and bolted, the room undisturbed. It was as if Arlene had not had time to even put up a struggle.

Suddenly the nape of Rowan's neck prickled, and she had a terrible thought: what if whatever had done this was still in the house? How stupid of her to dash up there alone. Her eyes fell to the bath chamber, and for a second, she felt sure she heard breathing coming from inside. Holding her own breath, her heart beating like mad, she slowly backed out of the room, one foot behind the other until something grasped at her shoulder.

Screaming, she turned to find Goi Tate glaring down at her.

"What might you be doing here, little Rowan?" But then he saw the body and took a step away.

Dr. Temper rounded the corner and upon taking in the sight of the room was moved to cover his mouth.

"Oh, good Goddess."

Goi Tate, suddenly on his guard, moved about the room like a cat. He peered in the bath chamber and then out the window.

"Rowan, did you see anyone?" he asked.

"Just Onsie Best, who found her."

"Right," he said, clapping her on the back. "This is no place for womenfolk."

"But," Rowan said, trying to contain a sudden surge of anger, "I've every right to be here that you have."

Goi Tate didn't seem to hear her. "Run along and fetch the duke, and then tell the elders another funeral will need to be arranged."

† † †

The strange thing about Arlene Blessing's body was that something had drained it of most of its blood. Her neck had been torn, her carotid artery severed, but aside from that, she bore no injuries. Of course, these things weren't said aloud. Such things never are. But Dr. Temper shook his head and said it was beyond his ken, and wouldn't it be best if Mama Lune had a look?

That was the day that the panic began. What had happened to the men on the hill, what had happened to the foreign girl who had wandered out into the woods, those were anomalies, inscrutable animal attacks suffered by people who were not truly members of the community.

But this was different. Not only had Arlene been struck down within the village boundary—within her own home as she slept behind a locked door—but Arlene Blessing wasn't some stranger. She had taught the little ones to mend and sew. She had helped teach new mothers to care for their babies. She was a kind woman, and when her husband had died, everyone had felt not only a deep sense of loss but also a fear that Arlene might follow in his footsteps, as aged widows are sometimes wont to do.

She was the sort of woman one wanted to die quietly in her sleep, surrounded by friends and family. She was the last person one would expect to die a violent death. At first no one discussed it outright. It was almost as if the truth of the matter was too horrifying to confront directly. Rather, it needed to be approached from the side. She was dead, and it looked like an animal attack, and therefore it probably was an animal attack. But everyone knew that no animal could have entered Arlene's house like that—walking through a locked door, only to escape through a high window it somehow managed to shut behind itself. And yet surely no human could have created that bite mark on Arlene's neck. No, it was best not to look straight at the truth of the thing. Only sometimes, truth has ways of revealing itself.

10. THE HANGED MAN

"You're going to do it, then?" Emily asked from her perch on the counter.

"Should you be sitting up there, really?" Rowan asked, arranging the flowers for her blessing wreath.

"Who's going to stop me?" she snorted. "They're my counters if they're anyone's. Answer the question. You're really going to do it? You're going to get married and leave me?"

"Don't make that pouty face," Rowan said. She was trying to seem strong for Emily, when inside she wanted to cry. "You'll be happy to be rid of me. Besides, it's not like I won't be visiting every day anyway. Also . . . also, it's not like I have a choice—not really."

"You could talk to your father. Get him to change his mind."

Rowan shook her head, trying not to blush. She hadn't told Emily she'd already done that and her father had refused her request. Revealing as much, even to Emily, would be too painful. "Why? Don't you like Tom?"

"Of course I like Tom. Who doesn't like Tom? And considering everything that's happened—Arlene and whatnot—I should think it's good to share a bed if at all possible. You'll have built-in security."

"Emily," Rowan said, embarrassed by the warble in her voice. "What do you think it is? What do you think is happening?"

"I don't know, Ro," she said. "I wish I did. A beast, I expect, like they say."

"But what kind of beast stalks the forest and mountaintops, eviscerating men like it's nothing, and then tiptoes into an old lady's house, leaving no sign behind but a bite on the neck?"

Emily shook her head. "Rowan, you keep this up and I'm not sleeping tonight. Let's get back to Tom and boys and weddings and such. That's beautiful, by the way," she said, pointing down to the wreath, her legs now swinging wildly. "He'll be blown away for sure."

Rowan nodded and concentrated on her work. Maybe it was the act of weaving the flowers, or maybe it was seeing Arlene's body—looking directly into the face of death—that was changing something inside her. Maybe these really were dark days. Maybe she should simply be happy to be alive.

Emily and Rowan's father walked with her over to the tavern to present the blessing wreath to Tom. The duke and Merrilee were invited to come to the festivities, but the duke did not seem enthusiastic. In fact, it seemed to Rowan that he had been avoiding her since her wrist had been bound—as if now that she was to be married, she was no longer of any use to him.

Tom nearly wept when he saw the flowers, and his mother proclaimed the wreath sublime.

"You'll have to keep them fresh, have to tend to them, my boy," Elsbet said to him. "You don't want to disappoint on the big day." And then, overwhelmed with emotion, she pulled Rowan to her bosom. "My daughter! My lovely daughter!" she cried.

The celebration went on into the evening, and the inn opened its doors to the public, so that their numbers might grow. Wilhelm even cleared some tables that there might be dancing, and Rowan and Tom took turn after turn on the floor, Rowan laughing in a way she hadn't for what seemed like an eternity.

Only Jude didn't appear to be enjoying himself. He stood in the corner, staring at Rowan with the oddest look, and for a moment, she thought she saw something like genuine affection in his eyes. When he noticed her looking, that affection seemed to be replaced with sadness, but still he met her eyes as if he were asking her an unanswerable question.

"What is it?" Tom asked, noticing she'd become distracted.

"This is going to sound strange, but I'm wondering if I should have a talk with Jude."

"With Jude? Now?"

"Now's as good a time as any. If I'm to be part of this family, I won't be made to feel uncomfortable within it."

Tom nodded, an anxious look in his eye. "Don't be too hard on him."

Rowan laughed. "I'll be a perfect lamb. I promise."

But just as she started over to the boy, Jude turned and, opening the back door, headed out into the snow. She slipped out behind him, and as she stepped into the yard, the coldness of the night stung her face.

"Jude, wait," she called, and he turned around just as the door to the inn closed behind her.

"Why are you following me?" he asked, his face unreadable.

They stood across the yard from each other, the snow silent between them, and Rowan realized that she had no idea what she wanted to say. Slowly she walked over to him, and she had the distinct feeling that she was approaching a deer in the wild and that at any second it might dart away from her and she would lose it forever.

"What is it, Ro?"

"I want to talk to you," she said, feeling a strange pull to him, a desire to reach out and take his hand, but the look in his eyes indicated that she should do no such thing.

"Talk, then," he said, sitting down on the stone wall at the edge of the forest.

"I want to start over," she said, the words coming quickly, her head a little muzzy from the ale. "I know that you don't like me. I know that you don't want me to marry Tom, but it's going to happen, so why not make the best of it? I mean, we can start over, can't we? We can try to be friends. Whatever it is I do that so bothers you, I'm sure I can work on it, and all the things you do that bother me, maybe you could stop doing some of those things too."

He snickered and shook his head but didn't answer.

"Say something," she pleaded, but he only shook his head again.

He looked up at her, and their eyes locked. From him radiated a frightening intensity. "Don't do it," he said.

"What?" she asked, confused, her head suddenly swimming.

"Don't do it," he said again. "Call off the wedding."

"You're joking," she said, but she could see in his eyes that he wasn't.

"I'm not. Don't do it. Don't marry him."

She laughed, but it was a pained kind of laughter. Why was this happening, just when she was finally beginning to feel she might learn to be happy with this marriage? The glow of the firelight and the sparkle of the ale had made her feel she was living in a kind of dream, but then as usual, Jude had to tear it all down and expose the harsh, cold reality of her life for what it was.

"It's not my choice," she said, touching a finger to her

nuptial twine. Soon it would be replaced with a wife's twine, woven of fine golden thread to show that the vows had been said. Her gut wrenched when she thought of it.

He shook his head. "There's always a choice."

"But there isn't," she said, stepping closer to him. "I've spoken with my father, and he's decided."

"You did that?" he asked, something like hope moving across his features. "You asked your father to let you out of it?"

Rowan froze when she realized the mistake she had just made by telling Jude. "Oh, please don't tell Tom. I was confused. I didn't realize what I wanted."

"You mean you didn't realize what other people wanted for you."

She closed her eyes. "Why do you always have to do this to me, Jude? Why can't you just be a friend?"

He looked her deep in the eyes. "Because I can't," he said.

She took a step back, the world suddenly spinning. "What do you want me to do?"

"I want you not to marry him."

Rowan was shocked. She knew the boy disliked her, yet to be so rude as to tell her not to marry his brother seemed extreme even for Jude. But she did her best not to appear upset. There was no point in giving him the upper hand. She cleared her throat. "I just told you that I have to," she said. "I've no other option."

"You could run away," he said, a strange note to his voice.

"You're telling me," she said, nearly choking on her rising anger, "that I should run away from my village rather than cause you the inconvenience of living in your home?"

He didn't respond. He just looked at her, and though she wanted to continue the argument, wanted to finally have the last word with him, he turned and walked away.

"You can't leave in the middle of this, Jude," she called after him. "Where are you going?"

But as she spoke, he hopped over the wall and disappeared into the night.

Rowan wandered inside, feeling as though something in her were injured and raw. And when she returned to the warmth of the inn, and the song and the dance, she couldn't help but notice that everything seemed somehow less beautiful.

✝ ✝ ✝

Just as Rowan was drifting off to sleep that night, the door swung open and there stood Emily with a candle lamp, the wick burning low.

"What are you doing?" asked Rowan.

"I've come to check you haven't left a window open, and there you are with yours wide as a grouper's mouth. Here I've bolted all the doors, and then as I was about to climb into my bed, I thought how you like to sleep with the window always cracked, no matter how cold the weather, and I decided I'd better come in here and close that fool window for you before something awful crawls inside."

Rowan cringed. "Lovely image, Emily. Especially just before bed. Thank you."

"Someone has to watch you," she said.

And as Rowan lay there, glad for her friend's presence, she couldn't help but admire her nightgown. It looked more of a sundress than a typical nightgown, and it was beautiful—white with eyelet lace, and at the base of the left strap an embroidered green flower.

"Emily, is that new?"

"Indeed," she said, showing it off. "Bill's mum made it for me. I'm hoping it means something good that she did."

Rowan sat up in bed, excited. "Oh, it has to. It can't be long before you two are wed."

"I hope so." Emily grinned. "Not that I want to risk leaving your father, but my guess is that if Mr. Rose will have him, Bill would love to come and work here as well. Then I'd be able to stay on." She pressed a hand to her heart, and a blush rose in her cheeks. "Listen to me prattling on like the vows have already been said, when all that's happened is his mother's made me a sleeping gown as a present."

Rowan squinted and leaned in. "It's lovely, Em."

Emily smiled and, kissing her on the cheek, she left Rowan and headed down the hall to her room. Before climbing into bed, Emily bolted the heavy wooden door and checked the latch on the window. Outside, the snow fell in steady waves, and she was glad for the warmth of the fire that was lightly burning in the hearth. She ought to have been able to relax into sleep, but she found herself uneasy still. She went to the closet and peered inside, telling herself she was making sure she'd hung up her skirt in such a way as it wouldn't show wrinkles tomorrow. She took a deep breath and made to pull back the covers, but she found herself paralyzed by a sudden inexplicable fear that she ought not to go to bed at all—that she ought to stay up all night keeping watch, back to the wall, eyes on the window.

But Emily was not a girl who gave in easily to her fears. She was a strong girl and a sensible girl. So with a quick dip and a check beneath her bed, which she told herself was for stray stockings, she eased her mind, drew back the covers, climbed in, and blew out the candle.

† † †

It was very dark when Emily awoke. So dark that she felt certain that an impenetrable cloud had passed before the moon, blotting out any light it might bring. She told herself that she ought to go straight back to sleep, but there was an odd kind of fear coursing through her veins, curdling her blood like poison.

And then she heard it: a steady *drip drip drip* from her bath chamber. Water, though she knew this was not possible. The water to the bath chamber froze in the evening, and they didn't begin the process of thawing it out and getting it flowing again until the morning. And yet ... *drip drip drip.*

Her heart seemed to sit in her throat. The noise grew louder, and she knew she would have to do something about it. After all, it was possible that there was a leak in the roof, and if that was the case, it would need to be dealt with.

Peeling back the covers and climbing out of bed, she lit the candle lamp, and the room erupted into strange shadows. They quivered as she walked, and for a moment, Emily almost thought she saw movement at the edge of the room, but she steadied her fear. There was no one in the room with her. It was a physical impossibility—the door was bolted and the window locked—and Emily didn't believe in ghosts or specters or whatever the villagers were talking about since Arlene's murder.

Slowly she took a step toward the washroom, her bare feet recoiling at the cold floor. She moved across the room with her heart beating a steadily increasing rhythm until she was at the door. Holding her breath, she stepped inside. In a fluid motion, she shined the light around the small room, making certain there was no one inside. She let out a long, relieved exhale.

And then from the corner of the room there was another exhale, mirroring her own, and Emily fought a scream. Thrusting her arm out, she bathed the dark corner in light. It was empty.

She was going crazy. She had to be. She was imagining things. There was no other explanation. But then she heard it again.

Drip ... drip ... drip.

It sounded as though it was coming from above. She raised her arm above her head, tipping the candle lamp at the ceiling, but she could find no source for the noise.

And yet standing there in the cold, she felt certain that what she sensed was something very like evil. She could feel it as surely as she could smell the wax from her candle. And then she felt breath on the back of her neck, and she froze. She closed her eyes and shook her head. It wasn't possible. She was letting a frightened mind get the better of her, and she refused to be owned by her fears like a child. So despite the sensory information to the contrary, Emily turned round utterly convinced that she was alone in that washroom.

The last thing she saw before her candle was extinguished by a thick, rotting breath, a breath that smelled of dirt and death, was the horrifying sight of the fangs just moments before they sank into her neck.

11. DEATH

IN THE MORNING when they found her, she was in her bed. Rowan, having thought her friend the worse for ale, had left her to sleep in, but when she became concerned, she'd gone up and pounded on her door, finally retrieving the skeleton key from the kitchen pantry.

She knew as soon as the key turned in the lock that there was something wrong. An odor wafted from the room, and stepping inside, Rowan found that she was overwhelmed by it. Something dank, earthy, rotten, and above all that, something starkly metallic.

Upon first examination, the room seemed undisturbed, but then Rowan noticed the misshapen lump in the bed.

People did not sleep like that. Whatever it was, it was not a person. She moved slowly at first and stopped a foot from the bed, her hand reaching out over the white downy covers, hesitant.

"Emily?" she called, though her voice was hoarse, and it came out as more of a whisper than anything else.

Silence.

She took a deep breath and then, stepping forward, pulled the sheet back.

It took her a moment to understand what she saw. An ivory shape, and beside that, a crimson stain—a perfect circle of blood soaking the bottom sheet, and even, it seemed, seeping into the mattress.

"Emily!" she said again, only this time it was a shriek as she reached out to shake her friend, her hand meeting with cold flesh, sticky with blood. She shook her head, beginning to cry. Emily's body was twisted and broken, seeming to curl in on itself at the wrong places, only to jut out again at even odder angles. Her eyes were wide open, frozen in a perpetual state of fear. She was naked save for the blood, and her neck . . . her neck had been ravaged beyond recognition.

"Father!" Rowan cried, and then she screamed, a high, piercing sound that caused her father to drop a cup and saucer in his study down below, the china shattering into slivers of white and blue.

The rest of the morning passed in a haze. People came and went. They made assessments. And how silly they all seemed to Rowan. There was only one assessment: Emily was dead. Nothing else mattered at all.

She sat in her father's study, drinking tea and staring out the picture window, not seeing. Footsteps sounded everywhere. People had descended on the house. She could hear them stomping up the stairs and down the hall to Emily's room. So much noise. It was hurting her head, hurting her soul. *Later,* she thought, *when Emily gets home, I will tell her. . . .* But she stopped herself when she remembered Emily would never get home.

And then she heard something that didn't make sense—footsteps overhead in what could only be her own room. There was no reason for anyone to be in her room. Her head swimming from the medicines Dr. Temper had put in her tea, Rowan lifted herself from the couch and started for the stairs. As she climbed, the walls seemed to expand and contract. The floorboards seemed to swell.

Before she even reached her room, she knew whom she would find inside, and when Rowan stumbled in, the world slipping like loose marbles beneath her feet, she could barely contain her anger. There she was, Merrilee, the back of her nut-brown hair facing Rowan as she stood at Rowan's desk.

"Get out!" Rowan screamed, and footsteps came quickly down the hallway. "Get out, you runt!" There were voices behind her, urging her to be kind to Merrilee, and then someone's hands on her shoulders. She pushed them off and, lurching across the room, grabbed Merrilee by her wool sleeves and spun her around.

"Get out of my room!" Rowan screamed again. "Get out!"

And then Merrilee raised her arms. She held something in her hands, and blinded by rage, Rowan grabbed it and dashed it on the floor.

There was a terrible crash, followed by weeping from Merrilee, and gasps from the onlookers. And on the floor lay broken glass and water, and flowers.

"They were for you," Merrilee wept. "I just wanted to make you feel better."

And then the girl ran past her, and the onlookers tut-tutted. Rowan saw faces glaring at her, glaring at wicked Rowan who makes children cry. Goi Tate, and Dr. Temper, and the old lady who lived near Arlene.

"Get out!" she screamed at the lot of them.

They backed away from her and out into the hall. She slammed the door and collapsed onto her bed.

Hours later, Rowan sat at the inn, a blanket wrapped around her shoulders as she sipped brandy and stared into the fire. There was a hollowness inside her. She kept trying to tell herself that Emily was gone, but she couldn't make herself believe it. Emily was always there. She always had been, and she couldn't just be gone all of a sudden. She kept feeling her cheek, knowing Emily would never give her another kiss goodbye. Her mind slowly moving through memories of their childhood together—playing in the stream, the warmth of the summer sun on their faces as Emily scolded her about going in too deep. Emily as a child, sitting on the counter, swinging her legs while Antonia cooked beside her. Or was that only the other night? This was wrong. This wasn't supposed to happen, she told herself. Emily was supposed to marry Bill Holdren and have ten babies she might scold to her heart's content. Her blond hair was supposed to fade to gray. The skin around her cat's eyes was supposed to wither and sag. Her face was supposed to happily line, and her body shrink. They were supposed to know each other's grandchildren. They were supposed to sit side by side as old ladies, Emily making jokes, Rowan quietly choking back her laughter.

It wasn't exactly that she had taken Emily for granted, but now that Emily was gone, Rowan felt somehow completely alone in the world. There were many people she loved, and who loved her, but none who knew every single one of her faults and loved her despite them. And there was no one who could drive her so crazy and whom she loved quite as much as she had loved—*still* loved—Emily.

She watched the flames dance before her, and took another sip of the brandy that Elsbet had given her. She enjoyed the way it burned her throat and took her away from her own thoughts . . . her pain. She felt a hand on her shoulder—Tom's hand, but she looked up to see Jude standing above her. He looked beautiful in the firelight, and for a moment, she forgot that she hated him.

"I'm sorry," he said, and then he sat down beside her and stared at the fire. They remained there for some time, side by side, watching as the fire slowly died.

Tom awoke with a start, a strange sense that someone was in the room with him. He lay there a moment, eyes closed, willing himself dead, willing the thing in the room with him, whatever it was, to kill him. To rip his heart out as it had done to his beloved.

He felt the energy of another entity. Heat. He felt heat, and then he felt the whisper of a finger against his lips. It was not what he expected. It was soft. And there was a scent of dewy, aromatic earth. And then he heard her faint laughter, and smelled her hair, the shining blackness that always seemed to emit the slightest hint of lavender. But it couldn't be.

He opened his eyes and flinched when he saw her crouching over him like an animal. Her eyes were wide and sparkling, a wildness in them he didn't remember from before. The skin of her shoulders and neck looked clean and alive, and her cheeks, though stark white, seemed somehow to be lit from within. Something about her dress was different. It was white instead of red, and it was a sundress, delicate straps revealing the taut muscles of her shoulders. And there was something feral about her, something within her that meant that it couldn't be her, not really. But then, he knew that already. There was no way it could be her because she was dead. He'd seen her lying in the snow, her heart ripped from her chest.

"Hi," she said, her voice lower than he remembered.

"This is a dream," he said, propping himself up on his elbows.

She shook her head and smiled, her lips wet and expectant. And then she leaned in and kissed him hard on the mouth. Overcome, on the verge of tears, he lifted his hands to her face and kissed her back, knowing that none of it could be real. His hands ran along the length of her body, and he could feel that underneath the white cotton shift, she wore nothing. He caressed the slope of her hip, the softness of her belly, and the more he reached for her, the more she seemed to stay just out of reach. And then she pulled away and looked at him with those pitch-black eyes—the eyes of a beautiful animal.

"Come on," she said, and she was off the bed and by the window. She cracked it open and a flurry of snow wafted in, coating her skin, but she didn't seem to mind it. Her skin that had been so rosy in life, in memory, was now the color of the snow that brushed against it. She swept her unruly hair over her shoulder and raised an eyebrow at him.

"You coming?" she said, and then, gathering his boots and pants from the floor, she tossed them in his direction.

He climbed out of bed and pulled on his trousers, but when he looked back up, she was gone. He ran to the window and looked out to the woods, certain he had lost her again forever, but she was still there, leaning against a tree, standing barefoot in the snow. She motioned for him to come.

He threw on his clothes and hurried downstairs. He opened the door and took his steps slowly. He was awake now. He was sure of it, and yet she still seemed to be there. It was nearly dawn, just the beginning, and the air was colored with lavender. The snow was coming down in gentle flurries like tufts of fur, or feathers kicked up from goose down pillows. But it was cold. And she was standing there in nothing but a sundress. And she was supposed to be dead.

"Come on," she said, hand on her hip, feigning annoyance.

The Fiona Eira he had known had been fragile and shy, but this new girl, this dream girl, was vibrant and bold, wild and free. She was warm. She looked at him like they were old friends, like she adored him, like he was worthy of being adored.

"I can't stand here all day. Do you want someone to see me?" She grinned as if it were a joke. As if the fact of her death were nothing but a humorous anecdote.

When he reached her, she took his hand in hers and pulled him into a gentle gallop.

"Come on, will you?"

And then he was running through the morning light, through the snow and the ice-cold air, still unsure what was happening, her hand so warm in his. She laughed and looked at him with so much excitement, so much love, that his veins seemed to expand, and more oxygen seemed to reach his brain, his lungs, making everything fantastically clear. Making it sparkle. And quite suddenly he felt as if the world had color again—as if he'd lived all his life without some key element that was now granted to him, which Tom knew he could never again live without. He'd never felt so himself before. It was as if with every step he took, he became more of the person he was destined to become. And he was sure he could conquer anything. He could be anything he wanted, and for a moment, he even thought he might understand Jude. His need for freedom. Was this what it felt like to run off into the wilderness alone? And surely he must be alone. The girl who ran beside him couldn't be there—not really. He wondered if this was what it felt like to be truly free. And for the first time in his life, he realized he could leave Nag's End. There was nothing stopping him. He could go out and see the world. See the wonders he'd only heard about.

The snow licked his face, and his nose was growing cold. He looked to his ghostly companion, stretched out an arm's length away, laughing, her teeth glistening white, her hair whipping around her in wild black waves. Only she was like no ghost he'd ever imagined. If anything, she seemed more alive than when she'd actually been alive. But he knew that she couldn't be there. He had seen her ravaged and dead. He had seen her laid out in her glass casket for all to gaze on her terrible beauty made colder, more perfect with death. This girl beside him was more alive than any girl he'd ever met. And so warm. Heat seemed to spill from her, warming him simply by his proximity.

And he knew this had to mean he was losing his mind.

Up in her room, Rowan dreamed of her mother again. Holding the wooden egg, she smiled at Rowan. Soft morning light filtered through the window, and her mother held her close. Rowan ran her little fingers down the length of her mother's arm, and at the base of her wrist, she found fastened a golden snake. Startled, Rowan screamed, and then began trying to squeeze her fingers between the snake and the flesh to free her mother, but that only made the snake squeeze tighter. Soon, the snake was burrowing in, cutting into her mother's flesh, breaking the skin. And then something happened—a blade slipped between the snake and the flesh, and with a quick swish, the snake split in half and fell to the ground.

"Ah," her mother sighed. "That's better." And taking Rowan into her arms, she held her.

In her dark bedroom, Rowan woke up crying, longing to be held as her mother held her in her dreams, knowing she never would be. With searching hands, she reached for Pema at the foot of the bed. She ruffled the dog's fur, and the warmth felt good against her fingers. Pema shifted in her sleep, and then Rowan lay back down again, and turning on her side, she shut her eyes against her pain.

They were inside the hollow of a tree. Tom didn't know how this could be possible, but there he was. They'd run for a long time, and now to him it seemed to be even more of a dream than it had before. It was all something of a blur. A luscious blur, and he kept trying to tell himself that he needed to remember everything about each moment, and that if he could do so, he could retain the knowledge, retain the vibrancy of the colors, retain the delicious taste that seemed to hang in the air, and he could take it with him back to reality. He could use it to become something new. Something powerful.

The inside of the tree was too large, and it seemed to recede impossibly far.

"It's a fairy tree, but they don't mind my using it," she said, taking a bite of her apple.

He wanted to tell her that he didn't believe in fairies. But he didn't speak. Instead, he took a bite of his apple as well—the fairies had left those too, the apples. Apparently they'd been in a hurry to lend her the place. The apple tasted otherworldly. It tasted like his mouth was lit on fire with thousands of shades of sweetness and tartness, and his tongue traced the apple before each bite, almost not wanting to lose contact with the fruit.

She was no longer wearing her sundress. Now she wore only her necklace and a purple satin piece of fabric draped lazily over her exquisite frame. Memories flooded his mind. Her face beneath him, above him, somehow around him. His hands surrounding her, bringing her to him, the fire within her warming the two of them. But that couldn't have happened. It was as if time was being difficult, refusing to unspool like it normally did.

She snapped her fingers in front of him, the air seeming to part for the pressing digits, sparks seeming to fly.

"You're going to have to keep it together if we're going to do this, Tom. I don't want to drive you over the edge here."

He bit into his apple. "You're not real," he said.

"Of course I'm real."

"No. You're not. You, this place, this apple, all of it, it's all just in my mind. I'm not even here right now."

"You're not?"

"No."

"Then where are you?"

"I'm back home in bed. I'm sick. I must be. I have a fever, and I'm dreaming all this."

She raised an eyebrow. "You dreamed what we just did?"

He nodded.

"That must have been one excellent dream, Tom."

"I think it was," he said. "Thanks."

And then without hesitating, she reached out and slapped him hard across the face. The burn was spectacular. He raised a hand to the pain.

"What about that, Tom? Was that a dream?"

He shook his head. And then she was crouching in front of him, his head in her hands, just like before, only now he had the distinct sense that he was in danger—that she had the capacity and possibly the desire to do him great harm. She held his eyes with her own black pools and spoke with great precision.

"Now listen to me, Tom. I am not part of your fantasy. I never was. I know you like to think that I am, but I am very much my own thing. I am something different now. I occupy my own space, Tom. Do you understand? I am real. I am here. I am more here than you are. Do you understand me?"

"But you . . . died."

"I didn't."

"But I saw you. Your heart was ripped out."

"Stop saying that!" she yelled, rage spilling into her eyes, and her grip on his face tightened. "What if I said that about you? What if I said that you were dead? How would that make you feel, Tom?"

"But I saw you. Your body was on display. How is that possible?"

She let go of his face, once again the sweet and sensual girl. Reclining beside him, she pulled the sheet around herself and took a bite of her apple.

"Maybe I wasn't supposed to die, Tom," she said, toying with the coin on the red ribbon she still wore around her neck. "Did you ever think of that?"

And then she kissed him deep and slow, and his urge to question ceased. After that, he followed her every command, and the hours went by strangely so that by the time she walked him back to the edge of the woods, the daylight that was only barely appearing when she'd come for him was already beginning to wane. He felt queasy, as if he'd had too much of something good, and in doing so had turned it putrid. He could feel it in his head, in his gut, the sick-sweet taste of shame. When they reached the edge of the woods, he stepped over the threshold, and she let go of his hand. He turned to see her, leaning into a tree as if she were a part of it.

"You're not coming?"

She shook her head. "I can't."

"Why not?"

"I can't leave the woods during the day."

A panic rose in his chest, and he reached for her. She took his hand, and as if pulling him through to another realm, she kissed him again.

"And, Tom," she said between kisses. "This is a secret. I'm sure I don't need to tell you that, right?"

And then, gently, as if she were dealing with a child, she pushed him away and leaned back into her tree.

"You're really staying here?"

She shrugged. "I have responsibilities, Tom. I have hungry mouths to feed."

He furrowed his brow. "I don't understand. Hungry mouths?"

"The forest is my home now. I have to stay."

"What—in that fairy hollow?" He felt ridiculous saying it, but then nothing in the world seemed to make sense anymore.

A strange smile spread across her lips, something powerful, something predatory.

"I don't think they'll be coming back anytime soon."

He stepped away from her, and then she looked normal again—a lovely, normal girl who somehow wasn't dead but wasn't quite alive either, standing half-naked in the snow.

"Go now," she said, shooing him with her hand. "I want to watch you as you walk away."

It was only then that he noticed her feet. In the hours since he'd been with her, he'd been pulled in by her strange beauty. He seemed to be covered in moss and dirt from their tryst in the woods, but she was perfectly clean, pristine, except now he saw that her feet and shins were caked with dirt and mud and a strange grayish substance. She noticed him looking, and then she was gone.

12. THE HIEROPHANT

THE NEXT MORNING, a small procession made its way
through the woods and up to Cairn Hill. It was a short walk
through the forest and then up a steep slope that let out
above Seelie Lake. There, at the Mouth of the Goddess, Emily's body, now wrapped in silk and anointed with oils of ce-
dar and hyssop, was placed in the snow, and then solemnly,
and with great care, the stones were laid atop. But Rowan
did not place a stone. Overtaken with grief, she departed
early. She did not even leave the customary offering of cinnamon for the Goddess. Her father would see to it that her
share was placed.

Wracked with sobs, she made her way through a

smattering of trees to the drop-off that overlooked Seelie Lake. A traditional place of mourning, it was called Lover's Leap, and though she had often heard people crying there, it was her first and only time at the edge. She sank to her knees and wept. A moment or so later, she felt a gentle hand on her shoulder and looked up to see the duke. She wiped her eyes, and gingerly, he helped her to her feet.

"It was good of you to come," she said, trying to pull herself together.

"Your father tells me this place is called Lover's Leap," he said. "I assume it's called so because lovers throw themselves off it after the death of their mate with some regularity."

"Yes," Rowan said, wiping her eyes. "That's why, and yet, I don't know that anyone has ever really done it."

"Really?" the duke asked, looking down at the ice-covered lake below them. "But it would be such a romantic gesture. I almost want to try it myself. I think I would if I weren't sure to break my neck and drown."

"They used to say there were water nixies in Seelie Lake," Rowan said, smoothing her skirts. "Tom's grandmother told him they were real, and when we were little, we believed her. She said they only came out at night, so how would we know the difference? It's strange to grow up and realize that so much of what you believed was a lie."

The duke sighed. "The pain will ease," he said. "With time, it will ease."

"I imagine you don't have nixie stories in the palace city," she said, trying to smile, grateful for his company.

He shook his head. "No, but I've heard them. I spent my childhood among the mountain folk, and the old grannies used to warn us to stay out of the water at night if we didn't want the nixies to eat us alive."

Surprised, she furrowed her brow. "How does a duke end up in the mountains?"

"Ah," he said, sighing, suddenly sheepish. "It's a long story. I'm sure you don't want to hear it."

"But I do," she said, looking up at him seriously, and after he considered her a moment, his shoulders fell.

"Fine. You know what a vicoreille is, right?"

Rowan nodded. The vicoreille was the advisor to the king—only, Rowan knew that in some sense the vicoreille held even more power than the king, for it was within the vicoreille's right to veto any law, although he seldom did. He usually served more as a religious figure, advising the king in spiritual matters, for his name meant "in place of the ear," and it was said that his was the only ear in the kingdom into which the sea god spoke.

"Well, my grandfather was the vicoreille to King Clement the Third."

Rowan tried to hide how impressed she was. The brother of the queen was one thing; the grandson of a vicoreille was quite another.

"Now, it so happened that my father's sister was quite beautiful, and the king decided he wanted to retire his first wife and marry my aunt. My grandfather refused, for my aunt despised the king. I don't know what you've heard about him up here in the mountains, but he was an awful, bloodthirsty man. Angered by the rejection, he had my aunt dragged through the streets and slaughtered in front of my grandfather. When my grandfather moved to stop the violence, the king had him ejected from the palace city. Our family was exiled to the mountains."

"That's awful," Rowan said, sick to her stomach at the thought. "How was it that you came to return to the palace city, and your sister to the throne, no less?"

He nodded. "When Lucius the Fourth came of age after his father died under, shall we say, questionable circumstances, and thank the sea god for that, my grandfather was pardoned and our family was brought back to the city. Lucius the Fourth had loved my grandfather and wanted to right the wrong his father had done, and so as a gesture of friendship, an offer was made to wed his son to my sister."

Rowan sighed, his family's tragedy heavy upon her chest. "I'm so very sorry."

He nodded. "But those years in the mountains taught me humility. They taught me kindness. That's why when Merrilee was brought to court—her parents were criminals; they had murdered a soldier for his gold, and the child was to be put in a workhouse—I couldn't let that happen. In her eyes, in that sorrow, I saw my grandfather, my family, and I agreed to take her on as my ward."

"She's a good child," Rowan said, ashamed of the way she had yelled at her after the incident with the vase. "I'm sorry if I hurt her feelings. I'm afraid I ruined any chance we might have had at a friendship."

The duke smiled. "I'm sure she will forgive you. She thinks the world of you."

"Really?" Rowan asked, surprised. "She does?"

The duke nodded and moved to speak again, but just then, Rowan heard her father call out from behind them. The ceremony was over. It was time to head back. A village meeting was in progress over at the inn. Usually such affairs were for men only, but Rowan accompanied her father and the duke, hoping they wouldn't dissuade her from coming, and was pleased when they didn't. Her father wasn't feeling well, and he excused himself when they passed their home, but the duke was eager for Rowan to come along.

When the two of them reached the inn, Rowan was surprised to see Jude standing out front.

He called to her, and when the duke continued inside, she reluctantly went to speak with him.

"What is it, Jude?"

"You don't want to go in there," he said.

"I don't?" she laughed, raising an eyebrow. "Since when have you been the arbiter of what I do and don't want?"

"It's about organizing another hunt," he said. "It's just Goi Tate yelling over everyone."

"When isn't Goi Tate yelling over everyone? Thank you for your concern, Jude, but I trust I will be fine."

"Suit yourself," he said with a shrug.

Rowan walked past him and pushed open the heavy wooden door. Inside, she found a large group of men in the midst of a fierce debate.

"This thing has taken three from our village. We have to

go out again," Goi Tate was saying, his face red with anger. "I'll not be held hostage in my own home."

Paer Jorgen nodded, his calm exterior a salve to the fury that surrounded him. "I understand your concerns. Since the duke has agreed to stay as the king's representative and lead the investigation, I think it's best to let him speak now."

"Please, gentlemen," the duke said from his position near the bar. "You must understand. This situation is a unique one. I urge you not to get carried away."

"Carried away?" Goi Tate said, crushing his fists into the table before him. "This thing, whatever it is, has taken lives. What's more, it's somehow gotten through the village barrier. The situation is dire. Whatever it is, we need to chop its head off and burn it, is what we need."

A roar of approval sounded when he had finished.

"I wonder," Rowan spoke up, but she could not be heard above the din. However, the duke flashed her a warm smile, then raised his hand to quiet the others.

"Please, everyone," he said. "The lady wishes to speak."

Clearing her throat, Rowan stepped forward. "I wonder," she said. "I wonder if we're hunting a monster at all. Goi Tate makes a good point. Arlene's and Emily's deaths were not like the others. They died in their homes—in their beds. I think we need to examine all possibilities." Noticing that the men were beginning to take her seriously, she grew confident and began to speak with more authority. "So we have the first deaths up on Beggar's Drift. Five men dead—one with his eyes and tongue gouged out, the others mysteriously dead after exposure to the elements. At the time, we wondered if it might be the work of a large predator—a wolf, many of us assumed. Next we had the strange case of my cousin's death. The girl was wandering about in the woods at night—unusual circumstances, to be sure. Few dare go into the woods at night during our best of times, and yet there she was, alone and wandering through the trees, when a beast struck her. As I'm sure you all know, it tore out her heart. So now we have two similar crimes, although not exactly the same, but what links them is their locations. Fiona Eira in the forest, and the men up in the mountains, they were all beyond the village boundary, out in the wilds and far from their homes. But Arlene's death, and my Emily's death, do not seem to match the others."

"Why are we listening to this chatter from a woman—and a child at that," groaned Goi Tate. "We need to get out there and find the beast. Chop off its head."

The duke raised his hand to silence the man. "Let her speak. Please, Rowan, go on."

"I think we need to separate the deaths based on their execution," she continued, her palms beginning to sweat. "We have two sets of attacks that were violently bloody in nature and carried out in the wilds. Then we have two more attacks that were quite different in nature. These took place within the village boundary, behind locked bedroom doors, and the attacks themselves were almost . . . neat. I saw the scenes myself. There was very little blood about because, well, because it seemed the victims had been drained of it."

The duke looked at her, something dawning in his eyes.

"So you think this might be the work of two separate perpetrators?" he asked.

"I don't think you should rule it out. Moreover, I think we need to look into the possibility . . . ," Rowan started, but suddenly, all eyes upon her, the words seemed too awful to say out loud.

"What is it?" prodded Paer Jorgen. "Speak, child."

"I just wonder if this second set of deaths was caused by something else—if it was the work of a person—of one of us."

Paer Jorgen seemed to seriously consider her question, and the room fell into silence, but a moment later, Goi Tate burst into laughter.

"A man who can walk through walls?" he mocked. "I forgot to tell everyone, that just happens to be one of my talents. Should have mentioned it."

Soon the others joined in with their laughter, and Rowan, annoyed, looked to the duke, who was staring at her intently but also seemed somehow miles away. Clearly, he had been struck by what she'd said. She met his eyes, and he nodded at her but was too lost in his thoughts to quiet the others. Frustrated, Rowan crossed her arms in front of her chest as Goi Tate went on, rising up to his full height as he spoke.

"People, we need to take action. There's something living in these woods. It's preying on our people, and it must be stopped."

Wilhelm spoke up, his voice hesitant. "I agree with Goi Tate. This thing, whatever it is, it must be stopped before it kills again. Whatever risk we take going out there is small in comparison to doing nothing in the face of this bloodshed."

"Easy enough to say when one of your own boys refuses to join the hunt," Tak Carlysle said.

Draeden Faez stroked his beard. "I must say, your son's reticence to join surprises me," he said.

Wilhelm looked shaken. "He's not been well, my boy. He's . . . not been well."

Rowan saw a few of the men exchange looks, and she fought back her growing anxiety. Surely they couldn't think Tom could have anything to do with the killings.

"And where was he again when Fiona Eira was murdered?" asked Goi Tate pointedly.

Wilhelm flushed a violent shade of red. "He was here at home. I . . . sent him out to gather firewood, and that's when he heard the scream."

"It's interesting, though, isn't it," Goi Tate continued, looking away from the older man. "That he happened to be the first to find the body, and now he seems to be losing himself to some mystery illness such that he's not content to join us in the hunt."

"What are you suggesting?" Wilhelm practically growled, starting across the room toward Goi Tate, but the duke held his hand against the man's chest, stopping him.

Rowan stood frozen, watching the scene as if it were taking place somewhere very far away.

The duke cleared his throat. "Goi Tate is making inappropriate suggestions. Your boy has had a shock. If he is unfit to hunt, then it is best that he stay home. This is not a forced labor, and we've numbers enough as it is. So," he said, clapping and looking around the room. "The beast seems to strike at nightfall, and that is when we shall hunt it. Let us hope we will have better luck this evening."

But they did not. Fifteen men, combing the woods in pairs until the early hours, did not find so much as a ground squirrel. It was as if the entire forest had gone into hiding. If there was a beast living in their woods, it was not going to make itself easy to find.

There was a moment, though, when Wilhelm, shotgun in hand, had a strange sensation. He was standing near an ancient yew tree, the kind his mother used to say was home to fairy hollows, when he was certain he felt movement beneath his feet, and for an instant, he nearly thought he heard Tom's voice. Distant, muffled, but Tom nonetheless. His entire body froze and his heart raced, and then, quickly, he pulled himself out of his trance and hurried away from the tree.

✝ ✝ ✝

The next day, Rowan was in the kitchen, pulling a tray of scones from the oven, when she noticed the duke leaning against the far wall.

"Thank you," she said, and after setting down the tray, she wiped the sweat from her brow. "Thank you for defending Tom like you did at the tavern."

"A mob of frightened men is a dangerous thing," he said. "They are like a pack of wild animals, and often they choose to sacrifice the injured of their herd."

She looked to him with pained eyes. "Tom couldn't have

had anything to do with any of this. He's a good boy. There is no one kinder. You don't suspect him, do you?"

He shook his head. "Of course not. The boy has had a shock is all. I'll do my best to help your fellow villagers see as much. Unfortunately, the gentle people of Nag's End do not share your love of logical inquiry."

His words made Rowan think of Goi Tate and Onsie Best, and she couldn't help but laugh, and when she did, the duke joined her.

"Ah, Rowan," he sighed. "How I wish I could take you with me to the palace city, and here you go and spoil it all by marrying a soulful village lad."

Feeling a blush rising in her cheek, she lined a basket with a towel for the scones. "I'm sure I wouldn't have been as much help as you suppose."

"Tell me," he said, pulling out a chair and taking a seat. "How are you doing? It seems to me your grief hangs heavy on you, my friend."

Turning back around, she met sympathetic eyes.

"Thank you," she said. "I'm trying to carry on with things. I reckon I'm a bit less of a mess than I was at the start. I just wish . . . ," she began to say, but then she shook her head, and turning back to her scones, she began placing them in the basket.

"Please," he said. "Go on. You can speak freely."

Suddenly, on the verge of tears, she gave in. It would feel so good to have someone to talk to again. "It's just some-times I wish I could get away from it all—from the grief, from the village."

"Ah, but there is," he said, rising, his warm gaze upon her. "You could come to the palace city with me as originally planned."

Rowan laughed, flustered. "You know I can't do that. My father's given my twine. I'm bound, and Tom isn't the kind who strays far from home."

Sighing, he said, "I fear this is all my fault."

"What do you mean?"

"Your father and I spoke about you coming to work with me, and I'm afraid he took it rather badly."

"He didn't seem pleased when I suggested it either. I can't understand it, because it's been his dream to return to the palace city."

"I know," he said. "He's made that clear for quite some time."

"He has?"

"Indeed, but I didn't really see a point. Your father is a diligent man, but he's not exceptional—not like you, Rowan. His kind of intelligence is like a sponge. It absorbs. It doesn't create. Your kind of intelligence is generative. It's much more exquisite. You're a rare bloom."

"Please," she said with a scowl. "You praise me and insult my father in a single breath."

"I'm sorry. I misspoke. I only mean to say that I am extremely eager to work with you, and I'm afraid your father might have misunderstood my intentions with you."

Rowan raised her eyebrows, unsure she wanted to hear more. And yet the duke went on. "Here's the thing, Rowan: I don't think you're going to be happy here. I think this marriage might be the death of you."

Rowan took a step away, but he only moved closer, taking her hands in his. "Come with me to the palace city, Rowan. Take a butcher's knife and slice off that hideous bracelet, and come to the palace city with me."

Stunned, she shook her head. "Even if I wanted to, I couldn't. It would be against the law."

He raised his eyebrows and smiled at her. "The law? Do you think provincial law matters when a member of the royal family is involved? Do you think we can't just take what we want whenever we want it?"

She grew cold. It seemed to her that this was a threat. "Please," she said firmly. "Please stop. I don't think I like where this is going. I'm to be married. If I disappear into the night with you, I'll look like—"

"If you're going to be conventional about it, I'll marry you if you like," he said, his eyes flashing, a strange, nearly mad smile on his face, and her heart contracted as much from fear as from flattery.

"Marry you?" Shocked, she pulled her hands away from his as if they were on fire. "But I don't love you."

He laughed, his grin growing even more odd. "I don't love you either, but I imagine it would sort itself out eventually. In the meantime, I could show you a world that would shock and delight you. I would shower you in jewels, and you . . . you would help me."

Rowan shook her head, her heart beating beyond her

control. "Please, you flatter me, but I don't want to be showered in jewels."

"Tell me this, then," he said, suddenly still, his expression intent. "Would you like to become the most famous woman in the history of the land?"

"What do you mean?" Rowan asked, confused.

"What if I told you I could guarantee that someday you would serve as first-ever female vicoreille?"

Rowan nearly laughed out loud at the idea. Not only was the position of the vicoreille always a man's post, but it was not something that could be offered, and Rowan knew this. Whatever the duke might say to flatter her, she knew now that they were empty words, for if he thought she would believe he had the power to appoint her vicoreille, then he thought her a fool.

Rowan stepped away from him, disappointed. It was clear now that he was not the man she'd supposed. He was handsome and rich, but reckless and deceitful. He was too much cake mixed with too much ale, and standing there looking into his dark green eyes, she felt that she might be ill.

"I'm sorry," she said, turning and quickly filling her basket. "But I have to go now. I'll be late. I'm to take these scones over to Tom."

Finally the duke moved away from her and folded his arms in front of his chest. "That sounds absolutely fascinating," he said, his tone no longer kind. "What a thrilling life you have ahead of you."

Without looking at him, she grabbed the basket and

hurried from the room. In the front hall, her hands shook as she fumbled with her cloak. It was only once she was outside and the cold air was smooth against her cheek that she felt she could truly breathe again, and as soon as she was out of sight of the house, she stopped and leaned against a tree to steady herself.

Her head seemed to spin as she tried to piece it all together. This was the second marriage proposal she'd received in the space of a fortnight, both of which came from men who did not love her. None of it made any sense. Clearly the duke wanted something from her, but to what end? Could it simply be her skill with the Midway translations? It couldn't be that, for the writings of the ancient Midway peoples were not considered especially important—the city people saw their legends as backward and their fallen civilization, a failure. No, there was something else that she wasn't seeing, and that worried her.

Rowan started along the path again, watching as the snow gathered on her deerskin gloves. It would be good to see Tom. He had been strange lately, it was true—haunted—and he may not love her as she loved him, but he was her friend, and being with him always made her feel grounded and safe.

When she reached the tavern, it was empty inside, but she heard sounds coming from the kitchen.

"Hello?" Rowan called.

"Out in a moment," Elsbet replied.

"I'll just go up and see Tom," Rowan said as she passed through.

She bounded up the stairs and burst into Tom's room, but she was surprised to find Jude, not Tom, within.

"Oh," she said. "I'm sorry."

Jude reclined on his brother's bed, barely looking in her direction. "You say that, but you're not."

"Excuse me?" she asked. She had been so in need of Tom—of his gentle reassurance—that she wasn't sure she could handle Jude at all.

"You're excused," he said, looking up at her now. "You didn't come to see me, I presume."

"You presume?" she echoed, annoyance already building in her. "Yes, Jude. After all these years, I wasn't suddenly consumed with a burning desire to come over here and see you. I think we're all astonished that that hasn't happened yet."

He bit his lip and looked out the window. "Touché, Rowan. Touché."

She looked to the bedside table, where her flowers languished, the life having drained from them, and a wave of sadness overtook her. Tom was supposed to be tending the blessing wreath for their wedding day. She tried to look away before Jude could notice she'd seen, but she was too late. She was always too late for Jude.

"I'd better be going," she said. "Tell Tom I dropped by."

Jude shook his head. "I will, but he won't hear me."

She narrowed her eyes at him. "What is that supposed to mean?"

"Please," he laughed. "You haven't noticed the change in him? You of all people should be able to see that there's something going on. There's something happening to him."

She put a hand on her hip as much to steady herself as to appear defiant. Whatever concerns she might have about Tom, she didn't want to reveal them to his brother. "Jude," she said. "I know you enjoy baiting me, watching me squirm, but *I* don't enjoy it, all right? To be honest, I don't enjoy anything about you. I think you are a blight on the face of humanity, and I want you to leave me alone."

He smiled and nodded. "I just think you should know."

"Jude, I don't want to play games with you. If you have something to tell me, just say it. Whatever it is, just say it."

She watched him closely, waiting for him to speak, and all at once he seemed different, almost desperate, as if he was trying to decide between two impossible choices. He furrowed his brow, then looked at her with eyes that seemed suddenly fragile, suddenly afraid.

"He didn't . . . he didn't come home last night. I was hoping to catch him as soon as he got in, but he still isn't here."

Rowan took a step back, her head swimming. "What?"

Jude looked at his boots. "He hasn't been sleeping here."

"No," she said. "No. I mean, that's not funny, Jude."

"I'm not joking," he said quietly. "He's gone all night every night, and sometimes part of the day. I don't know where he goes. And when he does bother to show up, he's not himself. He's angry. He's different."

"That can't be," she said, trying to sound reasonable, trying not to break down. "You're lying."

His dark eyes bored into her. "I'm not lying to you. I'm many things, but I'm not a liar."

Rowan tried to think of something to say. She even

opened her mouth, but her jaw started to tremble, and she found herself at a loss. Finally, she said, "I'm sure Tom has a rational explanation for it."

He nodded. "You're probably right."

"Don't agree with me if you don't mean it," she said, her voice ascending an octave, starting to warble. She was in danger of losing control of some aspect of herself, but she wasn't sure what it would be.

Jude shrugged, and Rowan felt rage burn within her. Maybe she could delay worrying about Tom, where he'd been, if she could focus her energy on hating Jude. Without thinking, she pushed at his shoulders, ground her fists into him, but he didn't move—his body was set firm against her blows as she came down hard against him with her hapless fists.

"What is wrong with you?" she screamed. "Does it make you happy? Hurting people? Does it make you happy?"

He didn't say a word, and this made the fury within her—fury she didn't even know that she had—rise to the surface, and she found herself beating against him with increasing force, as if she were a battering ram trying to break him, and with each blow, the tension within her seemed to ease, as if she were scratching an itch.

"I hate you!" she screamed, swatting at his face, and with the full force of her body, she slammed herself into him, and this time she met no obstacle, only receptive flesh as he softened his chest to her, and she tumbled forward, forcing him down onto the bed, finding herself suddenly on top of him, pressing into him, his lips a breath away from hers, and the room went silent as he gazed up at her. She could hear her own heartbeat and feel his chest seem to tremble beneath her. She knew she ought to move, to pull herself off him, and run from the room, but she didn't. She stayed where she was, staring down at him, at his softly parted lips, feeling his chest rise and fall beneath her, lifting her gently with each inhalation. And suddenly he seemed terribly weak lying there, vulnerable even. Anger mixing with heartache, she looked into his eyes, and she knew he was telling her the truth.

"Rowan?" he said, his voice much more calm and measured than she'd anticipated.

"Yes?" she answered back.

He looked at her with soft eyes, his face steady and relaxed.

"Rowan, I don't want to be rude, but would you mind getting off me?"

"Yeah," she said, lifting herself up to stand. "Yeah, sure. I . . ."

He propped himself up to rest on his elbows, and he watched her.

She began to pace, adjusting her sleeves, pulling them down on her arms. "You say you have no idea where he goes?"

Jude shook his head.

"When does he leave?" she asked.

Jude shrugged. "I'm not going to inform on my brother."

"It's a little late for that," she snapped. "The damage has already been done. Tell me when he leaves."

He sighed. "If he comes home at all, he'll leave again just after nightfall. He goes down the back way and out into the woods."

Rowan nodded and then started for the door.

"Don't do it," he said, his voice low and gravelly, stretched with emotion.

"Don't do what?" she said, turning to find him sitting up and staring at her, seemingly devoid of emotion.

"Whatever you're going to do," he said. "Whatever you're going to do, don't do it."

"Why not?" she said defiantly.

"Because I don't want to see you get hurt," he said, holding her gaze.

Glaring at him, unable to understand what she felt in her heart, she backed out of the room, and with great purpose, she stormed down the stairs and out of the inn.

13. THE STAR

THE HOUSE WAS quiet that night when Rowan stole out of bed and crept down the stairs. She knew that going outside the village barrier at the witching hour was inviting disaster, but she had to know what was going on with Tom. He wasn't just her betrothed; he was her best friend, and he was in some kind of trouble. She was sure of it. After choosing a black cloak from the closet, she retrieved a dagger from her father's study and slipped it inside her boot. She was fairly certain that a dagger would do little to protect her against whatever walked the woods, but the cold steel flush against her calf reassured her.

She made her way through the village, stealing past the

illuminated windows at the front of the tavern, and rounding the back of the inn, hiding herself among the shadows. A twig snapping caught her off guard, and she twisted her head to peer into the darkness behind her, but there was nothing more. No movement, no sound. She kept her eyes trained on the back door of the tavern, and when it swung open, her heart lurched, but it wasn't Tom. Old Petey Barnes came flying out the door and, falling to his knees, vomited straight into the snow. Rowan wrinkled her nose, gagging when a breeze caught the odor and sent it in her direction. Burping and wiping his mouth, the man nodded to himself, seemingly satisfied, and then tossed some snow over the mess. He picked himself up and wobbled back to the inn, opening the door and shutting himself inside.

Rowan shook her head. Tom wasn't coming. Jude had been lying. There was no way Tom was sneaking out into the forest in the dead of night. Tom was a good boy. Tom was the boy everybody trusted. Moreover, he was her best friend, and he would never hurt her. She knew that. So why had she doubted him? She wanted to cry, thinking about herself reduced to spying, standing out in the snow trying to catch the person she loved most in the world. She fought back her emotions, but they seemed to take root in her legs, weakening them, and before she knew it, she was shaking. She sat on the cold ground and pressed her knees to her chest to still them. She closed her eyes and leaned her head against a tree.

When she heard the door creak, her eyes flew open and she saw Tom shutting it behind him. He looked around, then headed off into the woods. She pressed a hand to her heart, and then she pulled herself up, trying to be as quiet as she could, and watched as he disappeared between the trees. On tiptoes she started after him. He wore white gloves, the fool, and as he moved, moonlight illuminated the fabric. She stole through the trees as silently as she could as he trudged ahead, seemingly oblivious to her and the rest of his surroundings. There was a weightiness to the way he walked that didn't seem like him, and at the same time he wore a generally frantic air, fidgeting with his hands and moving his neck in strange, uncomfortable-looking directions. To Rowan, he looked like an alcoholic forced to abstain, his body slowly rebelling against his mind.

Then there was a noise, a crack, and Tom froze. Rowan, not twenty yards behind him, did the same. And then Tom did something so odd, Rowan could barely believe her eyes. He turned suddenly in her direction and pinned himself against a tree, eyes shut tight to the world. In the moonlight, she could see that his face was pale, his features pulled taut with what looked like terror.

And then she heard it. A low rumble and then a sweeping sound, as if something large was moving through the forest, tearing down everything in its path. And yet the forest around her was still, as if the sound was not attached to anything, as if it were no more corporeal than a sigh. But then the noise intensified, as if it was overlaid with another, otherworldly sound like the rasping breath of a thousand dogs. Fear shot through her, laced with a kind of horrific intoxication. Involuntarily, she spun around and flattened her back against a tree, just as she had seen Tom do. She tried to bite back her scream as the wall of sound approached, but the fear began to tear at her chest. She shut her eyes as the moment of safety slipped away from her, pushing her farther back against the tree, and then it was all around her, but not just where she was. She could hear it yards away, where she knew Tom stood also like a trapped and helpless child. And she could hear it even farther than that, sweeping against the ground, pushing aside the very air that surrounded her, breathing in chattering shrieks like a legion of demons moving in tandem.

In her mind, she spoke to herself as a mother might to a child, telling herself that everything would be okay—that soon it would pass, and life, the world, would go back to normal. But even as she tried to speak these words within the confines of her mind, the noise, the movement, seemed to drown it out, as if the thing, whatever it was, was capable of pushing through the spaces in her brain, her body, her self, moving through her being as easily as it moved through the trees.

There was a crack and a gust of wind as something whipped through the air, and then the noise, the heaviness to the air, vanished, as if it had charged off somewhere very far away.

Rowan stood there another moment, her back pressed against the tree, her eyes still closed. She knew it was gone, but she couldn't bring herself to move. She realized that her entire body was shaking, as if trying to release itself from the bondage of her fear. Her breath coming in shuddering spasms, she turned her head to see if Tom was all right.

He was backing away from the tree slowly, staring into the darkness. He closed his eyes a moment as if in prayer and made the sign of the Goddess. Rowan peered out into the woods, trying to see what Tom saw, but found nothing. And then, as if receiving the signal he awaited, Tom turned and sprang in the opposite direction, darting into the trees faster than Rowan had ever seen him move. Pulling herself up, she lurched after him, then launched into a full sprint. She pushed herself as hard as she could go, but she couldn't keep up with Tom, and she cursed as he disappeared into the trees.

Her lungs were stretched beyond capacity, and the stabbing pain forced her to choke on the cold winter air. Up ahead, she could just make out the white of Tom's gloves as he seemed to heave himself over something, a fallen tree probably, and, knowing she was about to lose him, she pushed herself even harder, her legs shaking beneath her, and then her foot caught on a tree root, her ankle twisted, and she cried out as the pain shot through her leg, burning. Shifting her weight, she tried to keep herself from putting too much pressure on her ankle. She threw her body in the opposite direction, and suddenly the ground slid out from under her. She was on the side of an embankment, and losing her balance, she slipped in the snow and tumbled down a steep slope. For a second she had the sensation that she was falling off a cliff, falling a great distance into an abyss that awaited her below, but soon she hit solid ground, her shoulder taking the brunt of her weight.

Again she cried out in pain, and then she heard something like the howl of a monstrous creature and felt movement behind her. She tried to pull herself up, to turn to reach for her dagger, but something was upon her, the warmth of a body, a familiar scent and a hand over her mouth. The body pressed on top of her, crushing her into the snow, the hand silencing her cries. And then she felt lips against her ear.

"Don't move," he whispered, and terror swept through her. "It's coming back. If it knows we're here, it will kill us."

Jude's voice. Jude's scent. Her body relaxed, and then she heard it again. Over their strained breathing, she heard it coming, sweeping through the forest on thousands of legs crackling like fire. Jude's arm was around her, his body, she now realized, covering hers in an attempt to shield her, his face pressed into her hair. She could feel the sweetness of his breath sliding down her neck, violently hot at her ear, only to cool by the time it reached her clavicle, and for the first time in her life, she truly believed she was about to die, only to be discovered lying in the snow, frozen solid, the boy she despised most in the world pressed against her. And for some reason, she thought about her mother. She rarely allowed herself the luxury, but now she thought that she smelled her, could remember her smell, and without meaning to, she began crying silent tears that flowed forth, pooling in the snow.

The sound came closer, moving, scrambling, scraping,

until it seemed to sweep through the whole of her body, poisoning it. And then, as quickly as it came, it receded, moving back into the darkness, back into the trees, and slowly Rowan exhaled. She could feel Jude's breath, coming in quick bursts now, feel his heartbeat racing.

They lay there another moment, their bodies pressed close together, and Rowan realized she was shaking. Then, lifting their heads, they faced each other, and Jude nodded. She pushed herself up to sit, and when he reached out to touch her face, she didn't recoil. Gently, he brushed the tears from her cheeks, then let his hand linger there a moment before she pulled away.

"Is it gone?" she whispered, and he looked at her with something like hurt.

"How should I know?" he said, the edge returning to his voice, but they both knew the thing, whatever it was, had departed. She could feel it. The air was different now, thinner, normal.

"What are you doing out here?" she asked.

"The same thing you're doing. Only you fell in a pit and I saved your life, and we lost him, so good one, Ro. Real solid work," he said, standing up and dusting off his pants.

"You did not save my life," she said.

"I didn't?" he laughed, a defensive note to his voice.

"No. You clambered on top of me, and we hid together in a pit. If it had found us, we would have died together."

"I was trying to protect you," he said, but she just shook her head and pulled herself up to stand. He did not, she noted, offer his hand.

"Come on," she said, climbing up the embankment.

"Where are we going?"

"We're going to keep looking. We're going to find where he went."

"Rowan," he nearly yelled. "What is wrong with you? We've lost him. We need to go home."

"I'm not going anywhere."

"You're hurt."

"I'm fine," she said, and started walking in the direction she'd last seen Tom go.

"I'm not going with you," Jude announced, and she turned to see that he meant it.

"That's fine. I didn't invite you. You followed me."

"I followed Tom."

"Then go back home, Jude," she said, waving him off. "I don't need you."

"Don't do this," Jude said.

"Why not?" she said, more defiant than curious.

"Because whatever it is you're searching for, I have a feeling it's something that's best left unseen."

Rowan looked at Jude standing there in the moonlight, his chin lifted to the sky, and then she turned and headed deeper into the woods, determined to find Tom.

As she darted through the trees, the darkness closing in around her, she feared that Jude was right. She had lost Tom, but still she searched. He was out there somewhere, and she would find him.

The pain in her leg grew, and eventually she stopped. She chose a clearing near an ancient yew tree for her resting spot. She leaned against the tree's massive, twisting roots and tried to steady her breath.

That was when she heard it. Tom's voice somewhere far below the earth. Slowly she backed away from the tree, taking in its full breadth for the first time. She knew this tree. When she was a child, it had frightened her. Tom's grandmother had called it a fairy tree. She said it was a poison thing, thousands of years old. Erupting from the ground in a gnarled tangle of knots and eyes, it shot up, only to spring forth like a terrible insect in a multitude of twisted twigs and branches. The farther Rowan moved away from it, the more distant Tom's voice seemed to grow, and the tree itself seemed to whisper to her:

Death . . . death . . . death . . .

And then she heard it again, coming closer, moving through the trees. She was in its path. She could feel it—feel her insides begin to change, altered in the very presence of the beast. Darting to her left, she scrambled up a large rock and lay flat, her cheek pressed against its surface. She could hear it now, approaching fast. She willed herself to keep her head down, not to look, but she found that she couldn't. It was right below her now. She had to know. She had to see. She poked her head up and opened her eyes. What she saw was so vile, the sight of it made her feel foul, dirty.

It walked upright, clicking along on legs made of splintered bone. It had teeth like great needles and eyes like the blackest of pits. It moved in a jagged way, lurching forward unexpectedly, and then suddenly standing stiller than still, so still, in fact, that Rowan could not tell the beast from the forest around it. Just when Rowan was certain it had disappeared, it would spring forth again, chattering its monstrous teeth, arms spindly as branches searching before it like spiders closing in on their prey.

The monster paused, rising to its full height, and exhaled, clouds of gray vapor issuing from between its slivered teeth. Guiding its rotten head from left to right, it appeared to be looking for something. And then in a flash, it fell down on all fours like a grossly elongated and skeletal wolf, and with a horrifying noise like the grinding of saw against bone, it pushed off and disappeared deep into the woods.

Rowan's whole body shook. It was gone. It was gone, she kept telling herself, and she had to get home, get indoors. As she climbed down from the rock, her limbs were like rubber, and she nearly lost her grasp more than once.

When her feet touched the ground, her legs were shaking so badly that they nearly gave way. And then she was running, her ankle no longer a nuisance. It was only when she'd made it home and was safe inside that she really understood that whatever that thing out there in those woods was, it was something much more terrifying than she'd ever considered.

Tom tried to tell himself that his life hadn't gotten wildly out of control. He tried to tell himself that any man would make the same choices he was making. He tried to tell himself that he was somehow special, that he had been chosen for his exceptional nature, and that he was therefore uniquely capable of dealing with what was clearly an exceptional situation.

Since their first encounter, he had been spending every night with Fiona, and what nights they were. In the morning, there were always parts he couldn't remember, parts that seemed to run together, flashes of her red lips, her creamy thighs, the slope of her neck, and words that didn't match, words from another time. And always his memory of the previous night was disjointed, as if it existed outside of time. At home in his bed, lying in the light, begging the Goddess for sleep that refused to come, his mind would run over it all, and he would see Fiona laughing in the woods, spinning around, then suddenly howling and beautiful, and then he would be totally alone somewhere he didn't recognize, only to be back with her greeting him in the ghostly moonlight as he arrived, and then laughing while she showed him some new trick she had taught herself since their last meeting. And all the while, inside him, something seemed to be changing, twisting him, sucking the anger out of his cells and pulling it ever closer to the surface so that at any moment, he feared he might snap.

He was in the middle of the woods, near her tree, when he heard the whistle. It seemed to come from above, so he looked up. Ribbons of moonlight slipped between the trees, and he delighted in the way the snow seemed to dance through the beams. And then he felt her hands slide over his eyes from behind.

He always knew it was her because of the heat and because of her scent, that rich earthy scent she'd had since coming to him that first night. Sometimes he wondered if it had something to do with the way her feet and shins never seemed to come clean. Even when she washed, they always seemed to remain dirty.

"Guess who?" she purred into his ear, and he smiled wide, his heart nearly bursting with joy. She spun him around and there her face was, more radiant, more beautiful than ever. And then he was somewhere else—inside her tree hollow, warm and drunk on her beauty. With each passing day, she seemed to grow more exquisite. She smiled at him, and instantly, his body was on fire. He was suddenly awake, out of his daze, everything crisp and clear like it never was back home. He kissed her, and she pressed herself against him.

"I've missed you," she said.

"It hasn't been all that long."

"It's too much for me," she said, smiling up at him with those limpid eyes. "I don't know what to do with myself when you're gone."

"Then come with me," he whispered, burying his face in her neck, her hair.

"You know I can't do that, Tom. This is my home now. But maybe, somehow it could be yours too."

He held her face in his hands, and in that instant there was nothing more precious to him in the world. And then she paused and held a finger to her lips. "Quiet," she whispered, pointing to the forest above them. "Someone's up above."

He moved to ask what she meant, but Fiona held her hand to his mouth. And then he heard it as well—the beast, Fiona's beast—that thing he could never completely see, and yet which always seemed to be nearby. Sometimes it looked like the snow through the trees, sometimes like jagged bones, and sometimes it looked like death itself.

"It's safe now," she said, removing her hand from his mouth and kissing him. "The girl is gone. Come on." She pulled him to his feet. "There's something I want to show you, but first you must close your eyes."

And then they were up in the woods again, and though his eyes were closed, he knew they were moving through the trees, through the night. After they had walked for a while, Fiona told him he could open his eyes. He stood a moment staring ahead of him before he understood where he was. The air seemed to swirl around him, so cold and yet always bearable in her presence. In front of him stretched the icy expanse of Seelie Lake, laid out below Cairn Hill and Lover's Leap like white silk. It looked magical, somehow more real than nature had ever seemed to him before. It was as if the lake from his childhood, that lovely creature so filled with possibilities, had returned to him more beautiful and mysterious than ever.

He started laughing, though he wasn't sure why.

"Isn't it wonderful?" she asked, smiling like a child. "I had no idea it was here. And wait, here's the best part. You have to see this."

And with that, she let go of his hands and ran out onto the ice, and her bare feet sliding across it, she twirled until she fell down. Panic rose in Tom's heart, and he reached out to her.

"Don't!" he yelled. "The ice might give."

Fiona laughed and pointed to the ice below. "Look at them, Tom. Just look at them!"

And then he saw—swarming beneath the lake's frozen surface, spiny teeth and monstrous eyes, circling, hungry hands clawing at the ice from below. The water nixies, real as the night, thirsty for blood. But they couldn't be real. They just couldn't.

"Fiona," he said, trying to remain calm. "Please come away. I think you might be in danger."

"Because of them?" she laughed, tapping the ice to provoke the terrible nixies. "They're so hungry, aren't they? But the ice won't break, and it's fun to tease them."

Tom took another step toward her. "Please, Fiona. Come away from there. Those things, they're monsters."

She smiled, a shy kind of smile. "And what do you think I am, Tom?"

He closed his eyes, once again convinced this all had to be part of a terrible dream, and then she was laughing.

"My pet fears them too," she laughed. "But then, water is not his domain. See him over there between the trees? He doesn't dare come out on the ice."

Tom turned to look where she pointed, but he saw there only darkness and slivers of snow.

"Come on, Tom, please try it. It's magical, isn't it?" she crooned.

Staring at her, so beautiful, he felt a fire rise in him, and he realized he couldn't disobey her if he tried. He walked out to meet her, the nixies surging toward him as he did. He tried to ignore them there below the ice, to focus on Fiona. Sliding across the silvery whiteness, she twirled and danced into his arms. He kissed her.

"You have to try it," she bubbled. "Take off your boots."

"I can't take off my boots. I'll freeze."

"Come on," she teased. "Don't be afraid. You're with me now."

"Yeah," he said, smiling down at her face, which at that moment was as lovely as a summer rose. "A lot of good that will do me when I've lost a toe."

"Don't be like that," she said, and crouching down, she began to untie his laces.

"What are you doing?" he protested, but he didn't try to pull himself away.

In a moment, she had his boots off, and then his woolen socks, and his naked feet were planted flush against the frozen lake, the cold sinking into every crevice, and yet there was no pain. There was only delight at the extremity of the sensation.

Taking his hands, she pulled him across the ice, and together they began to spin.

"It doesn't hurt," he said, surprised.

"Of course it doesn't," she said. "I'll never let anything hurt you."

And he knew that no matter what happened, no matter

what the truth of the situation might be, that a part of him would always be out there spinning on the ice with her. The moment itself seemed to fill his veins, and he knew that she would be inside him. Always and forever. After feeling like this, there was no going back.

PART THREE

14. THE WHEEL OF FORTUNE

ROWAN DID NOT sleep that night, and at first light, she found herself at the inn, asking to speak with Jude. Elsbet was still in her dressing gown, and it was clear that the sight of Rowan unsettled her.

"I'll go get him, dear. The boys are sleeping for sure," she said, the lie evident in her eyes, and Rowan wondered where the woman thought Tom could be spending his nights.

A few minutes later, Jude appeared on the stairs.

"Hi," he said, his eyes wide. "I'm glad to see you're still in one piece."

She moved close to him, and without meaning to, she found that she'd taken his hands in hers.

"I saw it, Jude. I saw the beast."

His mouth opened, but it was clear he had no idea what to say.

"It was so close I could have reached out and touched it," she recalled. "It was enormous—I'd say three men tall, and awful. Just awful, Jude. I've never seen anything like it, even in nightmares. And the way it moved—it tore through a huge swath of forest, and yet it didn't seem to break any branches or destroy any foliage. It's like it was there but not quite of this realm."

Jude ran a hand through his hair, concern creasing his features, and then he seemed to decide something. "Come with me," he said, and without thinking twice, Rowan followed him up the stairs to his room. Once he'd closed the door behind him, he sat on his bed and stared at her intently. "There's something I need to tell you."

She took a seat at the end of his bed, and he shifted to face her, and suddenly she realized she was nervous to be so near him. Not her normal anxiety stemming from anger and frustration—it was something else. When she looked at him, he seemed somehow different—this strange, hard boy now curiously gentle—and she began to wonder about him, about who he really was.

"You must understand," he said quietly. "I'm telling you this in absolute confidence. Whatever differences there exist between us, you must put them aside for the moment. I need to know that I can trust you."

"You can trust me," she said solemnly.

"I also need you to trust me," he said, meeting her gaze.

"What do you mean?" She cocked her head.

His eyes were wide, insistent. "I know your father doesn't believe in forest things and witch powers, but I do. I've seen proof of such things myself."

"You have?" Rowan asked, moved by his seriousness.

"I have," he said, and his eyes lingering on hers, Rowan noticed they burned with a strange intensity. "These woods are my woods. I've spent a lifetime in them, and I've seen things that would amaze you. But you needn't just take my word for it. After what you saw last night, surely you must doubt your father's skepticism. I know you were brought up not to believe in any of this, but I'm asking you please, for just a moment, to put your prejudices aside and to consider the possibility that you and your father might be wrong."

Looking at Jude, she couldn't help but trust him. In truth, her heart had always strained against her father's beliefs. Deep down, she'd always sensed the magic in the woods, and she'd shunned the witches not for their deceptions but for their powers—powers she feared they truly did possess. She'd fought her instincts out of deference to her father, but of late, her father had become a stranger to her, and as much as it pained her to do so, she had to admit to herself that at this point she trusted Jude more than she trusted her father.

"I believe you," she said finally. "How can I not? After what I've seen, how could I deny that there are things in this world beyond my comprehension? But the witches, Jude, they frighten me. I've always avoided Mama Lune, and then the other day, she accosted me in the village. After a lifetime of ignoring me, she walked up to me as if we were old friends. She wanted to tell me again about her visitor—about Mama Tetri. She said . . . she said that Mama Tetri knew my mother and my uncle—that they'd grown up together."

"Really?" he marveled. "And you didn't know that?"

Rowan shook her head, and suddenly she thought she might cry. "It was the first I've heard of it. She told me that Mama Tetri came to Nag's End to say sooth when my mother was pregnant with me. I know that my father would never allow such a thing, and yet . . . when she spoke the words, I believed her. I feel like I no longer understand the world. What's happening, Jude? Do you understand what's happening?"

Jude sighed. "I can't say that I understand it, but I can tell you what I know." He paused to scratch his head. "Rowan, do you know what a Greywitch is?"

She raised her eyebrows. "I know what they were. They're all dead now, aren't they?"

He nodded, seemingly collecting his thoughts. "Well, they're supposed to be. Everyone thinks they are, but Mama Lune told me that she saw something that convinced her otherwise."

"What did she see?" Rowan asked, shocked.

"She said she saw Grey magic," he said.

"She *saw* magic? What does that even mean?"

"That's what I wanted to know," Jude said, smiling. "Mama Lune said that everyone can see magic, but that normal people like us aren't used to looking for it. She said that if you look closely, you can see its aftereffects. She explained it's like seeing smoke from a dying fire."

"And you believe her?" Rowan asked, leaning toward him.

"I do," he said.

"Then I do too," she said, and reaching out to him, she rested her hand on his arm. Her touch seemed to startle him, unsettle him even, and so she withdrew it as quickly as she'd placed it. "But what does it mean? If there is a Greywitch in Nag's End, what does it mean?"

Jude pulled his leg up to rest a shin on his knee. "If there is a Greywitch among us, it would explain a lot, but she said that just because she'd seen Grey magic here, doesn't mean that the witch is here. It could have been a spell performed a great distance away that is nonetheless affecting us."

Rowan's mind began working furiously. Standing, she began to pace. "If there was a Greywitch among us, would we be able to tell?"

Jude frowned. "I don't know. They are wicked souls, Rowan. Mama Lune says that if it is a Greywitch, that she wouldn't risk coming into the village openly and being discovered, but really so little is known about their ways. They haven't been active in any number for hundreds of years."

Rowan walked with careful steps, trying to make sense of it all. "So this creature, then—this beast I saw last night—do you think it is the work of a Greywitch? I was of the mind that there were two separate forces at work, but after seeing what I saw last night, I just don't know. I mean, that monster must be the thing responsible for the deaths, right?"

"I would think so," Jude said, concentrating hard. "But if it wasn't born of the Goddess—and let's face it, Ro, the thing you saw last night was not—then it couldn't very well cross the village boundary. It would be confined to the forest."

"But . . ." Rowan said, stopping in front of Jude. "But a Greywitch is born of the Goddess. A Greywitch could cross the boundary."

"Yes," he said, his eyes growing wide. "Yes, it could."

"Jude," she said. "I'm frightened."

"So am I," he said.

Out in the woods, Tom awoke to a harsh winter light. He was cold and alone. Shivering, he pulled himself up to stand, his head spinning. The sickness was starting to bore into him. Wrapping his coat around himself, he staggered through the trees. He needed to go home. He didn't know how long it had been since he'd last bathed. Days were slipping away from him. There was only Fiona, and when she wasn't beside him, taking a breath felt like inhaling razors, and walking sent pain tearing down his spine.

He was nearly to the village barrier now. As he crossed it, the low rock wall remained the only thing between him and his parents' inn. His head spinning, he brought his hands to his eyes, and that's when he saw it. Blood. His hands were covered in it—stained red with it. Sticky, metallic blood.

Horrified, he stumbled back, as if to escape himself, and tripping over a rock, he landed sprawled out in the snow. Quickly, he pulled himself up, and eyes darting this way and that, he slowly backed away from the inn—from his parents, from his people.

He would return to the woods; he would find Fiona. She would help him. He didn't know how the blood had gotten there. He didn't know what he'd done, but he feared the worst, and there was no going home. Not anymore.

That afternoon in the village square Rowan heard what was to be done with the glassblower. The elders had put forth their case, and the duke had decided. Seamus Flint was to be executed at dawn. The hangman's hood had yet to be worn during Rowan's short life, and she feared the spectacle the morrow would bring.

Although she wanted justice for Fiona and Lareina, she knew that there could be no such thing. What was done could not be undone, and punishing the guilty could never fill the void the dead left behind.

She took the long path home, and as the snow fell in shimmering waves, her thoughts lingered on Goi Flint. She wondered what it was that made one man go mad but left his brethren unscathed. The elders called madness the hunger moon disease, after the third moon of winter, when food was scarce and desperation often took hold. They maintained that right living could keep any man from it, but Rowan knew that a mind once rent at the seams could unspool in the most spectacular way—and once it was fully unwound, what remained could be as disparate as diamonds and snow.

She paused at her gate and stared deep into the Black Forest. Somewhere out there was a monster, she knew. She'd seen it with her own eyes. And yet the beauty of the place continued to leave her breathless. It was such a shame the things beauty could conceal. Shaking her head, she passed through her gate and into her yard.

That was when she remembered she'd need to fix supper. It seemed to her a cruel thing that she should be tasked with feeding everyone when she was the one grieving most. Every time she set foot in the kitchen, she thought of Emily, and her heart broke anew each time.

But when she walked in that night, she found the duke chopping winter herbs, and a pot of something boiling on the stove. She tried to hide her surprise. He smiled at her, that glittering beam of white teeth, and she did her best to forget the strangeness that had occurred between them the other day.

"Good evening," he said.

"Hello," she said. "You're making supper."

"I am. I don't see why I oughtn't pitch in."

"It's very kind of you."

"I wanted to apologize," he said, scooping the herbs into the pot of boiling liquid. "I offended you the other night. I did not mean to. I hope we can remain friends."

"Of course," she said, relieved to have the tension cut between them. "I imagine I might have been snappish with you as well. I'm sorry if I overreacted."

"You didn't," he said. "You were right to rebuff me. Your place is here with your people. Let's not speak of it again."

Smiling, she nodded, and then started into the dining room to set the table.

Seamus Flint awoke in his cell to the sound of someone lightly giggling. He sat upright, a sweat breaking out along his hairline, as he was gripped by an overwhelming sense of terror.

"Who's there?" he gasped, and then he saw a figure in the shadows.

"Hello," replied a girl's voice.

He could just make out a silhouette in the darkness. "Who are you?" he whispered.

The figure spoke to him as if he were a child. "It's me. Fiona. I've come for a friendly visit."

He held up his hands to her, making the sign of the Goddess, but nothing happened. "You're not Fiona. You're a thing from hell is what you are."

She laughed again—a high, tinkling laughter that made him feel like he might be sick.

"I've heard the news," she said. "I've heard that they're going to execute you, and I just can't let that happen."

"You can't?" he asked, and for a brief moment, he was moved to believe this demon crouching there in the darkness was there to help him.

"No," she said. "Not after what you tried to do to me . . . after what you did to Lareina." Fiona paused for a moment, then continued, "I want you to tell me something."

"Anything," he said, nodding.

"You knew my father well, didn't you? Back before you were drinking. You were young men together."

"Yes," Seamus said, his voice quavering. "I knew him well."

"Tell me, why did you marry his wife? Why did you bring us here away from our home?"

"To—to protect you," he stammered.

"And did you do that?"

"I did," he gasped.

"Think again, dear stepfather. Is that what you did? Were you really trying to protect us?"

"Okay," he cried. "No. That's not what I did. Your father, he received money from here, from Nag's End. From your uncle. I thought I could use the money, only it wasn't . . . it wasn't enough. But please, it wasn't just that. I also protected you. You and your stepmother would have been destitute if I'd not stepped in."

"Ah," she said. "And were you trying to protect me that night when you came into my room?"

He shook his head. "I didn't mean to. It was the liquor. It was only the liquor," he said, shaking now, violent shudders surging through his body.

"Poor Seamus," she mocked, stepping into the light now. "You must be so cold. And so scared. Are you scared? Do I make you feel scared?"

He looked away, afraid to see the creature that stood fully illuminated before him.

"Tell me," she said. "Tell me why Goi Rose was paying my father."

He shook his head, and then he felt a hand pull his jaw forward, a burning heat searing his face.

"Answer me!" she screamed.

"I don't know," he cried, still averting his eyes. "Please, I swear to you that I don't know."

And then the hand released him. "I believe you," she said, her voice sweet again, and he sighed with relief. "Now, we're almost finished here, and then I'm going to save you. Do you understand? I want you to thank me."

"Thank you," he whispered.

"Just one last thing," she said. "I want you to look at me."

"No," he wept. "I can't do that. Please don't make me."

"Look at me," she commanded.

Trembling, he looked up at her, and for a moment, she was the person he remembered—beautiful Fiona, an angel among girls. But then something went wrong. She began to change, and right before his eyes, she transformed into a monster, full of fury and hatred, filth and evil, and the last thing he remembered was the searing pain as her teeth tore into his flesh.

Fiona hadn't been in any of the usual places, and Tom had spent the day wandering, searching, and when night came, he could barely move for the cold that had gotten inside his bones.

Night was slipping into morning when he finally found her. She was back in her fairy hollow, having stolen past him at some point. At first he was relieved to see her, but something was wrong. She was curled up in her nightgown, and it was covered in blood. It was everywhere, all over her body, all over her hands and face, and to her hair clung bits of flesh and bone.

He rushed to her and took her into his arms.

"My darling," he cried. "My darling, are you hurt?"

She looked up at him, clearly only just realizing he'd entered the space. "Tom." She smiled, and he saw that her teeth were stained pink.

"What's happened to you?"

"I'm so glad you're here," she said. "I was hoping you'd come."

He searched her body for wounds, but he found nothing.

Reaching for him, she clung to him and wept. "I don't know what's happening to me."

"It's going to be okay," he said, his head swimming, knowing that whatever was happening, there probably wasn't a way that it could ever be okay.

Gathering water from the basin, and a cloth soft as petals, he started to wipe the blood away. Stroke by stroke he worked, the ivory of her skin beginning to peek out from underneath. When he had finished, he helped her change into a white shift he discovered under a blanket in the corner, and then he led her to the little bed she had made for herself. For an instant, he was startled to see something on top of the bed, something white and smeared with blood. His heart stalled for a moment before he realized it was only a stuffed lamb. Fiona, barely looking at him, climbed under the covers, and gripping the stuffed animal to her chest like a child might, she closed her eyes and drifted off to sleep.

15. JUDGMENT

THE NEXT MORNING, Jude returned from his hunt to find his father discussing something with his mother.

"Is everything all right?" he asked, and his father nodded, then apparently thinking better of it, he looked at his wife and shook his head.

"No, everything's not all right," Elsbet said. Standing, she placed her hands on the table in front of her and stared down her oldest son. "What is going on with your brother? He's not coming home at night. Where is he sleeping, Jude? I know that you know."

Jude raised his hands in the air. "Leave me be. He hasn't spoken to me in days."

"He's lying," she said, and stalked out of the room.

When Jude was alone with his father, the older man looked at him with pained eyes. "You mustn't mind her."

"I don't," he said, not wanting to discuss his mother. "But, Father, I wanted to ask you something."

"What is it?"

"Henry Rose's wife, what was her name?"

His father thought for a moment. "Brigid. A lovely woman. Tall and beautiful, with a kind face she was. A sad thing, her death."

"Did you know her?" Jude asked, taking a seat opposite him.

"No. Not more than to say hello. They weren't here long before she died."

"Do you know where she came from—what province?"

"I don't." His father looked at him with curious eyes. "Why all the questions?"

"Mama Tetri, the Bluewitch staying with Mama Lune, have you ever seen her in Nag's End before?"

His father nodded. "I have. Water witches tend to roam. I'm sure she's been through here a couple of times at least."

"Do you remember when?" His father shook his head, so Jude went on. "Do you think it's possible that she might have come through when Rowan's mother was pregnant?"

Wilhelm seemed to think for a moment, then squinted. "Aye. I think so. Yes. Well, Brigid wasn't pregnant anymore; she'd already gone to the Goddess during childbirth. Your mother and I missed the rites because Tom was quite ill." He held a hand to his heart. "I still remember that like it was yesterday. Here he was just walking, just starting to get his sea legs, when all of a sudden he can't lift himself up. Couldn't even crawl or move his head. Came on like a summer storm it did. We had to call Mama Lune. She said he'd caught an ill wind, and she fixed him up. We thought he was going to die, but she had him right in a few days' time. But yes," he said, confusion lining his face. "I remember the Bluewitch was with her. She played with you while the rest of us tended to Tom. Goddess, am I glad you boys are grown, and those days are gone—those days when you were small enough to die from a hint of wind."

Jude's father stopped, his face suddenly overtaken by sadness, and Jude knew that his father was thinking of how Tom was once again in danger. Both of them knew it, whether they wanted to admit it to themselves or not. And then something occurred to Jude.

"Father," he said, trying to piece it together. "You say that Tom was walking when Rowan's mother died in childbirth?"

"He was."

"So he must have been around a year?"

"Just about."

"But Rowan is three months older than Tom," he said, and the words seemed to stretch out in the air, distancing the space between father and son, and then the man winced and looked away.

"I . . . I must be remembering things wrong. My mind, you know, it isn't what it once was," he said, moving to stand. Jude reached out and placed a hand on his arm.

"Father, please. I need to know."

"It was so long ago," he said, looking away. "I've probably said too much already. Just let it go."

"Please. It might help me help Tom."

Wilhelm bowed his head and sighed, defeated. "There was another child after Rowan. A stillbirth. Went when the mother went."

Jude sat stunned. "But why lie about something like that?"

His father's eyes widened. "I don't know. I just did what I was asked."

"Asked of you by whom?"

"Henry Rose, of course."

Jude frowned, trying to understand what it could mean. "But what purpose could such a lie serve?"

"I don't know, Jude. Your mother was the one to speak with him," his father said, sadness in his eyes. "I'm just telling you what she told me. I'm an honest man. You know that. But a grieving father—a widower at that—shows up with a request, you do as he asks. So what if he doesn't want his little Rowan to know she had a dead brother or sister? So what?"

"You didn't think it odd?"

"I don't know that I thought much about it," he said, his voice straining. "That's women's business, for the most." He paused and looked down at his hands. "He also made a donation to the tavern."

"A donation?"

"Out of gratitude for our silence."

Jude leaned back in his chair and shook his head. He wasn't sure what Henry Rose was up to, but he was sure now that he didn't trust the man. He was about to question his father more, but the tavern doors burst open, and Goi Tate bounded in. His face was mottled, his eyes wide.

"It's Seamus," Goi Tate said, his voice shaking. "Something . . . something's got to him."

Jude had been shocked by the gruesomeness of the previous deaths, but they were nothing compared to what had been done to Goi Flint. While the creature had drained most of the blood from the two women, it had not seen to treat Goi Flint with such kindness. Beside him, Jude could hear his father gasp, feel his mother swoon. To say that the scene in the gaol was carnage would be to miss its true horror, because carnage brings to mind images of a quick death such as a fall from a great height or a swift blow to the back of the head. What had happened to Goi Flint had been slow and exact, and it was inaccurate to say that there was much bloodshed because it seemed that there had been nothing but bloodshed.

The duke, who had been called as soon as the remains were found, shook with disbelieving horror as he stared at the scene.

"It looks like he's been turned inside out," Tak was able to say before he vomited onto the toes of his boots.

Dr. Temper looked pained. "I daresay he was skinned alive."

"Oh Goddess," Jude said, stepping away and out into the cold, trying to fill his lungs with fresh mountain air.

"Doctor," the duke said, turning to the older man. "What . . . what happened here?"

"Like I said, I think he *might* have been skinned," Dr. Temper said, unable to take his eyes from the scene. "Before he was . . . taken apart."

The men made their way out of the cell and processed outside into the snow. The duke stared off into the forest as if searching for an answer. "I don't understand it," he nearly whispered.

"My lord," said Dr. Temper. "Under the circumstances . . . given the state of the body . . . I want to formally request that we be allowed to burn the remains. We cannot offer him to the Goddess in such a state, and given the nature of—"

But the duke cut him off with a raised glove. "Please, Doctor, I am in no mood to argue, and neither, I suspect, is your village. Do what you will with the body. I shall sequester myself from the vapors."

The villagers thought it best to burn the body immediately. There was nothing else to do, and they had taken enough chances with their dead in recent times so as soon as men could be roused and supplies gathered, a bonfire was started in the middle of the square, and the body was brought piecemeal over by wheelbarrow.

The day was already strong when Tom awoke. He propped himself up on his elbows. Fiona was gone. The blood was gone. Had he dreamed it? Rubbing his eyes, he pulled himself up to stand and quickly made his way out of the hollow.

When he saw her, his heart stopped for a moment. She stood in the snow, her eyes closed, dark spidery lashes kissing her cheeks, as she held her tongue out to catch the falling flakes.

"Hello, Tom," she said, her eyes still shut.

He walked toward her. "What are you doing?"

"Enjoying the beauty of it all," she said, and then slowly she opened her eyes, and when she focused them on him, it felt like coming home after a long journey. She ran to him and kissed him, but immediately she seemed to sense his hesitation.

"What is it?" she asked, looking him over as if trying to understand a riddle. "You look upset."

"Something is wrong with me," he said, his voice shaking.

She considered him a moment, and then dancing away from him, she kicked her pointed toes through the snow. "But, Tom," she crooned. "Nothing's wrong with you. You're perfection."

He held his hands to his face, fighting back the tears. "I think I've gone mad. I think . . . I think I killed someone."

She laughed, a strange, cutting sound. "You couldn't kill a rabbit."

"I had blood on my hands yesterday. I'm sure of it."

She shook her head. "That was the blood of a deer. Don't you remember? You were trying to save it. Trust me, Tom. You'd not hurt a person if your life depended on it."

"A deer?" he said, longing to believe her. "I was trying to save a deer?"

Images flashed through his head, Fiona's eyes—no, a deer's—and bleeding. It was injured. Something was injuring it—a wolf, blood on its incisors, feeding. Only it wasn't a wolf.

With a single raised eyebrow, she managed to assuage his earlier fear while raising yet a greater one.

"You were trying to save it. You mustn't do that again, Tom. You could get hurt."

And he knew. Just like that, he knew. Shaking his head, he backed away from her.

"We can't do this anymore," he said, his heart in his throat.

"Surely you must be joking," she said, spinning around with her arms held out to the sky. "We can do whatever we like."

"Last night," he said, stumbling over the words. "Last night I found you covered in blood. It wasn't your blood, and it wasn't a deer's, was it, Fiona?"

She stopped, held a hand to her milky-white hip, and observed him. "I hope you realize you're being no fun at all right now, Tom."

"Whose blood was it, Fiona?" he demanded, his voice straining with anger.

She stared at him, her face pinched as if she was caught

between two worlds, and then she smiled, fairly drenching him in her beauty. "You've had a bad dream, Tom. You must forget about it at once and come enjoy yourself with me."

The anger gradually drained from his eyes, and he looked at her with utter heartbreak. "I know," he said.

"What?" she laughed. "What do you know?"

Slowly he walked to her, and gazing at her with the love of a broken man, he said, "You can enchant me all you want. You can confuse me, and exhaust me, and drive me half mad, but I'm still a man, and I know what you are."

She stared at him, silent, her face devoid of emotion, and then it was as if something within her switched off, and her face seemed to crumble. Tears filling her eyes, she backed away from him. "Tom," she said, shaking her head.

"I know what you've done. I love you. I've never loved anyone or anything like I love you. Without my love for you, I don't even know that I'm a person anymore, but I have to let you go."

"No!" she shrieked, her face contorted, panicked. "You can't leave me! I'll stop it."

"You can't stop it."

"I can," she said, and flinging herself at his feet, she wrapped herself around his knees. "I promise you that I can."

Reaching down, he gently pulled her up to stand. He looked into her dazzling eyes. "Fiona."

"I can," she said. "I promise you. I promise you with everything that I am, that we are. I won't do it again."

"Please," he said, nearly crying, taking her hands and pressing them to his heart. "Promise me it will stop."

"I promise," she said. "No more. I promise."

He pulled her close to his chest and kissed her head, knowing that no matter what he might say, he could never leave her.

† † †

When Rowan awoke, she smelled an awful stench coming from the center of the village. A fire. A funeral pyre, she thought. Only, whose could it be?

"Tom," she gasped, and dressing quickly, she set out from the house, pulling the hood of her cloak down over her eyes.

When she reached the center of the village, she saw that everyone was already there, gathered round the pyre. She searched the crowd. Her father was engaged in serious conversation with Goi Parstle. Elsbet fanned the flames, while holding the ear of several of the older women. Jude sat alone, a short distance from the fray.

She rushed over to him.

"It's not Tom, is it?" she asked, desperate.

"Goi Flint," he answered, shaking his head. "He was to be executed tonight at sunset, but it seems someone has gotten to him before the elders and their noose."

"But who?"

"No one knows. The cell was locked."

"Where's Tom?" she asked, looking around, but Jude just shrugged.

"Missing, as usual."

Rowan put her face in her hands and tried to staunch the flow of her tears. Then something began to rise inside her, and she shook her head. "This has to stop. I'm going to find him."

"And how will you do that?" Jude asked.

"I have an idea where he is," she said, thinking back to the ancient yew in the woods.

"Do you want me to come?" Jude asked, and while Rowan appreciated the gesture, she wanted to speak to Tom alone.

"No," she said. "Thank you for the offer, but this is between me and Tom."

He nodded. "Be careful," he said, and with that, she turned and headed into the forest.

† † †

Jude watched Rowan disappear between the trees, his heart heavy with worry. He was deciding whether or not he should secretly follow her as he'd done the day he pretended to abandon her outside of the village barrier, when he saw Goi Tate approaching and realized his opportunity had slipped away.

"Terrible business this," Goi Tate said, whistling through his teeth.

Jude nodded, not bothering to rise.

"I've been wanting to speak with you," Goi Tate continued. "These meetings we've been having at the tavern, the ones where we make plans about how to stop the killings. I wanted you to know that there have started to be other meetings as well, ones we've kept secret from your family."

"Is that the case?" Jude asked, trying to hide his concern.

"It is. It was actually Tom's betrothed who put the idea in our heads. It was during that meeting. She wondered aloud if the thing we seek might not be a monster at all but a man who walks among us."

"What are you saying?" Jude asked, suddenly cold.

"I'm trying to do you a favor here," Goi Tate said.

"And what favor is that?"

Goi Tate leaned in close. "We know something is wrong with Tom. Everyone can see it, and we know he goes off into the woods nearly every chance he can get. We've tried to follow him, but we always lose him. He always seems to vanish."

"Why are you telling me this?"

"Because I like Tom, and I don't want to hang an innocent man, and that is what the others are just about ready to do."

"You can't be serious," Jude said, but he could see that Goi Tate was. He wondered if the elders had told the men what their oracles had seen—the darkness they'd seen over the inn—and his heartbeat began to speed up.

"My advice is that you find him," Goi Tate said. "Find out where he goes and clear his name while you still have the chance."

And with that, Goi Tate turned and headed back to the fire.

† † †

Rowan knew exactly where she was going. She weaved through the trees with long, purposeful strides. Earlier, she had heard Tom's voice out in the woods, seeming to emanate from the ancient yew tree. She didn't know what that might mean, or how it might be possible, but she was going to find out. She was tired of feeling helpless.

And yet, as she walked, fear seemed to bite into her, and with each step, she grew warier. When she was nearly to the clearing, she heard his voice again, only this time much more audibly. She stopped where she was and crept up toward the area, careful not to let herself be seen. As quietly as she could, she rounded the bend in the path, and they came into view.

What she saw shocked her. Tom stood in the snow. In his arms, he held a girl clad only in a white dress, and he was kissing her passionately, his lips traveling to her neck, her shoulders, and all the while he gripped her body with an intensity Rowan hadn't imagined Tom could possess.

So this was the source of Tom's secrecy? A girl? A hidden love affair? She could barely contain her relief. So Tom loved another. That was his great crime. He was no murderer. He was just a lovesick fool, and a reckless one at that, having risked the woods the previous night just to meet a girl. But who was she?

Rowan was stepping forward to get a better look when something about the scene struck her. The two had stopped kissing, and now Tom held the girl close to his chest, and on his face was the most beautiful look of complete and profound love. This was not a boy straying randomly, his infidelity catalyzed by fear at his approaching nuptials. This was something wholly different. This was how a man gazed at the mother of his child. This was something she knew she could never touch.

And that was when she realized who the girl was, who she must be, her long black hair falling wild down her back. The beauty tilted her face to smile up at Tom with a reciprocal ardor, a burning affection, and then Rowan knew with utter certainty that it was Fiona Eira standing before her.

Rowan turned and she ran, her mind no longer connected to her body. When she reached the village, her heart was hammering, and she felt like she was drowning. The thing she had just seen, she couldn't have seen. That girl . . . that girl with Tom. That girl was dead. Rowan had seen her lying pale and lifeless in that unholy coffin. She needed to talk to someone. She needed to tell someone what was happening. Only, she didn't know who would believe her . . . except perhaps Jude.

When she got back to the square, Jude was nowhere to be found, so she hurried to the inn, where his mother informed her he was out back taking apart a fox in the shed. Jude was digging his knife into the dead animal when she flung open the door.

He looked up from his task and smiled. "You're back," he said, and wiped his knife with a cloth.

"I'm back," she said, still trying to understand what she had just seen.

"What's going on with you? Are you okay?" he asked.

"I saw them," she said, her head still spinning. "Tom and . . . Fiona. They were in the woods. They were kissing. Jude—what's happening?"

Stunned, Jude dropped the knife and turned to her with wide eyes, his face utterly serious.

"Fiona Eira is dead," he said slowly.

"You have to believe me," she said, on the verge of tears. "I'm telling you the truth."

He nodded, appearing to collect his thoughts. He looked her straight in the eyes, and there was such intensity behind them that for a moment, Rowan wondered how she ever could have hated him. All she could think was how absolutely beautiful he was. He took off his gloves and laid them on the counter. Slowly he walked over to her, that intensity seeming to grow, and she found herself wondering what it might feel like to have his lips on her neck again.

"You're telling me that's where my brother has been? With a . . . a dead girl?"

Rowan nodded. "I know it's impossible."

Jude's breath caught. "But we saw her laid out. She was dead."

"It was her," Rowan said, still struggling to find the words. "It was her out there. She wasn't a rotting corpse. She was radiant. Jude, you have to believe me."

She looked to him with pleading eyes, and gripping her gently by the shoulders, he stared back into hers. "Rowan. Of course I believe you. I don't want to, but I do."

"How is it possible?" Rowan said, trying to find a solution where there was none. And then something occurred to her. She remembered Mama Lune's face, staring down at Fiona's dead body. "At the funeral, when Mama Lune looked at Fiona's corpse, she saw something there that frightened her. Do you think she knew what was going to happen?

265

Do you think it's possible that a Greywitch brought Fiona back?"

Jude considered her words and then spoke softly. "I don't know, Ro. I think we need to go and speak with Mama Lune and Mama Tetri."

Rowan considered. "If it's true . . . if she has risen, and we tell them, what will they do to her?"

Jude frowned. "I don't know. There's hardly a precedent."

Rowan cringed, a spike of fear suddenly upon her, for something inside her still trembled at the thought of any harm coming to her cousin. "You're sure we can trust the witches?"

Jude nodded. "I think we have to. We have no choice. I have to finish up here, and then I'm going to go speak with Mama Lune. Will you come with me?"

He held a hand out to her, and after a slight hesitation, she reached out for it, and pressed her own hand against it. The warmth of him caused her to lose her breath for a moment, and then, nodding, she backed away.

"I'll return in an hour," she said.

Jude stepped toward her. "You can stay here if you like."

"No," she said. "I have something I need to do."

He looked at her with suspicious eyes, and Rowan could tell he wanted to stop her, but he didn't. "Be careful," he said, holding her gaze.

"I will," she said, and then she turned and stepped out into the snow. Slowly she walked toward the woods. She recalled that beautiful girl she'd spoken with on the path, snow glittering in her hair. She'd seemed so fragile, so lost, a lifetime away from the boldness of the girl she'd seen with Tom in the woods. Rowan had to go back out. She had to see her again. She had to make sure.

But as she walked, fear was building in her spine, because if it was true—if Fiona Eira truly had come back from the dead, then there was something terrible she had to consider. For Fiona Eira, monster though she might be now, had indeed been born of the Goddess, and as such, she would have had no problem crossing the village boundary.

Wrapping her cloak tight around her chest, she quickened her pace, the forest seeming to close in around her.

16. THE FOOL

OUT IN THE woods, knife strapped to her leg, Rowan sat atop the large rock that overlooked the clearing and the ancient yew. Knees pulled to her chest, she was certain an hour must have come and gone. She should be heading back to Jude. Disappointed, she was beginning to climb back down when she heard a familiar voice.

"I know you're there," the voice called. "There's no need to hide from me."

Terrified, her legs threatening to give way beneath her, Rowan climbed the rest of the way down the rock.

Fiona stood in the clearing, arms outstretched, a ghoulish smile on her ruby lips.

"Come," the dead girl said. "Let's talk."

Trembling, Rowan approached, but paused when she felt her legs would carry her no farther.

"Closer," Fiona commanded, and Rowan, knowing she had no other choice, did as she was told, stopping when she was within arm's reach of the girl.

From such a close distance, Fiona looked different than she had in life—somehow more beautiful and more ghastly all at once. Her black hair hung in wild glossy waves, and she wasn't dressed for the weather. She was barefoot, her naked toes nestled into the snow, and she wore neither cloak nor dress. Instead, she wore a lightweight shift. Rowan thought it looked vaguely familiar, but she couldn't concentrate on it for too long because her gaze was drawn back down to the girl's feet, which seemed to be caked with a strange, horrible kind of mud.

"Hello," Fiona said, her quicksilver voice sliding through the air.

Rowan stared at her as if she were seeing something that wasn't there. That couldn't be there. "What . . . are you?" she whispered.

The girl smiled, and Rowan thought she saw the dying light catch and glimmer off the tip of an incisor. And then Rowan saw something she couldn't understand. Strung around Fiona's neck with a red ribbon was a coin, the design of which matched the drawing she'd found in her father's study.

"I'm just a girl," Fiona said, looking deep into Rowan's eyes. "And I want to be left alone. Do you understand me?"

Rowan nodded, her blood growing very cold. She knew quite all at once that this girl, this creature, could kill her in an instant if she so chose.

"I don't want to hurt you," Fiona said, and she seemed to mean it. Rowan backed away. "But if you tell anyone about me, I will. Do you understand?"

Speechless, Rowan nodded again.

They stood there a moment, staring at one another, and then the wind picked up, blowing a chill across Rowan's neck. She looked at the girl standing half-naked in the snow and wondered how it could be possible. And then Rowan remembered where she'd seen the shift the girl wore—white eyelet lace with a green flower stitched at the base of the left strap on the girl's dress. It had been Emily's. She'd been wearing it the night she died. Rowan began to grow sick at the thought, but then she heard something—something coming through the trees, fast, and Rowan knew it was the beast, the creature, and she was certain that she was going to die.

She closed her eyes as if that could stop it, but she opened them again when, with a crash, the monster came lurching through the trees, its gaping maw extended, its daggered teeth ready to devour. Rowan screamed, her body paralyzed with fear, but then the creature stopped abruptly directly in front of her, and with those empty eyes—the eyes of the dead—it stared into her, and it seemed to Rowan that it knew her every thought.

Fiona took a step toward the creature, and reaching up, she stroked it as one might a beloved pet, and then, at some unspoken communication between them, the beast retreated, backing away into the trees. Rowan's eyes were trained on it as it grew horribly still and seemed almost to become part of the whiteness itself, disappearing into the trees, into the snow. If it hadn't been for its steaming clouds of breath, Rowan would never have known it was there.

"Curious," Fiona said, turning her attention to her cousin, but Rowan was so petrified that she could barely feel her feet, let alone speak. "It didn't hurt you. It's so very hungry, you see. And yet it didn't hurt you."

The girl wrinkled her brow, seemingly disturbed by the idea, and then she turned to Rowan.

"What . . . what is that . . . thing?" Rowan whispered.

"A friend. And like I say, it's so hungry," she said, and reaching out, she tucked a strand of Rowan's hair behind her ear. "Incidentally, so am I. I think you'd better go now."

Rowan began to shake uncontrollably.

"I . . . can go now?" she asked, barely able to form the words.

The dead girl smiled at her, and then she nodded. "I think you'd better. But remember"—then she held a finger to her lips—"shhh."

† † †

Jude was cleaning up outside the shed when he heard approaching footsteps. Expecting Rowan, he dusted off his trousers but was surprised to see Tom. Tom, with that strange haze to his eyes, that simmering violence just below the surface, took a step back when he saw his brother.

"I don't want to talk," he growled, and headed for the inn, but Jude stopped him.

"I know," Jude said, grabbing Tom by the shoulders and holding him still. "I know where you've been going, and I know what she is."

Tom pulled away. "Leave it alone, Jude. You don't understand what's happening. You can't know."

"But I do know. I know exactly what's happening, and it needs to stop."

"Forget it," Tom snapped, turning toward the woods. "It was dumb to think I could come back here."

"People think it's you," Jude said. "They're probably combing the forest for you right now. They think you've lost your mind, Tom. They think you killed those people."

"Me?" Tom laughed.

"I'm trying to protect you," Jude said. "What are you becoming? Where is my brother who enjoys helping the elderly and who always has a kind word for his fellows? It drives me crazy, but that's the person you are. Come back to us. Even if you don't feel normal, you need to start acting normal or else the tide of suspicion that's already turned against you will grow. The elders came to talk to Father when this all started. They said their oracles told them there was an evil hanging over our house."

"An evil over our house?" Tom asked, his eyes seeming somewhere very far off. "When? When did they say that?"

"Right after the soldiers died. If they tell the others, that will be enough. They'll hang you, Tom. They will."

"That's ridiculous," Tom said, his eyes growing increasingly clouded. "You're being paranoid."

"Have you seen your face? Do you have any idea what you're doing to our parents—to Rowan?"

Tom spun around, his eyes suddenly alight with a haunting kind of fire. "I don't care," he said. "None of that matters anymore. Who I was before, that wasn't me. I didn't know who I was then. I know now. This is who I am. I've found the thing that every man seeks, and I'm not letting it go."

"It's unholy," Jude said, and Tom stared back at him with hatred in his eyes. "I'm sorry that she died. It was a tragedy, a horrific tragedy, but it's what was meant to be. She was dead. She's supposed to stay dead."

"But she's not dead," Tom said, his face slowly contorting so that when Jude looked at him, he saw little more than an animal. "Don't you see? She's not dead. She's here, and she loves me."

Jude shook his head. "No, Tom. She is dead. You found her dead in the snow with her heart torn from her chest. You saw her yourself laid out in that casket."

Before Jude could say more, Tom drew his fist back, and with all his fury, he hit his brother in the face, throwing him backward into the snow. Jude tried to scramble up, but Tom was on top of him, and Jude was blinded by the pain.

And then Tom released him.

Jude lay on the ground a moment, trying to understand what was happening. He heard footsteps, and then the shed door opening. Confused, his head throbbing in pain, he wondered what Tom could possibly want in the shed.

By the time Jude realized the answer, it was too late, and his brother was on top of him again, knee to his stomach, holding the hunting knife directly over his heart.

"No!" Jude screamed. And through the blood, Jude's eyes locked with his brother's, and in them he saw only evil.

Jude struggled, but Tom overpowered him. He hovered over Jude, knife held aloft, but instead of plunging it down, Tom tore open Jude's shirt and dragged the knife slowly across the skin of his chest. The pain was excruciating, and Jude cried out in agony.

It was as if the cry awakened something in Tom. Suddenly he stopped, his eyes grew wide for a second, they cleared, and then he looked at the knife in his hand in horror. He dropped it in the snow, and running off, he disappeared into the woods, leaving his brother writhing in agony.

† † †

When Rowan found Jude, he was washing the blood from his torso. His face was swollen but no longer bleeding.

"Goddess!" she cried. "What happened to you?"

He flinched when he saw her and then looked away, obviously ashamed. "Tom" was all he said.

Reaching out with trembling fingers, she touched his chest, careful not to aggravate the wound. "He did this to you?"

"He sure did," Jude said, unable to keep the anger from his voice.

With great pain, he pulled his shirt back on and began buttoning it up.

"But that needs dressing," she said, concerned.

"Mama Lune will help me. I was waiting for you, but I don't think you should come with me."

"What?" she said, hurt. "Why not?"

"We have to go through the woods to get to her, and I have no clue what's happening here. I don't know what to fear or how much to fear it. All I know is how much danger we're in, and how much happier I would be if you were safe, locked in your house, than out in the woods with me, especially so near nightfall."

"No," she said firmly. "I'm coming. Besides, being locked in a house did nothing to protect Arlene or Emily."

He started to argue with her, but when he saw the determination in her eyes, he knew it would be useless.

"Fine," he said, defeated. "But we have to hurry. It will be dark soon."

The two moved quickly through the woods, trying to make as little noise as possible. Rowan noticed that Jude winced with pain as they went, but he seemed intent on hurrying, so she didn't try to slow him. She smelled the smoke from Mama Lune's fireplace before she saw the cottage, and when she did, she increased her pace. It was a pretty stone thing with a thatched roof, set back against a mossy glade.

Before they could knock, Mama Lune opened the door.

Behind her, Rowan could see Mama Tetri, her dark skin even more lovely illuminated by the firelight within.

"You've come," Mama Tetri said, smiling. "I'm so pleased to see you."

Sweeping forward, the Bluewitch took Rowan by the hands. She looked at her as if she were looking at her own child, then pulled her close and held her in her arms. "Come," she said. "Come, my child. Sit with me by the fire, and we will have our talk."

Mama Lune's eyes moved to Jude's swollen face. "What happened?" she cried, and when he removed his coat to reveal his blood-soaked shirt, she gasped. "Who did this to you?"

"It's complicated," Jude said, looking away, and Rowan wondered whether he was protecting his brother or was ashamed.

"You come with me," Mama Lune said, putting her arm around him as if she were holding an injured bird. "This will need a plaster. Rowan and Mama Tetri have much to discuss. We will join them once we have you fixed up."

Rowan watched as he was ushered from the room, and she realized her heart was breaking for him, for no matter what he might say or do, the boy loved his brother, and to have his love met with such violence could not have been easy for him.

"He will be fine," said Mama Tetri, her voice soothing. Rowan had not expected witches to be like this. She had not expected mothering tones and quietly burning fires. She followed Mama Tetri to the hearth and took a seat in a comfortable wooden chair.

"I am so pleased you've finally come to hear. Mama Lune feared you never would."

Rowan shifted uneasily in her seat. "In the village, she told me something—something I could not believe—that you said sooth for my mother when she was pregnant with me."

"I did," Mama Tetri said, and Rowan fought the urge to argue with her, for whatever prejudice she had against the witches seemed moot now. "We were children together—your mother and her brother, Pimm, and I. When she found she was with child, it was only right that I should come say sooth for her. Do you know what sooth is, my child?"

"It's like a prophecy," Rowan said, squinting. "Right?"

The witch smiled. "A little. It's a blessing, really, but often there are bits of prophecy involved. Sometimes a witch will see things when she lays her hands. Sometimes these things cannot be easily explained. This was the case with you."

"What did you see?" Rowan asked, trying to keep the fear from her voice.

The woman pursed her lips. "It was strange. When I lay the hands, it was as if half of you was blocked from me. I had never seen the like, though I tried not to convey my worry to your mother. I stayed through your nesting—you know, when you were small, you had the most lovely red cheeks; they were like fires burning beneath your skin—and I tried to divine what I could not see in your sooth. I looked in the waters, but they did not speak to me. After your mother was settled, I moved on, and when I had the opportunity, I held conference with an older witch who was more experienced in birthing matters, and she helped me to understand. She explained that this could happen when siblings' destinies are extremely closely linked. I've seen it a few times since. If the path of the first child is determined by the birth of the second, then it will be impossible to see the complete picture for the first until the second has survived the birthing process. All became clear when your mother called for me to say sooth again within the year."

Rowan shook her head. "But my mother died in childbirth. I don't have a sibling."

Mama Tetri smiled. "Of course you do. If you didn't, we wouldn't be having this conversation."

"But I don't," Rowan repeated, her muscles tensing. I am an only child. My mother died in childbirth."

"Yes, my child. She died just after giving birth, but not to you. You were only a little over a year old. Tell me, do you sometimes dream of your mother?"

Rowan nodded, pain gripping her heart as she thought back to her dreams of her mother and the wooden egg.

"Those aren't dreams, child. Those are memories. You knew your mother."

"I did?" Rowan asked, a wisp of a memory floating past her mind's eye—her mother's warm breath upon her face, a slant of light through a diaphanous curtain.

"You did," Mama Tetri said. "The destiny I saw when I said sooth the second time was that together you and your sister would eventually bring the downfall of both your parents. By the time I reached your mother, when I said sooth for her, she was already ill, and with this second pregnancy, her fortune was set. I could see clearly now that both parents were destined to die as a result of it. I had to tell your mother. It was my duty. Your mother, she didn't believe it, and when your father talked of separating the two of you—of sending the baby to your mother's brother as soon as she was born—your mother wouldn't hear of it."

"The baby lived?" Rowan asked, the words tumbling from her lips like apples from a cloth sack.

"The baby lived," said the witch.

Rowan's eyes grew wide, the truth suddenly upon her.

"Fiona Eira?" Rowan said, the name wounding her heart as she spoke it. "Fiona Eira is my sister?" She was stunned, and yet on some level, she'd always known. She'd always sensed her absence, and that day standing on the path, she'd been so familiar. When Fiona had died, the grief had nearly torn her apart, although she'd had no idea why.

"She begged your father not to separate you, and he promised her he wouldn't, but still," continued Mama Tetri, "your mother, she feared for her children. She feared that with such dark fortunes, harm was bound to come to you both. So upon her deathbed, while she stared down at Fiona Eira's snow-white face, and while she caressed your rose-red cheeks, she spoke these words: *'You two shall have each other forever so long as you live. What one has she must share with the other.'* When your mother died, your sister's fate was sealed. Your father sent the girl away to your mother's brother, Pimm, and his wife, Malia, with instructions never to bring her to Nag's End."

"Why?" Rowan asked, shaking her head. "Why are you telling me this?"

"When I first returned to Nag's End, it was because I saw in the waters that the sisters were to be reunited, and I feared what might come of it. I wanted to speak to you because I thought you might listen, but since then, much has changed. Outcomes are very uncertain."

Out of the corner of her eye, Rowan saw Jude and Mama Lune standing at the edge of the room. Jude looked at her with deep concern in his eyes, and she wondered how much he'd heard.

"Do you know?" Rowan asked the witches. "Do you know that Fiona Eira walks again?"

Mama Tetri nodded. "We have discovered this, yes."

"We know about her," said Mama Lune, coming closer. "And we know about the beast she commands."

"I've seen it," Rowan said, shivering at the memory of it. "It's awful—a monster of death."

Mama Tetri nodded. "I've seen it as well—in the water, and we've heard it, moving through the trees at night."

"Tell me," Rowan said, a connection beginning to form in her head. "Was her rising the work of a Greywitch?"

"We think so, yes," Mama Lune said, but she averted her eyes, and Rowan knew she wasn't telling her everything.

"What was it you saw that day? You saw something at the funeral that frightened you—something that made you suspect that a Greywitch was among us."

The Greenwitch sighed. "Your sister, when her body fell, I saw that she wore a coin around her neck. This coin—I could see Grey magic trailing off it like ribbons of smoke. Death magic went into its making. Do you know what that means, child?"

Rowan's mind flashed back to the drawing of the coin she'd found in her father's study. She knew he was involved; he had to be, but she still didn't see how it was possible. She shook her head, trying to focus on the witch. "Death magic? I've heard of it, but I can't say that I know what it is."

"For death magic to work, innocent people have to die. They are sacrificed—were sacrificed—in order to create the spell that made that coin," said Mama Tetri.

"What is it, though?" Jude asked. "What is the coin?"

Mama Lune squinted her eyes, crow's feet fanning out from their edges. "I have seen its like before. It was a long, long time ago, but it is not a thing easily forgotten. Do you know what a talisman is, child?"

Rowan nodded. "I think so. It's a protective charm."

"No," the witch said, raising a finger to stop her. "It *can* be a protective charm, but in its essence, it is a placeholder. It is simply an object that can be used to hold the intentions of the witch who cast the spell into it."

Mama Tetri cleared her throat. "In old times, when the Greywitches ruled their sisters, talismans were used almost exclusively to summon ancient spirits, wicked things that they could command to do their bidding."

"I'm not sure I understand," said Rowan. "So the talisman summons a spirit?"

"It is a doorway," said Mama Tetri. "Each talisman is fashioned for the purpose of housing a specific spirit. It is only through the metal of the talisman—and it is always fashioned of metal—that the spirit may enter this world."

Jude ran his hand through his hair. "So this monstrous beast that stalks our woods, someone used this talisman to call it forth?"

Mama Tetri furrowed her brow. "Not just someone. A Greywitch. A most powerful Greywitch."

"Wait," Jude said, shaking his head. "But this beast does not live in any talisman. It is corporeal."

"Is it, though?" Rowan wondered aloud.

"Of course it is," he said. "You saw it yourself."

She shook her head. "But I've also seen it disappear among the trees, and we've both felt it move past us without seeing its shape. It's almost as if it is of this world and not of this world at the same time."

Mama Tetri nodded. "I think you may be right. You see, even if a spirit were made corporeal—and it would take an immensely powerful Greywitch to cast such a spell—its essence, its heart, would remain in the talisman. It is like the shell of a sea creature. It may wander forth without its shell, but it is not safe or whole unless it is in its true home, the talisman. A spirit is of no use to a witch if she cannot hold sway over it."

"But Fiona Eira has it," Rowan said. "She has the talisman."

"We know," said Mama Lune.

"But," said Jude, "Fiona couldn't have summoned that thing."

"No, she couldn't have," Mama Tetri said.

"Then how?" Rowan asked.

The witches looked at each other, and then Mama Lune spoke. "All we can say for certain is that somewhere out there, a Greywitch is missing a very important possession, and she can't be pleased about it. I would hazard a guess that she doesn't know who has her talisman, and therefore she doesn't know who has her beast. She must be searching for it, and yet we have not felt her walk our woods."

"But," said Rowan, trying to make sense of it all, "what about Fiona . . . what exactly *is* she?"

Mama Lune's eyes grew wide as she spoke. "She is a bloody one, child—the hungry dead. She needs to feed or she will die a second time, the pain of which you can scarcely imagine."

"And the beast," Jude said. "You say it is a kind of spirit?"

Mama Tetri pursed her lips. "It is an old thing—from long ago, when the world was a wicked place."

"And it is the coin that connects them because Fiona wears it around her neck," said Rowan.

"It could be more than that that connects them," said Mama Lune.

"What do you mean?" Rowan asked.

"The Greywitch must connect them both. It has to," the witch answered.

Rowan's mind felt alive as all the pieces of the puzzle began to click into place. And yet, there was a creeping fear, a sense of doom looming just above her, threatening to press down and crush the air from her lungs. "Do you think this Greywitch could still be in Nag's End?" she asked.

Mama Lune furrowed her brow. "If so, she is being very quiet. We have not sensed her."

"So . . . what do we do?" Rowan asked, galvanized. "There must be something we can do? Some kind of magic?"

Mama Lune scowled and put a hand on her hip. "We are not all-powerful, child. I am a Greenwitch. I make herbs and tinctures to heal. Mama Tetri is a Bluewitch. She works the water to divine. We don't go about fighting primordial monsters."

"But can't you divine how to kill it?" Rowan pleaded. "Can't you divine what to do?"

Mama Tetri pursed her lips. "I have tried, and I cannot see. The only thing we do know is that witches like us are powerless against this kind of magic."

"But you can't be!" cried Rowan, fear welling up in her heart. "There must be something you can do."

Mama Lune shook her head. "We are heading west. It is time for Mama Tetri to move on, and I shall go with her."

Rowan was shocked to hear the words, but looking at Jude, she saw that they hit him harder.

"What?" he said, stepping away from Mama Lune. "You can't leave now."

"There is nothing we can do," the Greenwitch said. "Mama Tetri has delivered her message, but we cannot stay and fight. Witches are a dying clan. We need to protect our ways. We must move on."

Jude stood stunned, his face crimson with anger.

"You're not going to help us?" Rowan asked, her mind spinning. "You're just going to leave us here?"

"This is not our battle. We cannot win it," Mama Tetri said, leveling her gaze at Rowan. "But there is a faint possibility that you might be able to do so. This connection you have with Fiona. See what that brings. You are connected to her, and she is connected to the beast. And therein lies your hope. Perhaps there is some way to use this connection to your advantage."

"You're both crazy," Jude spoke, fury charging his words. "You're telling us that you won't stay and help us, but that Rowan should risk her life?"

Mama Lune nodded. "I cannot make you understand the ways of the witches. Forgive me, child."

Jude shook his head. "That's all we get?"

"That's all you get," she said, pity in her eyes, and for a moment, Rowan felt certain that Jude was going to scream, but clenching his jaw, he turned and strode over to Rowan.

"Let's go," he said. "I'm sorry I brought you here."

Mama Tetri reached out to take Rowan's hands, but she backed away from the witch and walked out the front door with Jude.

Once outside, Rowan turned toward Jude, and he winced, pain written across his face. "I'm sorry," he said. "I don't know what we're going to do."

"It's not your fault, Jude," she said, upset to see him so hurt, wanting to soothe him somehow.

"I trusted them. I thought they would help us. I thought they would help you," he said, looking at her with desperate eyes.

And that was when they heard a man's scream—sharp

and otherworldly. They froze there, staring at one another, the same thought pulsing through them both—Tom. Without another word, they raced through the trees, back toward the village, toward the scream.

As soon as they saw the body, Rowan knew it wasn't Tom, but the sight was so horrific that she was overcome. There in the snow, his rifle beside him on the ground, Goi Tate lay splayed out, his chest a bloody cavern.

Some distance through the woods, Rowan heard movement—the snapping of branches, the crushing of snow.

Jude took her hand. "We have to go. Before it comes back. We have to get inside the village barrier."

17. STRENGTH

Out in the woods, Fiona kissed Tom between his eyes. He sighed and cocked his head.

"I think I'm changing," Tom said, but she only laughed. "I don't know who I am anymore."

"I know who you are," Fiona said, smiling. "And I think you're wonderful."

"This anger, this violence inside me," he said. "It grows stronger every day. I fear it will consume me." Gazing at the coin she wore around her neck, he remembered Jude's words. The elders had seen an evil in their house, and Tom knew they were right to have seen it, but the evil hadn't emanated from a person. It was the coin that they'd sensed. He took a step toward Fiona. "It comes from there. It draws me to it. I need it to stop. Please, Fiona, make it stop."

Fiona's face grew serious, and grasping the coin around her neck, she took a step away from him as if to shield it. "What would you have me do?"

He looked at the coin and then back to her face. "It makes me sick. It turns me inside out and makes me crave things—things that frighten me."

"What things?" she asked, her expression curious.

"Violence. Blood. I nearly killed my brother today. I stood over him, ready to plunge a knife into his heart, and I don't know why. It was as if there was no other choice. And I know it was that—that thing. It drives me to do things. Please, Fiona."

She shook her head, insistent. "There's nothing I can do about it."

"Yes, there is," he pleaded, moving to touch her. But just as he stepped toward her, she stepped away. "Get rid of it. Destroy it."

"You would have me destroy it?" she asked, shocked. "But I need it. I cannot live without it."

"Of course you can. Please understand, that coin, it will drive me to do things I will regret. Since the moment I found it, things have gone wrong. Up on that mountain, when I found it buried in the snow, somehow I knew. I just knew, but I took it anyway. Even when I forgot about it, when I packed my heavy coat away in the attic, the coin in the pocket, I believe I still felt it calling to me even then. And then, when I put it around your neck, everything changed. Don't you see? It was as if the world turned sour after that. If I hadn't found it, if I hadn't given it to you, maybe everything would be okay right now. Maybe it still could be. I am begging you to destroy it."

She moved close to him, and taking his head in her hands, she peered into his eyes. "I will help you. I will teach you how to control your urges as I am learning to control mine. When that girl, my cousin, came into the woods earlier today, do you think I did not want to tear her throat from her wispy frame? Do you think I did not want to consume her? But I fought the urge because I promised you I would not kill again."

Tom bowed his head. "Then we have to leave."

"What?" she asked, shocked. "Where would we go?"

"Up north," he said, a plan formulating in his mind. "Away from people. If I am to turn into a monster, then I want to be where I can do no harm to innocents."

"But we're happy here," she said, sad-eyed. "I can control it. I can help you control it as well."

And that was when they heard it—the crack, the scream, and Fiona's eyes grew wide.

"What . . . what's happening?" Tom drew near her, terrified she was injured, but then she sighed, and as she arched her back, a delicious smile spread over her face.

"Are you okay?" he asked, gripping her tightly.

Eyes wild and sparkling, she licked her lips. "I feel wonderful," she said. And then fear spread over her face. "Oh, Tom. Oh, Tom, no."

"What is it?"

"It has fed. Oh, Tom, I am so sorry."

"No," Tom said, understanding immediately. "You said it did what you bid."

"It does," she said, bewildered. "It *did.* But it was so hungry, Tom, and something strayed into the woods tonight."

"Oh Goddess, my Goddess," Tom moaned, pacing. "Is it my brother? Is it Jude?"

Fiona tilted her head, feeling what the beast felt. "No . . . I don't think so."

"We have to leave," he said, and this time when he spoke, he saw on her face that she understood he was right. "We are a sickness—a plague. We have to sequester ourselves, take that beast with us where we can hurt no man."

Fiona started to shake her head, but it was not worth fighting.

"I need to say goodbye to my family," Tom said, speaking quickly, as if trying to piece everything together. "Then we'll go away from here. We'll leave tonight. We'll start anew somewhere else. We won't hurt anyone."

Fiona closed her eyes, and then she nodded. "I need to say goodbye to Lareina. She is buried where you pointed out to me—on the cliff above the lake?"

"Yes," he said, relief consuming him. "That's right. Up Cairn Hill at the Mouth of the Goddess. I will meet you there, and then we will go."

Taking her hands in his, he stared into her eyes, and then, without another word, each went their own way into the night.

† † †

By the time Rowan and Jude reached her house, they were out of breath, their lungs bursting, and Rowan was on the verge of tears. Flinging open the door, she screamed for her father. She ran to his study but found it empty. Footsteps on the stairs sent relief flooding through her, but a moment later, when the duke emerged into the hall, she was overtaken by a sudden sense of uneasiness.

"What is it?" he asked, concerned.

"There's been another attack," Jude said, breathless. "In the woods. Goi Tate. I'm afraid there's nothing we can do."

The duke ran a hand through his hair, thinking for a moment before he spoke. "Jude, you come with me. We'll go to your father's tavern and gather what men we can. Perhaps we can catch the beast while it's still afoot. Rowan, you lock the door behind us. Don't let anyone in."

"Okay," Rowan said, confused and terrified. "Where is my father?"

"I'm sorry," he said. "But I don't know. Merrilee is asleep upstairs. Will you keep an eye on her for me?"

Nervously, he wrung his hands, the silver rings catching the moonlight and casting a glittering veil over Rowan's eyes. She turned away, a tightening in her chest, and suddenly, though she couldn't say why, she was newly afraid.

"Of course," she said, though the words came out as no more than a whisper.

"Thank you," the duke said, and then, turning to Jude,

he added, "Come along. I suspect we have a full night ahead of us."

She watched them leave, the heavy oak door shaking the house when the duke pulled it closed behind him. Once they had gone, Rowan stood alone in the hallway, feeling very much as if icy hands were gripping her shoulders. Shivering, she tried to understand the source of her fear. She stood very still, listening to the old house creak and breathe, settling into its foundations, as Emily used to say. Her teeth began to chatter, and her thoughts fell to the rings the duke wore on his left hand. That was what had frightened her, what continued to frighten her, though the reason she could not place.

A creak from the floorboards above startled her, and she did her best not to cry out. Merrilee. She needed to check on Merrilee.

Slowly she took the stairs one at a time, her knuckles growing white from gripping the banister as she went. Above her, the second-floor landing was lit only by the radiance of the moon cascading through the picture window, and the house was so quiet that she could hear her own breathing echoed back to her by the walls above.

She took the last step and pulled herself up onto the landing. The moonlight illuminated about a quarter of the hallway, but gradually the darkness took over until it seemed to consume the length of it. Nearly frozen, Rowan peered down into the shadows to the far end of the house where her mother's old room lay. She moved slowly, running her fingers along the walls, careful to keep her feet silent as she went. She watched her fingers disappear as she moved out of the moonlight and into the darkness, and from then on she was guided only by memory, and by the lines of light beneath each wooden door. When she reached Antonia's old room, where Merrilee slept, she caught her breath and opened the door as silently as she could. Light streamed in through the window and kissed the sleeping child, who was curled up on the bed like a tiny animal. Rowan breathed a sigh of relief.

Turning, she pulled the door closed behind her, and then let her attention fall to her mother's old room, where the duke was staying, and again she felt uneasy.

She crept across the hall to his door, and quietly she opened it and stepped into the bedchamber. Unsure what exactly it was she sought, she looked around for anything that might stand out. Reaching for the matches over the fireplace, she lit a mounted sconce, and a warm, quivering light flooded the room and danced upon the walls. The chamber was neatly kept, the bed expertly made. Oddly, though, his personal belongings were nowhere to be seen. It was as if no one was occupying the space at all. She tried the closet door but found it locked. Remembering that Emily kept keys in the top drawer of the dresser in each room, she gently pulled the drawer open, but inside she found nothing.

Rowan leaned against the wall and swept her eyes over the room once more. If the duke had the key on him, then she was out of luck, but perhaps he'd hidden it. If she were going to hide a key somewhere, she wondered, where would she hide it? She scanned the space again, and then they alighted on the wooden bedposts. Rowan grew very still as she stared at the round wooden finials. They looked like . . . eggs—like wooden eggs. In her dream, her mother held one of those wooden eggs in her hand. But if the witches were right, then those dreams weren't really dreams; they were memories. And if it was a memory, then that meant that those finials could be removed. Could there be space inside them large enough to fit a key?

Hesitant, her heart beating wildly within her chest, she took a step toward the bed. With shaking hands, she reached out and began twisting the round finial nearest the window, near where the light had streamed in in her dream. It gave way easily, and she turned it until it came loose from the post.

Her heart gave a start as she realized what this must mean. The witches were right. It was true—she *had* known her mother. Her mother had held her and loved her, and Rowan remembered it all. The dream wasn't just a dream; it was a memory. She fought back tears of joy as she thought of it. Carefully removing the wooden egg, she reached inside the post. It was a space definitely large enough to hide a key. She let out a joyful gasp, overwhelmed by what this meant, and then her fingers brushed against something metal. The key.

Smiling, she pulled it out and headed to the closet. She slipped the key into the lock and turned it, and the door eased open to reveal a most unexpected sight. Three trunks lined the base of the closet, their lids shut and padlocked, but the shelves, instead of being filled with clothing, were hidden by lengths of thick black velvet cloth. With a shaking hand, she reached up and pulled off one cloth, and then another, and another, and behind each gleamed mass of sparkling silver after mass of sparkling silver. Strewn along every surface—forks, knives, spoons, serving implements, dashed together carelessly, and at the center of the mess was a large silver bowl. Rowan found herself stepping away, clutching at her chest as the meaning hit her.

It was him. All along it was him. Although she'd had moments when he'd made her feel odd, she'd never suspected he could be the Greywitch. She'd assumed that all witches were female, but apparently she'd been wrong.

The light from the dancing candle seemed to animate the glittering mass of silver, sending it into a rapturous dance, and even as her gut cinched in upon itself, she found herself reaching out for the riches. But just before her fingers grazed a gleaming chalice, she came to her senses and jerked her hand away.

She needed to get out of there. If the duke found out what she'd discovered, they'd all be in terrible and immediate danger. She tossed the cloths back over the silver and locked the door.

She stole back to the bedpost, but when she shoved the key down inside, she felt it hit something. She pinched whatever it was with her fingers, pulled it out, and replaced the key.

At first when she pulled it out and stared at it, she didn't understand what she saw. It was twine—yellow twine—

twisted and frayed. And then it was upon her, and her knees nearly gave way.

The golden snake. It had been her mother's marriage twine, but why was it in the bedpost? Why had her mother removed it? She thought about the golden snake, the way it had cut into her mother's flesh, and then suddenly she remembered her mother's belly, swollen, about to burst, the skin of her wrist swelling along with it. As her second pregnancy had progressed, the twine must have cut into her wrist, so she had removed it. Rowan had heard that that happened sometimes, and in such cases, arrangements could be made, the elders could be consulted, and the twine could be replaced. But her mother hadn't consulted anyone—hadn't sought anyone's approval. She had simply slipped a knife blade between her skin and the bracelet, and severed it, freeing her flesh, freeing herself.

Just then, she heard the front door open, and she was jerked back to the present. Quickly, she replaced the twine in the bedpost and secured the finial atop it. And after extinguishing the candle, she closed the door silently behind her and hurried downstairs.

Rowan found her father in the hallway, brushing the snow off his boots. Her first instinct was to run to him, to press her face to his chest and cry, for standing there, he seemed the very image of safety, and yet she knew that was all it was—an illusion of safety. He was mixed up in this somehow; she was certain.

"Goi Tate is dead," she said to him, and he nodded, grief carving its way along his lined face.

"I've heard. I met Jude and the duke on the path just now. Tragic."

Walking past her, he continued down the hall and into his study, but Rowan followed, anger rising in her chest. He took a seat behind his desk, and Rowan approached him.

"I've been to see Mama Tetri. She . . . she told me things. Things I couldn't believe. Things about my mother. Things about my sister."

Henry Rose opened his mouth to speak, and for a moment, time seemed to be suspended, and in his eyes, Rowan could see him trying to decide what to do. He furrowed his brows, angry, but then he shook his head, and his cheeks flushed.

"You know," he sighed, and grasping his hands in his lap, he shut his eyes tight as if to block out the truth.

"It's true, isn't it? Fiona Eira was my sister." The words came out strange and shaky, and even though she knew them to be true, she wanted him to tell her they weren't. She wanted him to tell her it was all some terrible misunderstanding.

But he didn't. "Yes," he said, his voice like a gust of wind.

"I had a sister, and you sent her away?"

He nodded. "I did what was best for our family, Rowan. I did what was best for you."

"Don't blame your choices on me. You sent her away because of a prophecy?" she asked, her voice choked with sorrow. "You don't even believe in divination."

He looked out the window into the heavy black night beyond. "Of course I don't."

"But you sent her away because of what the witch told you," she said, and standing before him, her fists clenched at her side, she resisted the urge to beat them upon his chest. "You can't believe and not believe at the same time. You have to decide."

"Rowan," he said, looking up at her with pleading eyes. "How can I explain this to you? I am a man of reason. I never believed in witches or goblins—in the things we can't explain. But your mother did believe, and when she invited that witch here, I have to admit, I was swayed. I liked her. She was so taken with you. She said you were destined for greatness. What father wouldn't want to believe that? But when she came back, when your mother was pregnant with Fiona, her tune was quite different. She spoke of illness, of death—of that vile prophecy. Hateful, that's what it was. What woman needs to hear she is going to die before her labor has even begun? Sometimes I sit up at night wondering what would have happened if that witch hadn't said those things to her. Would she have found the strength . . . would she have made it through alive? Do you see now why I hate them? Do you see why I've kept you from their lies?"

Rowan shook her head, trying to understand. Taking a step away from her father, she leaned against the window seat and ran a finger along the rose stripe of its cushion. "But," she said, "but she did die."

He nodded. "She did die. She left me alone with an infant and a child of no more than a year. What was I supposed to do? I sent Fiona Eira to your uncle Pimm and your aunt Malia. I knew he was a good man—that he would raise her as his own. It's not as if I abandoned her."

Rowan felt a pressure growing in her chest. She thought of Fiona Eira, an infant, her mother dead, forced from her home by a father who didn't want her. Rowan's heart ached for her, and it ached for herself, for the sister she'd never known. All those times when she'd instinctively reached out for someone, she was reaching for someone who was very much alive, someone who was supposed to be there beside her.

"And when she came back?" Rowan said, meeting his eyes. "You wouldn't see her. How could you refuse to see your own child?"

He looked away, but not before Rowan could see the tears filling his eyes. "I was . . . I was frightened."

"Frightened?" Rowan laughed, bitterness pinching at her throat. "Frightened of what? Of the prophecy? But you said you didn't believe in the prophecy."

"I didn't," he said, his chin quivering. "I don't. But Rowan, life is unkind, and sometimes we tell ourselves we believe things because we need to believe them. An infant dies in its sleep, and the mother tells herself that the goblins took him. That is what she needs to believe, and so she does. Don't you understand, I don't know if any of these things are real. I don't know if the prophecy is real, but I need to believe that it isn't. For my own sanity, I need to believe that it isn't."

"You . . . you took my sister away," she whispered. "My mother was dead, and you took my sister away."

"I did what I thought was best for you. Best for the two of us." He held out his hands to her, but she didn't take them. "Please, Rowan, you have to forgive me. You have to understand that not a day has gone by that I haven't questioned my decision. I know that if I hadn't done what I did, that Fiona Eira would probably be alive today. I know that in my heart, and it kills me. It eats away at me night and day."

Rowan looked into her father's pleading eyes, and she saw that she had the chance to know his mind—that the secrecy that had kept him from her in recent times was slowly abating.

"I need to ask you something," she said. "And I need you to tell me the truth."

He looked her straight in the eyes and nodded. "Anything."

She inhaled, as if preparing herself for the worst. "I want to know who the duke is—who he really is. I want to know why he's here."

He stared at her a moment, and then exhaling, he dropped his face into his hands.

"Rowan," he said. "He's a dangerous man. A very dangerous man."

"Why is he here?"

"I suppose it's best if I tell you from the beginning," he said, his voice so soothing that Rowan sank into a nearby chair like a child settling in for a bedtime tale. "I've known him for a while now—since before he took over the job of conservateur. I knew of his interest in Midway texts, and I knew he'd recently unearthed a new cache of them, which, I heard, he was guarding quite closely. When those soldiers came through Nag's End, I wondered what they were after. There is little to interest the king up here, but the mountains behind us were once home to a sect of the ancient Midway peoples. I thought immediately of the duke. When the soldiers died, I sorted through their things over at the inn, and I discovered their captain's logbook, and when I saw mention of the duke, when I read that he had commanded the mission, I decided to take the book for myself, to read it through." Suddenly he let out an embittered laugh.

"What?" Rowan asked, taken aback. "What is it?"

He shook his head. "Perhaps I should have listened to the villagers. Perhaps I have incurred the luck of the dead after all."

"May I see it?" she asked, her mind racing. "May I see the logbook?"

"You've already seen it," he said. "When I yelled at you over the papers you held. Those were loose sheets from the logbook—schematics. But I'm afraid I no longer have it. It disappeared from my locked drawer. I am assuming the duke figured out some way to reclaim it."

"What did it say? What did you find between its pages?"

"I don't know exactly what I expected to find in there," he said, running a hand through his hair. "But I was unprepared for what I did find. I thought perhaps it was an archaeological expedition for which the duke hadn't secured approval. I thought at most it might be a bit of a scandal, but what I found between those pages stank of treason."

"Treason?"

"According to what the captain knew, the men were on that mountain to find a weapon—an ancient weapon of great power that the duke believed was buried in the vicinity of Beggar's Drift."

"My Goddess," Rowan sighed, trying to piece it all together.

Her father nodded. "From what I could glean, one of the duke's precious Midway texts had been translated to reveal the location of this weapon. Now, I knew the duke. I knew the hatred he harbored in his soul—the revenge he's longed to seek against the throne. A secret trip to find a weapon of mass devastation did not look good for him—it was not something he would want the king to know about. So I wrote to him and explained that I had read the logbook, and asked if he'd like to discuss its contents with me. I also sent him your translation work. I knew he would be impressed, and I suppose I hoped that my knowledge of the contents of the logbook, coupled with your skills with the Midway dialects, might be enough to secure me a position in the palace city. I thought at the very least it might yield a profit of some kind."

Rowan recoiled. "Blackmail?"

He grimaced. "Oh, I know it was base of me, but man *is* base, Rowan, and I pretend to be nothing more than a man."

"Tell me about the weapon," she said quietly. "Did he tell you what it was?"

"You won't believe it," he said, his eyes wide. "Once he got here, he told me this weapon he claimed to have found was no weapon at all. It was a creature, he said—a great slumbering god that he said he could awaken through some magical nonsense. He intended to transport it in a massive wooden cart—that was the other sheet of paper you saw among my things—schematics for his ridiculous mobile prison. Of course, as soon as he told me this, I knew that he'd gone mad—dangerously mad, but it was too late by then. I went along with what he said because how could I not, but monsters and magic? It's insanity. He arrived babbling about how his monster had been lost, and how he needed some coin—how if only he could find the coin, then he'd be able to set it all right again."

Rowan cleared her throat, not yet ready to show her hand. "So he has no idea where the coin is? Has he . . . has he found the monster?"

"Rowan," he laughed. "Use your head, my girl. There is no monster. Madness is the monster—the madness is driving the duke to kill."

Rowan shook her head. "I think you might be wrong about that, Father."

"Rowan, the blood fairly drips from his bejeweled fingers. I've been wracking my brain, trying to figure out a way to stop him, but I come up with nothing. He is the queen's brother. I cannot accuse him of murder. You know how this royal lot is. What is a handful of slaughtered villagers to them? So I have been trying to obtain proof. When he goes out at night, I follow him, but each time, I come up empty. I've even started looking for this coin myself, thinking that if I could find it, that I could send him on his way, but the task is impossible. It's utter lunacy."

"There is a coin," Rowan said gravely.

"What did you say?" He looked up at her with a raised eyebrow.

"There is a monster as well."

He stared at her a moment before laughing and shaking his head. "Don't be ridiculous."

She held his gaze. "I've seen it, Father. I've seen it in the woods. I've seen it as plainly as I'm seeing you."

Her father stared at her, the blood slowly draining from his face. "You're serious."

"What the duke told you is true, and he's far more dangerous than you know. He did summon a monster. It stalks these woods. It's killed and killed again, and it will keep on killing."

Her father laughed and shook his head. "No. You can't be serious, child."

"Father, when will you trust me? When will you listen to me? Maybe there *are* goblins and fairies. Maybe there *are* monsters. Maybe these simple village folk from whom you've always sought to separate yourself know more about the world than you do. Maybe their beliefs aren't as backward as you think."

Her father paused a moment, his face a muddle of emotions, and then he leaned in. "You say . . . you say you've seen it," he said.

"I have. I swear to you that I have. It's an ancient thing, a horrible thing—summoned from the bowels of the earth by a terrible magic. You say the duke is dangerous, but you don't know the half of it. He's a Greywitch, Father."

Henry Rose sat there, stunned, and Rowan could see the enormity of it wash over his face, and color slowly began to trickle back into his cheeks, as if what he was hearing was on some level a relief.

"I can't ... I can't believe it," he said slowly.

"Then believe me. We are in danger. We are all in danger. The duke is a wicked man. He committed heinous acts to summon that monster. If he is able to get it under his control, the rivers will run with blood."

Her father scratched his beard, his quick eyes focused, thinking. "You say you've seen the coin as well."

She nodded.

"And the duke believes that the coin controls the beast. So it would seem we have only one option." He met her eyes. "We need to get that coin."

Rowan's mind flashed to Fiona Eira's pale chest, to the red ribbon around her neck, to her glittering incisors. "Listen, Father, I know who has it, but it's not going to be easy to get, or for that matter, to explain."

"What do you mean?"

"There is no simple way to say this." He waited patiently for her to continue, and there in his eyes, she saw trust, and she knew she had to tell him. "Fiona ... Fiona Eira has it."

He looked at her with a mixture of surprise and fear. "Excuse me?"

She nodded. "Fiona Eira. She walks among us. She wears the coin around her neck like a bauble."

He looked at her with a blank expression, as if trying to make sense of the incomprehensible, and then he shook his head. "My child . . . Fiona Eira is dead."

"I know. But I've seen her. Out in the woods, I've seen her."

"But that can't be," he said, astonished. "No," he whispered. "That's not possible. She was dead. We saw her in the casket."

"Father, she wears the coin around her neck."

A relentless knocking sounded at the door, jolting Rowan to her feet before her father could answer. She started from the room, her father at her heels, but was surprised to find Merrilee just outside the door, her face swollen from crying, her little body pressed against the opposite wall.

"Merrilee," Rowan said, rushing to her. "Are you all right?"

The girl shook—clearly she wasn't. "I'm afraid," she said, trembling. "I think something bad is going to happen."

Rowan reached out and stroked the child's cheek. "Shhh, now. Don't worry. I'm going to answer the door. You go sit with my father in his study, and I'll be back in a moment."

Rowan looked to her father, who nodded. "Careful now, Ro," he said.

Rowan hurried to the front hall. Through the eyehole she saw Jude's flushed face, and when she opened the door, something inside her surged with happiness. Without thinking, she threw herself into his arms, and hesitant at first, he seemed to freeze, but then he pulled her close. She pressed her face into the warmth of his chest, inhaling his scent, flooded with relief. She looked up at his shocked face, and laughing, she stepped away from him.

"I'm sorry," she said. "I don't know what came over me."

"Don't be sorry," he said, his eyes still wide with surprise. .

"Jude," she said, grabbing his hands. "It's the duke. The duke is the Greywitch. I should have seen it. I should have known. He's the one who summoned the creature. He wants to use it as a weapon to depose the king. If he gets control over it, who knows how many will die. But the coin is the key. If we get the coin, we can take control. We can stop the bloodshed. We can get Tom back."

"Tom's leaving," he said, and when he stepped closer, she could see heartbreak in his eyes. "He says he's headed up north. I know he means to go with her, and I can't let him. He can't go off into the wilds with that monster. I have to stop him."

"He told you this?"

"No," he said softly. "I just missed him. He came to say farewell to my parents. My mother said she saw him slip some cinnamon into his pocket before he left. She wondered if he might be heading to Cairn Hill to pay his respects to our dead before he goes. I'm heading up there now to see if I can catch him. I have to stop him, Ro. He'll die up there. He'll die."

Jude's words surged through Rowan. Coin or no coin, they had to find Tom. He was her best friend. She couldn't let anything happen to him. "I'll . . . I'll go with you," she said, but he shook his head.

"No. I'm going alone. I just wanted to say goodbye in case..." Reaching out, he held a hand to her face and looked into her eyes. "Rowan," was all he said, but there was such tenderness in the word, that even amidst all the pain and fear in her heart, something fluttered to life. And his hand warm on her cheek, he gazed into her eyes. "Rowan," he said. "I want you to know... I never hated you. I ... I think you're wonderful."

She looked up at him, and he stared down at her with a new sort of intensity, one with a soft edge that both confused and thrilled her.

Warmth rushed through her as he said the words, and all at once everything became very clear. "I'm going with you," she said.

"No. Rowan, please stay here."

"I'm coming," she said firmly. "I'll do whatever it takes to save Tom."

"Because you love him?" he asked, his voice trembling.

Rowan looked into his eyes and realized that for him the weight of the world rested on her answer.

"No," she said, excited and frightened all at once. "Because he's my friend."

Standing there in the snow with Jude, she felt deliciously free, and suddenly she knew what to do. Her mind flashed back to her dream—to the golden snake that cut into her mother's flesh, and to the blade that freed her from it. Smiling at Jude, wildly giddy, she reached into her boot and retrieved her dagger.

He raised his eyebrows at her, confused. And then in

one fluid movement, she slipped the blade between her flesh and the red twine, and she sliced.

Just like that, she was free.

Jude took a step away from her, shocked, staring at the severed twine that lay mangled in the snow. Rowan reached down to retrieve it, and smiling at Jude, feeling wonderfully alive, she hurled it as far out into the night as she possibly could.

And then he stepped toward her, and his deep brown eyes flashing, he reached for her, her body swaying to curve against his.

"Jude," she whispered.

Pulling her to him, he kissed her, and a wave of emotion swept through her. She yielded to him, her body flush against his, her breath coming more quickly, her legs beginning to shake, and then she stepped away, overwhelmed.

"I've been wanting to do that for a really long time," he said, confusion in his eyes. "I'm sorry if I . . ."

Rowan shook her head, slowly returning to her senses. "Don't be," she said, and then taking his face in her hands, she kissed him deeply, a different kind of kiss, a hungry kiss, and he leaned into her, matching her passion, and it seemed to Rowan that the world spun wildly around her. And then he was lifting her up, her hungry fingers holding fast to his shoulders.

And then, dizzy, she leaned her head back, and he set her down. They stared at each other, stunned.

"Right," Jude said, still shocked but grinning now. "Where does your father keep his weapons?"

18. THE TOWER

IN THE STUDY, Henry Rose handed them each a rifle and took a third for himself. Rowan tucked her dagger into her stocking and looked over at Merrilee, who sat huddled up in the window seat, knees to her chest.

"Don't be frightened," Rowan said, walking over to the little girl.

Merrilee wrapped her arms around her legs. "I don't want you to die," she said.

Rowan exhaled. "I'm not going to die. No one is going to die."

"Can you promise me?" the girl asked, a tremor to her voice.

Rowan sighed. "That's not really something you can promise. But I give you my word that I'll do my best to make sure everyone returns safely."

"Especially your father?" Merrilee asked, looking at Henry Rose with love.

The gesture stirred Rowan's heart, and she was overcome with sympathy for the little orphan. "Especially my father," she said. "Now listen to me. I want you to go up to your room and lock the door. Don't open it for anyone, do you understand?"

"Not even for the duke?" asked Merrilee, her voice quavering.

"Definitely not for the duke," Rowan answered firmly.

Merrilee nodded, and after hopping down from the window seat, she shyly kissed Rowan on the cheek, then hurried out of the room and up the stairs.

Then, together, Rowan, her father, and Jude headed out into the woods. Night was already upon them, but a fat moon hung in the sky, illuminating their way. Rowan could feel the fear growing inside her as they passed through the village boundary and crossed into the woods. The forest was a different place at night. She knew that now. Devils stalked between the trees, and somewhere out there, a Greywitch walked among them.

As they approached Cairn Hill, she couldn't shake the feeling that they were being watched, followed. She looked to Jude, but his countenance gave nothing away.

As if sensing her trepidation, her father turned to her. "Steady now, Rowan. We're nearly there."

But the words did little to assuage her fear. The moon cast strange shadows, making monsters of the trees, and as they trudged through the snow and up the steep slope to Cairn Hill, Rowan had a feeling that something very bad was about to happen.

When they reached the top of the hill and entered the Mouth of the Goddess, Rowan's eyes swept the burial ground for signs of movement, but there was only stillness.

They approached with their weapons raised, and Jude, spotting something, hurried to the ceremonial altar at the far end of the sacred place.

"They've left the cinnamon offering," he called. "They've already come and gone."

Rowan looked to her father, desperate for a plan.

"We'd better head back down," he said. "Maybe we can still catch them."

Rowan paused, a strange feeling upon her, and she looked out past the trees toward Lover's Leap and Seelie Lake. "Let's go that way."

"But there's nothing out there," her father insisted. "Only the drop-off."

"I think...I think I can feel her," Rowan said, surprised by her own words. But it was true. She'd felt it every time she'd seen Fiona. There was that energy between them, a link.

Heeding Rowan's instincts, the three traveled a short way through a sparse wood and out toward the edge of the cliff, toward Lover's Leap. Rowan spotted Tom and Fiona before they saw her, and her heart flooded with relief.

They sat in the snow, his head in her lap. He looked

unwell—pale, nearly green—but Fiona stroked his hair and gazed at him with such love—like a child admiring her favorite doll. The sight shook Rowan, but there was something else, something she couldn't put her finger on. Something was making her feel especially uneasy.

"Raise your weapons," her father said, and he stepped out into the clearing. Jude and Rowan followed.

Sensing them, Fiona looked up, but Tom didn't notice. He continued staring up at her, while Fiona only gave them a pleasant smile.

"Not the farewell I'd hoped for," she said, still smiling, but narrowing her eyes.

Tom, startled, scrambled to his feet and stepped in front of Fiona as if to shield her. "What are you doing?" he yelled, horrified. "Put your weapons away."

"Tom, please listen to me," Jude said. "You need to come home. You're in danger."

Tom glared at his brother. "Get out of here, Jude. Leave us alone."

Rowan's father cleared his throat. "Tom, you know we can't do that. Your brother's right. Your place is with your family."

"You're sick," Jude said. "She's made you sick."

Tom flushed crimson. "She's done no such thing. I'm fine."

"Fine?" Jude laughed. "You tried to kill me today."

Tom looked away, ashamed, and Rowan's heart broke for him. He was different now, there was no question about that, but he was still Tom, and to see him in such pain was excruciating. Her eyes traveled to Fiona. Rowan kept expecting her to join in, to speak, but she only sat watching from her place on the ground, placid and beautiful, her hair falling in black waves down to the snow.

"Please," Tom said, looking at his brother's gun trained on Fiona. "I love her. And we're leaving tonight. We're going north to the Old Territories, away from people. We only came up here for a final farewell."

"And what about that creature—that beast?" Jude asked.

"She's taking it with her," Tom said, stumbling over the words. "It won't hurt anyone again. Neither of them will. They will feed on moose and northern bears. Just let us go."

"You would choose such a life?" Jude said, his voice breaking. "She's bewitched you. She's a monster."

"She didn't ask for this," Tom cried. "She's a victim. You can't punish her for choices that weren't hers to make."

"People are dead, Tom," Rowan said. "People we knew and loved, they are dead because of her."

"At least let her defend herself. Tell them, Fiona," he said, turning to her. "Tell them what happened."

"Why?" she said calmly. "I owe these people nothing."

"Please, Jude!" Tom pleaded. "Put down your guns. Please, give her a chance to speak. As my brother. As my friend. Do this for me."

Jude considered a moment, his face strained with emotion, and then he signaled to Rowan and her father that they should lower their weapons.

Tom turned to Fiona, but she looked away. "I . . . don't want to tell them," she answered.

"Then tell *me*," he pleaded, kneeling beside her. "Tell me what happened to you. Because if I'm going to risk death up there in the north, then I need to know. If you love me, you will tell me. You will help me understand what it is that I'm walking into."

She looked at him with a desperate kind of love, and then, pain marring her face, she nodded. "I don't like thinking about it," she said, her voice soft. "I don't like thinking about anything anymore."

"Start with the night in the woods," he urged. "Do you remember what happened?"

She nodded. "It was the coin," she said, running her fingers over the necklace. "My pet, it was far—very far from here, but the coin connected us. It had been up there, you see—up on Beggar's Drift, slumbering, ancient. And then something woke it, and at first it didn't want to answer. It wanted to stay sleeping, but then the call became unbearable. When it emerged, it sought the coin, but it had been in such a dark place for such a long time and without a heartbeat to follow, the beast was like a blind infant, searching in vain. First it headed north, where the animals are large and warm and fresh. But then my heartbeat, it called it back down here, back to me, because I am its master. I was born and I died that I might be its master. That night when it found me in the woods, it was wild then, it was filled with longing and death, and in lunging for me, for its new master, it didn't mean . . . well, you know the rest."

Her voice cracked, and she blinked as if fighting back

315

tears. Tom touched her arm, gently urging her on, and she nodded.

"After that, I remember very little except for cold and the sense that I was very alone. And then something changed. I heard . . . digging. And then I remember gasping for breath, clawing my way out of the mud. I remember the night sky above me—how beautiful it looked as the pain shot through me, and my body came to life. Next I was in the woods. It was with me, waiting for me. And we were hungry, so hungry. The hunger, it burned inside us. Tom, you can't know what this hunger was like. There are no words for it."

"We?" Rowan asked, her thoughts turning to the abomination she'd seen with Fiona.

Fiona narrowed her eyes at Rowan. "Yes, we," she hissed. *"We."*

"So," Tom said, his voice shaking. "So it was the beast that killed the villagers?"

Fiona hesitated a moment and then shook her head. "You have to understand. When it woke me, when it pulled me from the clutches of death, it gave a piece of itself that I might live. And we were so hungry, and it couldn't cross into the village, so I had to do it. I didn't want to. It wasn't a choice."

"That thing. That thing did this to you?"

Fiona's eyes were wide with emotion, and it seemed to Rowan the girl was desperate to make Tom understand. "We are bound. I gave it my heart, and it gave me its soul. We share our hunger, our thirst . . . our mortality."

"Your mortality?" Tom asked, his voice breaking with

316

sorrow. "Tell me you're not serious. Tell me your life isn't yoked to that creature's."

"We need each other, Tom," Fiona said. "The beast and I, we are not whole without the other. But no one has to die anymore. I grow stronger every day. If we can just get far enough away, then no one has to die. We'll find something else—something big and warm. We just have to leave, Tom, and we have to leave soon. Because given our current situation," she said, looking to the others, "I can't promise anything."

"Tom," Jude said. "Don't go with her. She'll kill you."

"She won't," he said. "I trust her."

"Then you're a madman. You really don't think she'll turn on you eventually when that monster of hers gets tired of eating bears?"

"If I'm a madman, then let me be mad. I'm going with her."

"Listen to your brother," Henry Rose said, taking a step toward Tom. "You're a good boy, Tom. You always have been. Go home to your family."

Rowan thought of the witches, to the connection they believed existed between her and her sister. It didn't seem likely that she could have much effect on Fiona, but she needed to try. She stepped toward her. "Please. I beg of you, listen to reason. He'll die if he stays with you. Let him go."

Fiona laughed, and Rowan, startled by the movement, raised her gun and trained it on the girl.

"Rowan, no!" cried Tom.

Slowly Fiona Eira pulled herself to her feet, and naked

arms outstretched, she started walking toward Rowan. "You think you can kill me?"

"Send him away," Rowan said, feet planted firmly in the snow. "He won't leave you on his own. You have to make him go. Please, make him go."

"Don't be stupid, girl, and don't threaten me again," Fiona said, anger beginning to transform her porcelain face. "I'll only give you one more warning."

But there was to be no further warning, only a flash of movement as Fiona darted across the snow, and a crack and an echo as Henry Rose fired his rifle, the bullet lodging in a nearby tree. And a moment later, Fiona had Rowan's body in her arms, holding her like a rag doll, as her bared teeth drove into the flesh of her neck.

"She's your sister!" Jude screamed, desperate, and Fiona froze.

Pain split into Rowan's being, clouding her vision, and then faded to a throb as the teeth retracted.

"What?" Fiona said, her arms still wrapped around her prey.

"She's your sister!" Jude cried. "Please don't hurt her."

Fiona let Rowan's body drop to the ground. Pain traveled from her neck, coursing through her, alighting every nerve in her body. She reached for the wound to stop the bleeding. With shaking legs, she pushed herself up to stand.

"What did you say?" Fiona asked, her gaze shifting to Rowan, something like recognition in her eyes, and Rowan felt it welling up within her as well—that person she was always reaching for, that twin soul, was right beside her.

"Put the gun down," Tom pleaded with his brother.

"My sister?" Fiona said, confusion and grief breaking the fragile ice of her features.

"Yes," said Henry Rose, clearing his throat. "Your sister. And I am your father. I beg of you, please, let the boy go. He's done no wrong in the world. Whatever evil called you forth from your grave, try to throw it aside and find your humanity."

For a moment, no one spoke, and a heavy silence filled the air. And then Rowan realized what was making her so uneasy. The beast. It was nowhere in sight, and yet, why not? Weren't Fiona and Tom leaving with it? Shouldn't it be nearby?

Fiona shook her head, agony in her eyes. "But I love him."

"If you love him," pleaded Henry Rose, "then let him go. Take your beast and hide yourself away. We won't try to stop you."

"Please," said Rowan, meeting her sister's gaze with kindness, her voice gentle. "You're killing him. Haven't enough people died already? Please spare Tom."

Fiona stared at her sister, her eyes growing soft, and it seemed to Rowan that she was beginning to reach the girl—to touch the place where her heart ought to have been. Fiona turned to Tom and looked at him with great sadness. Then, cutting through the silence, there came a rustle in the trees and the sound of approaching footsteps. Rowan turned to see the duke emerging from the woods. How had he known where they would be? When she heard Merrilee's

319

whimpers, she had her answer. Stepping out into the clearing, dragging the girl by the wrist, he gave them all a magnificent smile.

"Should I be hurt that I wasn't invited?"

Rowan held tight to her rifle, ready for anything.

"Merrilee!" Henry Rose exclaimed, but as he started toward her, the duke pulled the child in front of him and pointed a gun at the back of her head.

"No!" screamed Rowan.

"I won't hurt her," the duke said, his face utterly calm. "I won't hurt her as long as I leave here with that coin." He gestured to Fiona, who glared back at him.

"What does the child have to do with this?" Henry Rose pleaded, horror in his voice. "Let her go."

"No," the duke said, as if speaking to a group of small children. "I would very much like that coin. And something tells me that it will not be easy to reclaim on my own. I am rather fond of my throat, you see. But you are all good people. You don't want this little girl to die. So I would suggest you all start trying to convince your friend here to hand over her necklace to me."

"Why?" Rowan cried, desperate to draw out the man she'd seen before, the man she'd thought so charming and kind. "So you can overthrow your king? So you can overthrow your own sister? Why are you doing this?"

"Why?" he asked, his face contorted with anguish. "Do I need to tell you why? Haven't I told you enough? I told you what these people did to my family, and when my sister married into their lot, she became one of them. They are murderers, all of them. They should no more be running a kingdom than should a pack of wild dogs."

"And *you* should?" Rowan asked, trying to keep from sounding as incredulous as she felt.

"No, Rowan, *we* should." He held her gaze, and for a moment, she lost herself in his eyes, in what could have been. "I tried to tell you that day in the kitchen. I tried to make you understand that together we could rule. Don't you see, Rowan, the things we could accomplish? You know about the documents I've unearthed. Your father has told you. You've seen for yourself the wonders they hold. You've seen the power they contain, but it took me months to decipher that one page of ancient script. I need you, Rowan. I need your gifts. Together we will change the world."

Rowan took a step back. "By unleashing monsters on it?"

"I can control it. I know how to control it. I promise you."

"You knew what you'd awakened, and yet you let it descend upon our village? You knew it had killed your soldiers, and you didn't warn us?"

"You think the monster killed my soldiers?" he laughed. "Oh, but how very wrong you are. You think it gouged out that man's eyes? No, my love, my monster was still sleeping then—stirring, perhaps, but still sleeping, I assure you. It didn't awaken until after they were all already dead."

"Then how?" Rowan asked, her mind suddenly cold with the possibilities.

"You really haven't figured it out yet? Think, Rowan. The captain's eyes were torn from him. The other soldiers' fingers were stained pink."

"They killed him," whispered Jude. "They killed him, and then they removed their clothes to wash the blood from their bodies."

The duke smiled. "The boy is brighter than he looks."

"But why?" asked Rowan, the horrible truth of it washing over her in waves.

"Why?" he asked, smiling at her with the eyes of a madman. "For the same reason I have a gun pressed to a child's head. For the same reason your friend Tom is heading off to the tundra to be consumed by death's mistress."

"The coin?" Rowan asked. "It's a talisman, a spell of some kind. But what is it to you? Why does it have this hold over you?"

"Can't you hear it?" he asked, his wide eyes growing stranger by the moment. "Can't you hear it calling to you? It's beautiful, like nothing else in this world. When my monster began to stir, when it began to push open that doorway to this world, the call became irresistible. Those men had no choice but to do what they did. We mustn't blame them. We are the same."

"A doorway? That's what Mama Tetri said—that the coin is like a doorway."

"My darling," he said, his face alight with a rapturous smile. "It's that and so much more. Can't you feel it? It's not just any doorway. It's the doorway to the underworld—the doorway to hell—and what beautiful music it makes, what glorious symphonies of lust and longing and death. Don't you want to follow it? Don't you want it to be yours? The only thing that stands between us and that beauty is the talisman around a dead girl's neck. Join me. Help me remove it, and I will show you wonders beyond your wildest dreams."

Rowan wanted to tell herself that there was no truth to his ramblings, that he was simply a madman. But she knew that she couldn't, for she had heard the melody as well, had perhaps always heard it—that distant music that haunted her sleep and awakened in her bones, a horrid longing to sink into the earth and meet death face to face. But she also knew instinctively that it was a trick, a lure, and that the call must always be refused.

Without meaning to, she took a step away from the duke.

His face grew hard, his eyes suddenly cold. "You stupid girl. I'm offering you the world." He pressed the gun harder against the base of Merrilee's skull, and the child cried out in pain.

"Let her go," Rowan said, her breath catching. "Let the girl go, and I'll come with you."

"Rowan?" Tom said, meeting her eyes with fear, but it passed quickly, for he knew his old friend, and he began to see what she was doing.

"Listen to me," Rowan said to the duke. "Let Merrilee go, and I'll give you whatever you want. I'll join you. I'll help you retrieve the coin. Just don't kill her. She's only a child."

She took a step toward him, and he held out a hand to her, his features cut with the strange and exquisite longing of a man who thinks he might not have to die alone.

"Rowan, no!" her father said. "This is not for you to handle. I have brought this fate upon our house. This battle is mine to fight."

But before she could communicate her true intentions to her father, it was too late. He moved quickly toward the duke, who shoved Merrilee aside and pointed the gun at Henry Rose.

"Father, no!" screamed Rowan.

And then something caught her eye. She stared in disbelief as Merrilee seemed slowly to change. A smile graced the child's lips, and she withdrew something from her sleeve—a flash of moonlight on silver, the sharp tip of a hunting blade. In Rowan's mind, she saw the image of Merrilee standing over the candelabra, sliding her greasy fingers over the silver, and she understood. Merrilee hadn't been looking into the forest; she had been looking into the silver. The duke wasn't the Greywitch. It was Merrilee.

"Father, no!" she cried again, but he didn't seem to hear, so intent was he on rescuing what he thought to be a helpless child.

It happened too quickly. One moment Merrilee was flinging herself into Henry Rose's arms, and the next there came a terrible sound as the child plunged her knife deep into his body, and with the strength of a man, she tore upward through his flesh, splitting him open, rending the fabric of his being.

Henry Rose tried to gasp, tried to cry out, but when Merrilee plunged the knife into his heart, there was no longer any more of him to scream.

Covered in blood, Merrilee stepped away, wrinkling her nose as if offended, and observed as her victim, opened up, ribs and viscera exposed, fell face-first into the snow.

Rowan screamed. Her world seeming to spin, she ran to her father, to where he lay motionless, crimson flooding out around him. Her hands moved against his shoulders as she shook him, tried to stir him, but her frantic fingers met only an empty vessel. She held his lifeless body, refusing to believe he was gone. Around her she could hear disbelief, screaming—but the cacophony seemed to flow past her as she sat shocked and silent. Soon Tom was beside her. He turned her father's body over, searching in vain for a way to save him. A moment later, Rowan felt Jude's hands on her shoulders, pulling her away from her father, pulling her into his arms.

"Rowan," he whispered. "Oh, Rowan."

The duke looked on, his face drained of color. "Merrilee, what have you done? Great god of the sea, what have you done?"

"I'll do what I like," Merrilee said, her tiny voice a bizarre companion to the darkness in her face.

Rowan stared at the child, unable to comprehend that this small creature could be capable of such evil. And then her eyes fell to her father's rifle, now abandoned in the snow. Before Rowan could move to retrieve it, Merrilee was upon it. Rowan scrambled to find her own weapon, but it was too far away to reach in time.

Gingerly, Merrilee lifted the rifle from the snow. She held it awkwardly, as if she meant only to keep her fingers to the metal, to avoid touching any wood. Gun in hand, she moved toward Tom.

"Tom!" Rowan screamed, and he jumped up to face Merrilee just as the child swung the butt of the rifle, cracking it with great force against his knees.

The sound of bones shattering echoed through the night, and Tom cried out, crumpling to the frozen ground. Distaste upon Merrilee's face, she hurled the rifle into the trees. Her knife in hand again, she grabbed Tom from behind, and pulling him to her with a relentless, otherworldly kind of strength, she pressed the blade flush against his throat. Rowan knew then that Merrilee was no child.

Fiona, who had been watching from a distance, sprang to attention, anger burning in her eyes.

"Let him go!" Rowan cried. "Please, let him go."

But Merrilee ignored Rowan and turned her attention to Fiona. "I want you all to understand something," she announced. "There are only two outcomes possible tonight. Either I leave here with that coin and I let this boy live, or I leave here with the coin and he dies—probably along with the rest of you."

"What are you?" Jude screamed, his face contorted with pain. But then his gaze connected with Rowan's, and she saw comprehension dawn in his eyes. He realized that whatever they were up against might be something they couldn't overcome.

Merrilee ignored him, her attention focused solely on Fiona and her necklace. "The dead girl gets to make the choice," she said, and then, dragging Tom through the snow like a rag doll, she made her way closer to Fiona. "Do you even know what it means to die a second death? Do you have any idea what that's like? Do you know what it is to have darkness consume you anew each night?"

Rowan looked on in wonder as Fiona snarled, her face suddenly contorted into a fiendish mask. She was a monster. Rowan knew this, but still something in Rowan's heart struggled against it. Her father was gone now. She had no family, except for this girl. Fiona, monster or not, was her sister, and she found that she didn't want to lose her just yet.

Rowan tried to push through the pain and grief that clouded her mind. She needed to think. Something wasn't right. Clearly Merrilee would stop at nothing to get what she wanted, and yet she wouldn't directly challenge Fiona. If she wanted the coin, why not kill her and take it from her? What power did Fiona hold over the girl? And then Rowan remembered what Fiona had said about her connection to the beast. If the beast died, Fiona died. Perhaps it was the other way around as well. And Merrilee needed the beast alive.

"Give me my coin," Merrilee growled, and with a hand on Tom's shoulder, she pulled back and twisted, the bones shattering beneath her grip as Tom wailed in agony.

Jude turned and ran to his brother's side. Enraged, he pointed his gun at Merrilee, but she pressed the knife into Tom's flesh, beginning to draw blood.

"Put your gun down or I kill him. You have three seconds."

Jude dropped his gun.

"Not just you," she said, looking around. "Everyone throw your weapons over the side of the cliff. Do it now, or the boy dies."

Shaking, Jude flung his gun over Lover's Leap before gathering the other weapons and heaving them over as well. For a split second, he stared into the woods where Henry Rose's gun now lay, but then he looked away and threw his arms into the air, though not until after giving Rowan a quick glance.

"They're gone," he said. "Now let him go. I beg of you; let my brother go."

"You too," Merrilee said to the duke, ignoring Jude. "You know the things I'll do to you if you refuse me."

His breath coming in raspy bursts, the duke tossed his weapon over the cliff, and the Greywitch turned back to face Fiona, a bright smile now on her face.

"The beast belongs to me," Merrilee said. "It's mine."

There came the sound of branches twisting, snapping, as behind them something moved. And turning, Rowan saw it—back at the Mouth of the Goddess, at the outcropping of forest, the creature hidden among the branches and snow.

Merrilee narrowed her eyes and turned to see what it was that moved among the trees.

Carefully Rowan made her way through the snow to Fiona Eira, and when the girl saw her, her expression transformed from suspicion to surprise. Looking into each other's eyes, the sisters suddenly knew each other. Fiona held out her hand to Rowan. Rowan reached out as she'd done a thousand times before, only this time cold fingers reached back, and clasping at her warmth, Fiona Eira pulled her sister to her side.

Hatred burning inside her, Rowan stared at the child who had just killed her father. "I'm not frightened of you," she said.

"Rowan," the duke said, his voice shaking as he walked slowly through the snow to the Greywitch. "Don't be stupid."

Merrilee turned her focus to him.

"Are you frightened right now?" the Greywitch asked. "Are you frightened of what I might do to her?"

"Stop, Merrilee, please!" cried the duke. "You promised that no one would die. You swore to me that no one would die."

She raised her eyebrows. "Promises have ways of getting broken. You think I don't know about the promises you've been making to Rowan?"

He shook his head, terror transforming his features. "I haven't . . ."

"I see," she said simply. "This is why you bought me from my parents, why you took me from my home? So I could work the magic that you cannot, and then once you have my beast, you could abandon me?"

"I'm not abandoning you, Merrilee," the duke said, his face pale with fear.

"You are," she said, furious. "You would take *her* to the throne. I will not have it. I do not like your change of plans, and I am tired of hearing your voice."

She turned her back to the duke and flashed a terrible smile at Fiona. "The coin," she said. "Now."

Rowan looked at the duke, who stared at her, pain in his eyes, and then he began moving slowly toward Merrilee. Rowan's heart gave a start as his intentions became clear. Approaching from behind, unseen, raising his hands as if to catch a violent cat, the duke descended upon the Greywitch. For a moment, Rowan was certain that he would save them all, but then, with one swift motion, without ever taking her eyes from Fiona or removing her grip from Tom, Merrilee thrust the knife behind her, plunging it directly into the duke's heart.

Rowan screamed as the duke's eyes grew wide. He shook his head and then took a single step before falling forward into the snow, crimson rivulets spilling from him, feathering their way through the powder.

With the knife once again pressed to Tom's throat, Merrilee drove her fingers deeper into Tom's already broken shoulder, shattering it even further. Tom screamed as his arm seemed to tear away from his body, hanging at an inhuman angle. Rowan looked at her sister, and all at once Fiona's expression grew calm. Any indication of the monster within seemed to melt away until only the clear, beautiful face of the living girl remained. She closed her eyes, and as if deciding something, she nodded.

Fiona turned to Rowan and squeezed her arm. Rowan stared into her sister's coal-black eyes, and within them she saw longing and grief, the vast tragic emptiness that had been the dead girl's short life. And then Fiona smiled, and her dark eyes filled with tears.

"Goodbye," she whispered.

In one fluid motion, Fiona Eira tore the necklace from her throat and flung it high in the air, far out over the edge of the cliff, down to the frozen lake below.

Merrilee looked on in horror, and then ran to the edge of the cliff as behind her there issued the terrible noise of trees torn asunder. The beast, atop jagged bone legs, surged toward the cliff and the coin. Fiona pulled Rowan back and out of the path of the beast just in time for Merrilee to turn and see the gaping wounds of its eyes, and the needle teeth lining its mouth as it clamped down on her, and the two of them hurtled out and over the cliff, the beast intent on the coin that lay on the ice below.

Rowan could barely breathe as she ran to the edge of Lover's Leap just in time to see the ice break beneath the enormous creature. To her shock, the starving water nixies—vast schools of them—swarmed upon the beast, pulling it and the Greywitch it held in its jaws down and down and down, their sharp teeth tearing and chewing as they went.

Stunned, Rowan backed away from the carnage below. She turned, then nearly fell to the ground as she took in the devastation before her. Her father—his body—lay lifeless in the snow. Gone from her so soon. Tom sat broken and in pain, staring up, terrified, at Fiona Eira beside him.

"What have you done?" he cried. "What have you done?"

"It's better this way," she said, and Rowan could see her

sister's once-lovely skin pull in on itself as Death began to suck the life from her. "It's better."

"No!" he howled. "You can't leave me. Please, no!"

But she only held a finger to her lips. "Shhh," she whispered, and then she closed her eyes.

Rowan watched as Fiona faded before her, shriveling, twisting as if burning from within, and then an awful cloud of smoke rose from the ground, and Rowan had to turn away and cover her mouth to keep from choking on the fumes. When she looked again, Fiona Eira was gone, now nothing more than a mound of white ash piled atop the snow.

Reaching into the ash with his good arm, gasping at the pain, Tom swept his hand through it, looking for something, anything. And then, collapsing completely, he curled into a ball. Hands to his face, he wailed, a cry that would ring in Rowan's ears for years to come.

19. THE HERMIT

AFTER PLACING THEIR cinnamon at the Mouth of the Goddess, Rowan and Jude made their way down Cairn Hill to Seelie Lake. It had been three months since Rowan had laid her father to rest, and still she experienced the pain of his loss as if each day he were torn from her anew.

They were leaving Nag's End, invited by the queen herself to the palace city. Rowan, hesitant to leave her village, had promised her brethren that they'd return shortly, but Jude had a sense that the journey that lay ahead of them would bring a grander adventure than either could anticipate. He, like Rowan, was hungry to see the world, and so certain was he that her destiny was larger than the limits of

Nag's End that he was simply happy to go where the winds might take them.

Hand in hand, they made their way along the banks of the crystalline lake, their boots slipping through the fresh green shoots of grass. Above them, the trees were waking, stretching out beneath the warmth of the vernal sun.

Tom was healing well, and walked now with the help of a staff, but still Jude worried for his brother. The villagers, sympathetic to the plight of the broken boy, had helped him build his own small cottage at the base of Lover's Leap. He was intent on the spot, for it was atop that fated slate rock, where nothing ought to grow, that there had come to sprout a bright green sapling. It grew fast and it grew wild, and already rich red roses blossomed upon it.

As soon as Tom's cottage came into Rowan's view, Pema burst out of the front door. Eyes glittering, tongue wagging, and bounding across the fertile banks of the lakeshore, she threw herself at Rowan and licked her face.

A moment later, Tom appeared, shuffling toward them with his walking stick, and Rowan couldn't help but feel he'd aged a lifetime since Fiona's death. It wasn't just his injury. The eyes that looked out from that now-wizened face were those of a man who already knew things about the world that most people never learn.

"Heading off now?" Tom called.

"We are," Rowan said, rubbing the dog's head. "You and Pema getting along well, then?"

"Aye," said Tom, turning back toward his cottage. "Birds of a feather."

Pema, spotting a large crow, set off after it, and Jude and Rowan followed Tom to his cottage. Inside it was pleasant and warm. On the small wooden table, Tom set out tea and lemon cake, and together the three ate and enjoyed one another's company.

When they'd had their fill, they said their farewells.

"Take care of each other," Tom said.

Rowan felt a stab to her chest, and she couldn't help but wonder who would take care of Tom. And then something caught her eye.

"There's a white one," she said, pointing up to the rose tree.

"What?" Jude asked, trying to see what she meant.

"On the rose tree," she said. "Among the red blossoms, there's a single white rose." And as soon as the words graced her lips, she understood.

"You'd better be off now," Tom said, looking at Rowan with the smile of a man who has had his fill of adventure and is now eager for his friend to have hers.

She hugged him close, her heart breaking for the boy he'd once been. And then, letting go, she took Jude by the hand. Together, the pair set off through the trees.

From the front of his cottage, Tom watched the lovers go, his spirit filled with joy. He looked up at the young rose tree that arched over the edge of the cliff, and he closed his eyes. There are some men who love only once, and Tom Parstle was such a man.

335

A turn in the weather caused Tom to open his eyes just in time to see the solitary white rose among its red sisters drop a single petal. Caught on a breeze, it flitted through the air, dancing in the morning light before landing in the palm of his hand. Tom smiled to himself, and gently folded his fingers around the petal. Then, slowly, with the solitude of a man whose tale was never told, he went inside, closing the door behind him.

ACKNOWLEDGMENTS

Enormous thanks to:

Krista Marino, the most astoundingly brilliant editor a girl could dream of having. This book is every bit as much her doing as it is mine. To Beverly Horowitz, Angela Carlino, and the rest of the amazing Delacorte Press team. To Kate Garrick, Brian DeFiore, Madelyn Mahon, and everyone else at DeFiore and Company.

Thanks to all the writers, teachers, and friends who helped with the book: Keith Abbott, Duncan Barlow, Jocelyn Camp, Julie Caplan, Camille DeAngelis, Sam Hansen, Patricia Hernandez, Kristen Kittscher, Jay Kristoff, Jennifer Laughran, Alex Raben, Isak Sjursen, Teddy Templeman, and Andrew Wille.

MCCORMICK TEMPLEMAN holds a BA in English literature from Reed College and an MFA in writing and poetics from Naropa University. *The Glass Casket* is her second book for young readers. She lives and writes in Santa Barbara, California. Visit her at McCormickTempleman.com.